Praise for Atiq Rahimi

Earth and Ashes

"Anyone seeking to understand why Afghanistan is difficult and what decades of violence have done to its people should read Atiq Rahimi. He is a superb guide to a hard and complex land."
— Ryan Crocker, former U.S. ambassador to Pakistan, Iraq, and Afghanistan

"The blasted dreamscape of Rahimi's story and his tightly controlled prose make this a sobering literary testament to the horrors of war."
— *Publishers Weekly*

"It has the feel of a book of great antiquity and authority; you could more readily level the Afghan mountains than damage the dreaming culture that *Earth and Ashes* both embodies and silently trusts."
— *London Times*

"With this novel Rahimi picks up a shard of broken glass and sees the whole truth of his devastated country."
— *Der Spiegel* (Germany)

A Thousand Rooms of Dream and Fear

"The language has the rhythm of a Sufi prayer; the novel offers an insight into the deepest fears of the people of Afghanistan."

"That sense of losing one's identity, of being subsumed by a greater, if illogical, power, is a key theme in Atiq Rahimi's taut, layered novel . . . *A Thousand Rooms of Dream and Fear* is the intimate narrative . . . of an entire desperate, anguished country."

— *Washington Post*

"An intensely intimate portrait of a man (and by extension his country) questioning reality and the limits of the possible . . . full of elegant evocations . . . *A Thousand Rooms of Dream and Fear* resonates deeply because, no doubt, Rahimi has written a true and sad account, but the story could easily be that of any other Afghan, of any other denizen of this modern, anarchic state. In the end, we are left to wonder whether Rahimi has presented us with a story, a dream, or a nightmare, though it is likely all three."

— *Words Without Borders*

"Rahimi's tale of confused nationality, indiscriminate punishment, desperate survival, and no clear way to safety depicts decades-old events, but it feels especially poignant amid the U.S.-led war in Afghanistan that's spanned the greater part of the past decade."

— *Flavorwire*

"An original and utterly personal account of the pressures a totalitarian society exerts on the individual in 1979 Afghanistan, before the Soviet invasion . . . A flawless translation does justice to Rahimi's taut, highly calibrated prose."   — *Publishers Weekly*

"In prose that is spare and incisive, poetic and searing, prizewinning Afghani author Rahimi, who fled his native land in 1984, captures the distress of his people."   — *Booklist*, starred review

"Rahimi is an author known for his unflinching examination of his home country as much as the experimental styles in which he writes . . . *A Thousand Rooms of Dream and Fear* takes risks in its structure . . . But Rahimi's carefully controlled new novel exploits these uncertainties, joining the past to the present and legend with fact,

creating an appropriately surreal narrative, one that rings through
with truth." —*ForeWord Reviews*

"A taut and brilliant burst of anguished prose . . . both a wonderful
and a dreadful little book." —*The Guardian*

"A beautiful piece of writing." —Ruth Pavey, *The Independent*

"Short but powerful . . . The beauty of the language lends this work
a haunting clarity." —*The Herald*

"The novella is verbal photography . . . [it] seems the real thing . . .
seamlessly translated." —Russell Celyn Jones, *London Times*

The Patience Stone

"[*The Patience Stone*] is a deceptively simple book, written in a spare,
poetic style. But it is a rich read, part allegory, part a tale of retribution, part an exploration of honor, love, sex, marriage, war. It is
without doubt an important and courageous book."
—From the introduction by Khaled Hosseini,
author of *The Kite Runner* and
A Thousand Splendid Suns

"*The Patience Stone* is perfectly written: spare, close to the bone,
sometimes bloody, with a constant echo, like a single mistake that
repeats itself over and over and over." —*Los Angeles Times*

"Powerful . . . an expansive work of literature." —*New York Post*

"In this remarkable book Atiq Rahimi explores ways through
which personal and political oppression can be resisted through
acts of self-revelation. He reveals to us the violence we are capable
of imposing upon ourselves and others in our personal as well as
political and social relations. In his stark and compact style, Rahimi

recreates for us the texture of such violence, its almost intimate brutality as well as its fragility. Although the story happens within the context of a particular time and place, the emotions it evokes and relationships it creates have universal implications and could happen to any of us under similar conditions. *The Patience Stone* is relevant to us exactly because, as Rahimi says, it takes place 'Somewhere in Afghanistan or elsewhere.'"

—Azar Nafisi, author of *Reading Lolita in Tehran* and *Things I've Been Silent About*

"With a veiled face and stolen words, a woman keeps silent about her forbidden pain in an Afghanistan marred by men's foolishness. But when she rediscovers her voice, she overcomes the chaos. Atiq Rahimi tells the story of this woman's heartbreaking lamentation to awaken our consciences."

—Yasmina Khadra, author of *The Swallows of Kabul*

"[A] clever novel . . . readers get a glimpse of daily life in a country terrorized by conflict and religious fundamentalism. Rahimi paints this picture with nuance and subtlety . . . [His] sparse prose complements his simple yet powerful storytelling prowess. This unique story is both enthralling and disturbing."

—*San Francisco Chronicle*

"Rahimi's lyric prose is simple and poetic, and McLean's translation is superb. With an introduction by Khaled Hosseini, this Prix Goncourt–winning book should have a profound impact on the literature of Afghanistan for its brave portrayal of, among other things, an Afghan woman as a sexual being."   —*Library Journal*

"A slender, devastating exploration of one woman's tormented inner life, which won the 2008 Prix Goncourt . . . The novel, asserts [Khaled] Hosseini in his glowing introduction, finally gives a complex, nuanced, and savage voice to the grievances of millions."

—*Words Without Borders*

Atiq Rahimi was born in Afghanistan in 1962, and fled to France in 1984. There he has become renowned as a maker of documentary and feature films, and as a writer. The film of his novel *Earth and Ashes* was in the Official Selection at Cannes in 2004 and won several prizes. *A Thousand Rooms of Dream and Fear* has also been adapted for the screen. His latest adaptation, for *The Patience Stone*, winner of the 2008 Prix Goncourt, was submitted for an Oscar in 2013. Since 2002 Rahimi has returned to Afghanistan a number of times to set up a Writers' House in Kabul and to offer support and training to young Afghan writers and filmmakers. His new novel, *A Curse on Dostoevsky*, is forthcoming from Other Press. He lives in Paris.

Three by Atiq Rahimi

EARTH AND ASHES

TRANSLATED BY ERDAG M. GÖKNAR

A Thousand Rooms of Dream and Fear

TRANSLATED BY SARAH MAGUIRE AND YAMA YARI

The Patience Stone (Sang-E Saboor)

WITH AN INTRODUCTION BY KHALED HOSSEINI
TRANSLATED BY POLLY MCLEAN

Other Press/New York

Production Editor: Yvonne E. Cárdenas
Text Designer: Jennifer Daddio/Bookmark Design & Media, Inc.
This book was set in 11.9 pt Cochin by Alpha Design & Composition of Pittsfield, NH.

1 3 5 7 9 10 8 6 4 2

LIBRARY OF CONGRESS CATALOGING-IN-PUBLICATION DATA

Rahimi, Atiq.
[Novels. Selections English]
Three by Atiq Rahimi.
pages cm
ISBN 978-1-59051-630-0 (pbk.) — ISBN (invalid) 978-1-59051-631-7 (ebook)   1. Afghanistan—
History—Soviet occupation, 1979-1989—Fiction.   2. Fathers and sons—Fiction.   3. Muslim
women—Fiction.   4. Islamic fundamentalism—Fiction.   I. Rahimi, Atiq. Khakistar va khak.
English.   II. Rahimi, Atiq. Hazar khanah-i khvab va ikhtinaq. English.   III. Rahimi, Atiq.
Syngué sabour. English.   IV. Title.
PK6878.9.R34A2 2013
891'.563—dc23
2013010938

Contents

✤

Preface

What man thinks, he becomes.

—THE VEDAS

It feels strange seeing my three novels, which were written at different stages in my life, brought together in a single volume. For a long time I felt that each of my books was a distinct literary entity, distinct in terms of structure as well as thematic content. But I now feel they constitute only a *single* work. Single and short. Short for ten years of literary life! A dispiriting realization that forced me to spread my life before me and, to reassure my troubled mind, re-examine the context in which my three pieces of writing were conceived. This was absolutely not with the intention of justifying my laziness. For that I will appropriate Rilke's advice: "To write a single verse, you need to have seen a lot of people, places, and things." My honor is intact!

Revisiting the context in which I wrote has been an opportunity to locate myself on the spidery web of creativity that held me captive as its prey for ten years. So I need to trace each of those thousand-and-one imperceptible threads in order to establish connections between my books and reveal their textual coherence . . . and all this in the hope of finding some existential cohesion between my life and my writing.

Camus says, "Every artist has . . . deep within him a unique source, and throughout his life it sustains who he is and what he says." Where is this source? What sort of water flows from it?

My first book, *Earth and Ashes*, was written in 1996, the year that the Taliban took power in Kabul, and that I had recently become a father for the first time. Before these events, Afghanistan had been just a sad recollection in the recesses of my memory, a memory traumatized by my brother's killing six years earlier, at the very beginning of Afghanistan's civil war. My family hid this tragedy from me for two years, so I did my mourning later, in the solitude of exile, wondering about my family's silence, about what had kept them from telling me about my brother's death. That was when I embarked on an unvoiced, inner conversation with my relations. I wrote *Earth and Ashes* for them; it is a space for mourning, where death can think things through and work. It thinks through life, my life, and it works a language, the language of my native land, a land first trampled underfoot by the Red Army, then destroyed by a fratricidal war of revenge before ending up lacerated and flogged by the "army of darkness," the Taliban. At the time, writing in Persian, my native language, was the only way I could share in my country's suffering. And the source from which my pen's ink flowed over those melancholy pages of exile went by the name of nostalgia. A very private text, then. One without a future and without any hope. It never occurred to me to that it might one day be published. But, one day, it did happen. And, one day, I became a writer, an identity launched into history. I had little choice but to undertake that journey to the wonderland of words and, to paraphrase R. Tagore, "to explore, discover, and share the best of me": to write with hatred about war.

Then came September 11.
Still in exile, I was right in the middle of writing my second novel, *A Thousand Rooms of Dream and Fear*, and busy cradling my second child, who was just six months old on that fateful day.

Long after the Soviet-Afghan war, the eyes of the world were turned once again on my native land, which had now become the very face of terror. How to explain such human savagery from a place that was once the land of mystic horsemen and epic poets?

Through the misadventures of one young Afghan man over the course of twenty-four hours, I tell the story of twenty-four years in the life of my country as it shifts from the red terror of Communism to the black terror of fundamental Islamists. Because on this earth we do not live *in* time, we simply *live* time; history is not written in time, but in space. You need only travel from one town to the next to cover the country's history. It is a labyrinthine reading/writing of Afghanistan in which we go from dream to terror and from terror to nightmare. It is therefore not a geopolitical analysis of this historical journey, but an intimist crossing, rather as I myself experienced on a drunken night in the streets of Kabul in 1982. Having been stopped and given a drubbing by some soldiers because I had forgotten the curfew, I floundered in a state of inner confusion while my anxious conscience was brutally confronted with a reality I wanted to deny. I brought this state of turmoil into my character Farhad's dream, during which all these different worlds are resolved in the brooding ruminations of his grandfather, a figure who represents ancestral and religious traditions. And that is when fear comes to roost in the young Afghan's mind. With fear comes terror. This progression illustrates not only the young man's life, but also the story of Afghanistan. In 1984, on the Afghan-Pakistani border on my way to exile, I came across dark, mysterious men like those I describe in *A Thousand Rooms*. They were handing out the much-publicized Book of the Dead to all young men. This book cultivated fear in our naive minds, eradicating from our memories the love once extolled by our great mystics, such as Rumi, Attar of Nishapur, Khayyám . . .

This cult of fear is what created monsters like the Taliban, and what produced their first victims: women. It is in homage to women that I wrote my third book, *The Patience Stone*. A less nostalgic book; a severing book. I wrote directly in French, after returning to my native country, and this aroused anger in my fellow Afghans. They cried treason! And yet . . .

In 2005 I was invited to a literary festival in one of our major cities, Herat, in western Afghanistan. A city renowned for its rich cultural history, for its poets and enlightened intellectuals. A week before I was to leave, I received a telephone call. The event had been canceled because the young Afghan poet Nadia

Anjuman had been killed by her husband. She had contributed actively to the organization of the festival.

Distressed, disgusted, and outraged by this killing, which was widely referred to as a family affair, I went to Afghanistan to carry out my own investigation. But I was told other stories, far more frightening and horrifying, about women's lives in this so-called enlightened place.

I wanted to meet the poet's husband in prison. But he had injected gasoline into his bloodstream, and been transferred to hospital. I saw him from a distance. He was in a coma. Right then, I would have liked to be a woman. To go over to him. And speak in his ear. Tell him everything. The most terrible, horrific things. Like what he had done.

And it was after that visit that "words attacked me," as Duras said. I wanted to write a story, a different one, not that poet's story. I wanted to write a shocking story, about a woman who needs to take revenge. Out of love or hate. With all her strength and weaknesses. And for that I needed an extreme situation, one that would be unlikely, but possible. A tragedy.

When I started writing I just wanted to get inside that man's skin, the paralyzed man who could hear everything but could not respond or move. I wanted to describe what he might be thinking now, this man who had never let his wife talk of her dreams and desires, her suffering. But something strange happened: the woman was the one who wormed her way inside me. She took my voice, my words. As if she wanted me to talk about her alone. To say that, like women all over the world, she has a body. A body full of desires, dreams, fantasies, secrets. But society, war, religion, and tradition have reduced this body to a bruised, repressed, forbidden thing, shameful and wounded. How to put all that in words? In countries such as Afghanistan that are dominated by prohibition and taboos, and therefore by censorship and self-censorship, all forms of thought and artistic creativity are determined by what is secret and left unsaid. And so speaking out becomes a political act, but also an existential one. The question then becomes not "to be or not to be," but "to say or not to say."

And in order to say all this I had to change languages. Because my mother tongue, Persian, still imposed its taboos and prohibitions on me, even if only for its name. The language of intimacy that taught me about life, love, and suffering. The language of propriety that established too many emotive, incestuous links. So adopting another language meant choosing freedom, not betrayal!

. . .

And so,
by writing, I allowed myself to grieve, renouncing
    revenge;
by writing, I set sail into history, denouncing terror;
by writing, I revealed my true self to myself.
Today, although I my doubt my books' power to
    change anything in my readers' lives, I am abso-
    lutely convinced that writing has changed a great
    deal about me. I have become what I write.

                                    Atiq Rahimi
                                    February 2013

Earth and Ashes

TRANSLATED FROM THE DARI BY

Erdag M. Goknar

For

MY FATHER

and other fathers who wept during the war

He has a great heart, as great as his sorrow.

—RAFAAT HOSSEINI

A Note on the Text

⚜

Reference is made in *Earth and Ashes* to the great eleventh-century Persian epic, the *Book of Kings* (*Shahnama* in Persian) by Ferdusi. This famous poem interweaves Persian myths, legends, and historical events to tell the history of Iran and its neighbors from the creation of the world to the Arab conquest in the seventh century. Even today, storytellers can recount large parts of the *Book of Kings* from memory. The characters mentioned in *Earth and Ashes* are:

ROSTAM, son of Zal, the great hero of the epic, who, in a battle, kills his son, Sohrab, whose existence he did not know about.

SOHRAB, son of Rostam, born from Rostam's secret union with Tahmina, daughter of the King of

5

Samengan, who finds himself on the opposite side from his father in battle and is killed by him.

ZOHAK, the legendary tyrant of the epic, who ruled with serpents who fed off the brains of the young men in his kingdom.

Earth and Ashes

✤

"I'm hungry."

You take an apple from the scarf you've tied into a bundle and wipe it on your dusty clothes. The apple just gets dirtier. You put it back in the bundle and pull out another, cleaner one, which you give to your grandson, Yassin, who is sitting next to you, his head resting on your tired arm. The child takes it in his small, dirty hands and brings it to his mouth. His front teeth haven't come through yet. He tries to bite with his canines. His hollow, chapped cheeks twitch. His narrow eyes become narrower. The apple is sour. He wrinkles up his small nose and gasps.

. . .

With your back to the autumn sun, you are squatting against the iron railings of the bridge that links
the two banks of the dry riverbed north of Pul-i-
Khumri. The road connecting northern Afghanistan
to Kabul passes over this very bridge. If you turn left
on the far side of the bridge, onto the dirt track that
winds between the scrub-covered hills, you arrive at
the Karkar coal mine . . .

The sound of Yassin whimpering tears your
thoughts away from the mine. Look, your grandson
can't bite the apple. Where's that knife? You search
your pockets and find it. Taking the apple from his
hands, you cut it in half, then in half again, and hand
the pieces back to him. You put the knife in a pocket
and fold your arms over your chest.

You haven't had any *naswar* for a while. Where's
the tin? You search your pockets again. Eventually
you find it and put a pinch of naswar in your mouth.
Before returning the tin to your pocket, you glance at
your reflection in its mirrored lid. Your narrow eyes
are set deep in their sockets. Time has left its mark on
the surrounding skin, a web of sinuous lines like thirsty

worms waiting around a hole. The turban on your head is unraveling. Its weight forces your head into your shoulders. It is covered in dust. Maybe it's the dust that makes it so heavy. Its original color is no longer apparent. The sun and the dust have turned it gray . . .

Put the box back. Think of something else. Look at something else.

You put the tin back into one of your pockets. You draw your hand over your gray-streaked beard, then clasp your knees and stare at your tired shadow, which merges with the orderly shadows cast by the railings of the bridge.

An army truck, a red star on its door, passes over the bridge. It disturbs the stony sleep of the dry earth. The dust rises. It engulfs the bridge, then settles. Silently it covers everything, dusting the apples, your turban, your eyelids . . . You put your hand over Yassin's apple to shield it.

"Don't!" your grandson shouts. Your hand prevents him from eating.

"You want to eat dust, child?"

"Don't!"

Leave him alone. Keep yourself to yourself. The dust fills your mouth and nostrils. You spit out your naswar next to five other small green plugs on the ground. With the loose flap of your turban, you cover your nose and mouth. You look over at the mouth of the bridge, at the road to the mine. At the black wooden hut of the guard posted at the road barrier. Wisps of smoke fly from its little window. After hesitating for several seconds, you grab hold of one of the bridge's rusty railings with one hand and grip your bundle with the other. Pulling yourself to your feet, you shuffle in the direction of the hut. Yassin gets up too and follows you, clinging to your clothes. Together you approach the hut. You put your head through the small, paneless window. The hut is full of smoke and there's the smell of coal. The guard is in exactly the same position as he was before, his back against one of the walls, his eyes still closed. His cap might have been pulled slightly further down, but that's all. Everything else is just the same, even the half-smoked cigarette between his dry lips . . .

Try coughing.

Even you can't hear your cough, let alone the guard. Cough again, a bit louder. He doesn't hear that either. Let's hope the smoke hasn't suffocated him. You call out.

"Brother . . ."

"What do you want now, old man?"

He can speak, thank goodness. He's alive. But he's still motionless, his eyes closed under his cap . . . Your tongue moves, preparing to say something. Don't interrupt him!

". . . You're killing me. I told you a hundred times. When a car comes past, I'll throw myself in its path, I'll beg them to take you to the mine. What else do you want? Till now have you seen any cars? No? You want someone else's word?"

"I wouldn't dream of it, my good brother. I know there's been no car. But you never know . . . What if you were to forget us . . ."

"How on earth do you expect me to forget, old man? If you want I can recite your life story. You told it to me enough times. Your son works at the mine, you are here with his son to see him."

"My God, you remember everything . . . It's me who's losing my memory. I thought I hadn't told you. Sometimes I think others forget the way I do. I'm sorry I've bothered you . . ."

The truth is, your heart is burdened. It's been a long time since a friend or even a stranger listened to you. A long time since a friend or stranger warmed your heart with their words. You want to talk and to listen. Go on, speak to him! But you're unlikely to get a response. The guard won't listen to you. He is deep in his own thoughts. Preoccupied with himself. Let him be.

You stand silently in front of the hut, gazing away from it at the pitch and roll of the valley. The valley is dried out, covered in thorn bushes—silent. And at the end of the valley is Murad, your son.

You turn away from the valley and stare back inside the hut. You want to tell the guard that you're only waiting here like this for a vehicle to pass because of your grandson Yassin. If you were alone, you'd have set out on foot a long time ago. For you, walking four or five hours is nothing. Each and every day you're on your feet working for ten hours, or longer, working your land. You're a courageous man . . . So what? Why tell the guard all this? What's it to him? Nothing. Then let him be. Sleep in peace, brother . . . We're off. We won't bother you again.

But you don't go. You stand there quietly.

The click of colliding stones at your feet draws your attention to Yassin. He is squatting down, crushing a piece of apple between two stones.

"What are you doing? For God's sake! Eat your apple!"

You grab Yassin by the shoulders and pull him to his feet. The child shouts:

"Don't! Let me go . . . Why don't these stones make any noise?"

The smell of smoke escaping from the hut mingles with the roar of the guard's voice:

"You're killing me! Can't you keep your grandson quiet for one minute?"

You don't have the chance to apologize, or rather, you can't face it. You take hold of Yassin's hand and drag him to the bridge. You drop back down to the ground against the iron railings, put the bundle by your side, and, wrapping your arms around the little boy, scold him:

"Will you behave!"

To whom are you speaking? To Yassin? He can't even hear the sound of stones, let alone your feeble voice. Yassin's world is now another world, one of silence. He wasn't deaf. He became deaf. He doesn't realize this. He's surprised that nothing makes a sound anymore. Until a few days ago it wasn't this way.

Just imagine. You're a child, Yassin, who heard perfectly well just a short time ago, a child who didn't even know what deafness was. And then, one day, suddenly you can't hear a sound. Why? It would be idiotic to try and tell you it was deafness. You don't hear, you don't understand. You don't think it's you who can't hear; you think others have become mute. People have lost their voices; stones have lost their sound. The world is silent . . . So then, why are people moving their mouths?

Yassin hides his small, question-filled face under your clothes.

Your gaze is drawn over the side of the bridge, to the dried-up river that has become a bed of black stones and scrub. You look above the riverbed to the rocky mountains in the distance. They merge with Murad's face.

"Why have you come, Father? Is everything all right?" he asks.

For more than a week now, this face with this question has haunted your days and your nights.

Why have you come? The question gnaws at your bones. Can't that brain in your head find an answer? If only there were no such question. No such word as "why." You've come to see how your son's doing. That's all. After all, you're a father, you think about your son from time to time. Is it a sin? No. You know why you've really come.

You look for your box of naswar, tip a little into the palm of your hand, and put it under your tongue. If only things were simple, full of pleasure—like naswar, like sleep . . . Your gaze rises above the summits of the mountains to the sky . . . But Murad's face still mingles with the mountains. The rocks are slowly becoming hot; they're turning red. It is as if they have become coal and the mountains are one great furnace. The coal catches fire, erupting from the mountain and flowing down the dry riverbed toward you. You are on one side of the river, Murad is on the other. Murad keeps asking, "Why have you come? Why have you come alone with Yassin? Why have you given Yassin silent stones?"

Then Murad starts to cross over to you.

"Murad," you shout, "stay where you are, child! It's a river of fire. You'll get burned! Don't come!"

You ask yourself who could believe such a thing: a river of flowing fire? Have you become a seer of visions? Look, Murad's wading through the river without getting burned. No, he must be getting burned, but he's not reacting. Murad is strong. He doesn't break down. Look at him. His body is covered in sweat.

"Murad," you shout again, "Stop! The river's on fire!"

But Murad continues to move toward you, asking, "Why have you come? Why have you come?"

From somewhere, you're not sure where, the voice of Murad's mother rises.

"Dastaguir, tell him to stay there. *You* cross the river. Take my apple-blossom-patterned scarf with you and go and wipe away his sweat. Take my scarf for Murad . . ."

Your eyes open. You feel your skin covered in cold sweat. You're not able to sleep in peace. It's been a week now since you've had a restful sleep. As soon as you close your eyes, it's Murad and his mother, or Yassin and his mother, or fire and ash, or shouts and wails . . . and you wake up again. Your eyes burn. They burn with sleeplessness. Your eyes don't see anymore. They're exhausted. Out of exhaustion and sleeplessness you keep falling into a half sleep—a half sleep filled with visions. It's as if you live only in these images and dreams. Images and dreams of what you've witnessed and wish you hadn't . . . maybe also what you yet must see, wishing you didn't have to.

If only you slept like a child, like Yassin. Yassin?

No, like any other child but Yassin, who whimpers and moans in his sleep. Maybe Yassin's sleep has become like yours, full of images, dirt, fire, screams, and tears . . . No, not like Yassin's. Like any other child's. Like a baby's. A sleep without images, memories—without dreams.

If only it were possible to begin life again from the beginning, like a newborn baby. You'd like to live again, if only for a day, an hour, a minute, a second.

You think for a moment about the time Murad left the village, when he walked out through the door. You too should have left the village with your wife and children and your grandchildren and gone to another village. You should've gone to Pul-i-Khumri. Never mind if you'd had no land, no crops, no work. May the land rot in Hell! You would have followed Murad. You would have worked in the mines, shoulder to shoulder with him. Then today, no one would be asking you why you've come.

If only . . .

Over the four years Murad has worked at the mine, you haven't had a single chance to visit him. It's been four years since he entrusted his young wife and his son Yassin to you and left for the mine to earn his living.

The truth is, Murad wanted to flee the village and its inhabitants. He wanted to go far away. So he left . . . Thank God he left.

Four years ago your neighbor Yaqub Shah's unworthy son made advances toward Murad's wife, and your daughter-in-law told Murad. Grabbing a spade, Murad ran to Yaqub Shah's house, demanded his son come out and, without asking questions or waiting for answers, brought the spade hard down onto the crown of his head. Yaqub Shah took his wounded son to the village council, and Murad was sentenced to six months in prison.

After he was freed, Murad collected his things together and left for the mine. Since then he has returned to the village only four times. It hasn't even been a month since his last visit, and now you're going to the mine to see him, holding his son by the hand. He'll definitely wonder why.

"Water!"

With Yassin's shout, your eyes drop from the mountains to the dry riverbed, and from the riverbed to the parched lips of your grandson.

"From where should I get water, child?"

You glance furtively toward the guard's wooden hut. You don't have the nerve to ask him for water again. This morning you took some from his jug for Yassin, and if you ask him again . . . No, this time he'll get angry and bring the jug down on your head . . . Better ask elsewhere.

Shading your eyes with your hand, you scan the other end of the bridge. This morning you stopped at a little makeshift shop there to ask the shopkeeper the way to the mine, and the man was kind. Go there again and ask him for water. You start to rise, but then remain nailed to the ground. If a vehicle goes past and the guard doesn't see you, all this waiting will have been for nothing. No, you'd better stay put. The guard isn't the sort of man to wait for you, or call out to you . . . No, Dastaguir, stay just where you are.

"Water, Grandfather, water!"

Yassin is sobbing. You kneel down, take an apple from your bundle, and hold it out to him.

"No, I want water, water!"

You let the apple drop to the ground, heave yourself up, grab Yassin with one hand and the bundle with the other, and hurry off toward the shop.

. . .

The shop is just a small wooden stand with three
mud walls. At the front, four uneven planks form a
window that is covered with plastic sheeting. Behind
a small opening sits a black-bearded man. His shaven
head is hidden by an embroidered cap and he wears
a black waistcoat. A large pair of scales almost completely obscures his thin torso. He is bent over a book.
At the sound of your footsteps, he raises his head and
adjusts his spectacles on his nose. Despite his pensive
expression, his eyes, magnified by the thick lenses, are
strikingly bright. He greets you with a kind smile and
asks, "Back from the mine?"

You spit your naswar onto the ground and respond
meekly.

"No, my good brother, we haven't gone to the mine
yet. We're waiting for a vehicle to pass. My grandson
is very thirsty. Would you be kind enough to give him
a little water . . ."

The shopkeeper pours some water from his jug
into a copper cup. On the back wall of the shop there's
a large painting: behind a large rock, a man holds the
Devil fast by the arm. Both of them are watching an
old man who has fallen into a deep pit.

. . .

The shopkeeper hands the cup to Yassin and asks, "Have you come far?"

"From Abqul. My son works in the mine. I am going to see him."

You keep your eye on the guard's hut.

"It was a bad state of affairs over there, wasn't it?"

The shopkeeper tries to begin a conversation but you keep your eyes fixed on the hut. You remain silent, as if you haven't heard anything. If you are honest, you did not want to hear. Or rather, you don't want to answer. Come on, brother, let Dastaguir be!

"I hear the Russians reduced the whole village to smoke and ashes last week. Is it true?"

You'll have no peace. You came for water, not tears. A mouthful of water, nothing more. Brother, by the grace of God, don't pour salt on our wounds.

What is this, Dastaguir? Moments ago your heart was heavy. You wanted to talk to anyone about anything. Now, here is someone who'll listen to what lies in your heart, whose look alone is a comfort. Say something!

Without taking your eyes off the hut, you answer, "Yes, brother. I was there. I saw everything. I saw my own death . . ."

You fall silent. If you get involved in a conversation, you might forget about the vehicle.

The shopkeeper takes off his glasses and pokes his head out the window to see what interests you so much. As soon as he sees the hut, he understands. He sits back behind his large pair of scales.

"My good brother, it's still too early. A vehicle always comes by around two. You've got two hours ahead of you."

"At two? Why didn't the guard say anything?"

"Probably because he isn't too sure himself. It's not his fault. The cars and lorries come at odd times. Besides, what's on time in this country that transport should be? These days . . ."

"Grandfather, jujube fruits!"

Yassin's words interrupt the shopkeeper. You take the copper cup from Yassin's hands. He hasn't finished it.

"First drink your water."

"I want jujubes, jujubes!"

You put the cup to Yassin's mouth and gesture impatiently for him to finish. Yassin turns his head away and continues in a voice choked with sobs, "Jujubes! Jujubes!"

The shopkeeper reaches out through the shop window and passes Yassin a handful of fruit. The child grabs it and sits down at your feet. And you, cup of water in hand, try to keep your temper. God help me. You sigh.

"That child will make a madman of me."

"Don't say that, father. He's a child. He doesn't understand."

You sigh again, more deeply than before and say, "I'm afraid, brother, the problem isn't that he can't understand . . . The child has gone deaf."

"May God heal him! What happened?"

You finish the remainder of your grandson's water and continue, "He lost his hearing during the bombing of the village. I don't know how to make him understand. I speak to him the same as before. I still scold him . . . It's just habit . . ."

As you talk, you pass the copper cup back through the window. The man takes it and looks sympathetically at Yassin, then at you, then at the empty cup . . . He prefers silence. Like a ghost, he withdraws into the shop. His hand reaches for a small bowl on one of the wooden shelves. He fills it with tea and hands it to you.

"Take a mouthful of tea, good brother. You're exhausted. You still have plenty of time. I know all the vehicles that go to the mine. If one comes, I'll tell you."

You glance over at the guard's hut and, after a moment's hesitation, take the bowl of tea, saying, "You're a man with a good heart. May your forebears rest in peace!"

The sound of your sipping brings a kind smile to the shopkeeper's lips.

"If you're feeling cold, come inside; your grandson also looks cold."

"God bless you, brother, it's fine here. There's sun. We don't want to disturb you anymore. What if a car were to come. I'll drink my tea and we'll be gone."

"Father, I just told you. I'll let you know if a car comes. You can see them pass from here. Now, if you don't want to stay, that's another story."

"I swear to you, brother, it's not a matter of wanting or not wanting. That guard isn't the kind of man to make a car wait."

"Dear father, it takes a long time for him to issue a pass and then open the barrier. And he isn't a bad man, that guard. I know him. He comes here a lot. It's sorrow that has ruined him."

. . .

The man falls silent. He puts a cigarette into the corner of his mouth and lights it. Then he goes on:

"You know, father, sorrow can turn to water and spill from your eyes, or it can sharpen your tongue into a sword, or it can become a time bomb that, one day, will explode and destroy you . . . The sorrow of Fateh the guard is like all three. When he comes to see me, his sadness flows out in tears. If he remains alone in his hut, it becomes a bomb . . . When he steps out of the hut and sees others, his sorrow turns itself into a sword and he wants to . . ."

You don't hear the rest of the shopkeeper's words. Your thoughts pull you inward, to where your own misery lies. Which has your sorrow become? Tears? No, otherwise you'd cry. A sword? No, you haven't wounded anyone yet. A bomb? You're still living. You can't describe your sorrow; it hasn't taken shape yet. It hasn't had a chance to show itself. If only it wouldn't take shape at all. If only it would fall silent, be forgotten . . . It will be so, of course it will . . . As soon as you see Murad, your son . . . Where are you, Murad?

"Good father, where have you drifted off to?"

The shopkeeper's question brings you back from your interior journey. You reply humbly:

"Nothing, brother, you were talking of sorrow . . ."

You finish the tea in one gulp and give the empty bowl back to the shopkeeper. You pat your pockets, take out your box of naswar and put a pinch into your mouth. Then you go and sit at the base of one of the wooden posts propping up the shop's corrugated-iron roof. Yassin plays silently with the stones from the jujube fruit. You take him by the arm and pull him to your side. You want to say something, but the sound of footsteps silences you. A man in military uniform approaches.

"*Salaam*, Mirza Qadir."

"*Waleykom Salaam*, Hashmet Khan."

The soldier asks for a pack of cigarettes and engages Mirza Qadir in conversation.

At your feet, your grandson is busy playing with an ant attracted by the naswar you have spat out onto the ground. Yassin mixes the naswar, the earth, and the ant together with a jujube stone. The insect squirms in the green mud.

The soldier says good-bye to Mirza Qadir, and walks past you.

Yassin digs with his jujube stone at a footprint left by the soldier.

The ant is no longer there. Ant, mud, and naswar are stuck to the boot of the departing soldier.

Mirza Qadir abandons his spot behind the scales and withdraws to a corner of the shop to perform his midday prayers.

It has been a week now since you've been to the mosque or prayed. So, have you forgotten about God? No, your clothes are not in a fit state for prayer. This same pair of clothes has been on your back day and night for a week. Yet, God is merciful . . .

Whether you pray or not, the reality is that God isn't concerned with you. If only he'd turn his attention to you for a moment, if only he'd come to your side . . . No, God has forsaken his subjects. If this is how he looks after his subjects, you yourself, in your absolute ruin, could be lord of a thousand worlds!

God help me! Dastaguir, you're committing blasphemy. Damn the temptations of Satan. Damn you.

Occupy your thoughts with something else. But what?

Aren't you hungry? Spit out your naswar.

"My good man, your tongue will wear out. Your

insides will wear out. For days naswar has been your bread and water."

You hear the words Murad's mother would say to you before you sat down to eat. When Murad was in prison, you would make up excuses to avoid coming to the table. Naswar under your tongue, you'd disappear into the little garden saying that you wanted to catch the last rays of daylight or that you had weeding to do. You would sit among the plants, and open your laden heart to the earth and flowers. Your wife's voice would boom out into the courtyard declaring that, after your death until the Day of Judgment, your mouth would fill with earth and your body would turn to earth from which a tobacco field would grow. In Hell you would burn in an inferno of tobacco leaves . . . forever.

You have yet to face Judgment Day and you are already burning. Who needs the flames of Hell and a bonfire of tobacco?

You spit out your naswar. You take a piece of bread out of the bundle and share it with Yassin.

Your teeth aren't able to chew the bread. No, they are. It's the bread that is at fault. It is days old and hard. If there's one thing that's still all right, it's your teeth. You have teeth, but no bread. If only you had the right to choose: teeth or bread. Would that be free will?

. . .

You take an apple from the bag and recommence
your conversation with God. You request that He
lower himself from the heavens. You untie and spread
out the apple-blossom scarf as if to invite him to share
your dry bread. You want to ask him what it is you
have done to deserve such a destiny.

"The soldier says the Russians destroyed the village."
Mirza Qadir comes between you and God. You
bless him for asking you a question that prevents you
from continuing your argument with God. You ask
for divine mercy and respond to Mirza Qadir.

"Don't ask, brother. They didn't spare a single
life . . . I don't understand why God saw fit to punish
us . . . The village was reduced to dust."

"Why did they attack?"

"My friend, in this country, if you wonder why
something happened, you have to start by making the dead talk. What do we understand? A while
back a group of government troublemakers came to
our village to enlist fighters for the Russians. Half
the young people fled, the other half hid. On the pretext of searching the houses, the government soldiers
wrecked and looted everything. In the middle of the

night, men from the next village arrived and killed the government soldiers . . . The next morning they left with the men who had hidden to avoid serving under the red flag . . . Not even a day had passed before the Russians came and surrounded the village. I was at the mill. Suddenly, there was an explosion. I ran out. I saw fire and clouds of dust. I ran in the direction of my house. Why wasn't I killed before I reached home? What wrong had I committed to be condemned to witness . . ."

Your throat is seized with sobs. Tears well in your eyes. No, they are not tears. Your grief is melting and overflowing. Let it flow!

Mirza Qadir, stunned into silence in the entrance of his shop, looks like a portrait, as if he has become part of the scene on the wall behind him.

"I ran toward the house through the dust and fire. Before I arrived, I saw Yassin's mother. She was running, completely naked . . . She wasn't shouting, she was laughing. She was running about like a madwoman. She had been in the bathhouse. A bomb had hit and destroyed it. Women were buried alive and died. But my daughter-in-law . . . If only I'd been blind and hadn't seen her dishonored. I ran after her. She vanished into the smoke and flames. I came to the house, not knowing how I'd found it. There was nothing left . . . The house had become a grave. A grave for my wife, a grave for my other son, his wife, and their children . . ."

A sob constricts your throat. A tear drops from your eye. With the loose flap of your turban, you wipe it away:

"Only my grandson survived. But he doesn't understand what I say. I feel like I'm speaking to a stone. It tears me to pieces . . . It's not enough to talk, brother. If your words aren't heard, those words turn to tears . . ."

You hug Yassin's head against your body. The child raises his eyes and looks at you. He stands and calls out, "Grandfather's crying. My uncle's dead, Mummy's gone . . . Qader's dead, Grandma's dead!"

Each time Yassin sees you crying, he repeats these words. Each time, he goes on to describe the bombing, miming it with his hands:

"The bomb was huge. It brought silence. The tanks took away people's voices and left. They even took Grandfather's voice away. Grandfather can't talk anymore, he can't tell me off . . ."

The child laughs and runs toward the guard's hut.

You call to him. "Come back! Where are you going?"

It's useless. Let him play.

Mirza Qadir, who has been silent till now, as if unable to find words to lessen your suffering, mumbles something under his breath and offers you his condolences. Then he starts to speak, in a calm, measured way:

"Venerable father, these days the dead are more fortunate than the living. What are we to do? We're on the eve of destruction. Men have lost all sense of honor. Power has become their faith instead of faith being their power. There are no longer any courageous men. Who now remembers the story of the hero Rostam? Today, it is Sohrab, his son, who murders his very own father and, excuse the expression, screws his own mother. We are once again at the mercy of the tyrant Zohak's snakes—snakes that feed on the minds of the young . . ."

He breaks off to light a cigarette, points to the scene painted on the wall and adds, "Actually, it is today's youth who are Zohaks. They're on the same path as the Devil, pushing their own fathers into a pit . . . and one day soon their own snakes will devour their minds."

. . .

He gazes into your eyes. Your eyes are fixed on the entrance to the shop. The interior has become a spacious room at the far end of which your uncle sits by his water pipe. You are a child of about Yassin's age. You sit at your uncle's feet as he recites Ferdusi's epic, the *Book of Kings*. He speaks of Rostam, of Sohrab, of Tahmina . . . He tells of the battle between father and son, of the talisman that saved Rostam, of the death of Sohrab . . . Your younger brother starts crying and rushes from the room to go and lay his head on your mother's lap.

"No, Sohrab is stronger than Rostam!" he sobs.

Your mother says, "Yes, my child, Sohrab is stronger than Rostam."

And you cry, too, but you don't leave the room. In silence, with tear-filled eyes, you remain at your uncle's feet, waiting to know whether Rostam will go on fighting after Sohrab's death . . .

Mirza Qadir's cough brings you back from your childhood.

The shop returns to being small. Mirza Qadir's head appears in the window frame.

"Are you going to the mine to work with your son?"

"No, brother, I've come only to see him . . . He knows nothing of the misfortune that has struck the family. On the one hand, there's the misery of the bombing, on the other, the misery of telling such a thing to my own son. How should I tell him? I don't know. He's not the type to take it quietly . . . You'd be able to take his life before you offended his honor. He has a temper . . ."

You bring your hand to your forehead and close your eyes.

"My son, my only son will surely go mad. It would be better if I didn't tell him."

"He's strong, father. You must tell him. He must accept it. One day or another he'll find out. It is better that he hear it from you, that you tell him you are with him and share the burden of his sorrow. Don't leave him alone. Make him understand that man's fate contains such things, that he is not alone, that he has both you and his son, that you are his source of strength and that he is yours. These hardships are everyone's fate, war has no mercy . . ."

Mirza Qadir moves closer and lowers his voice.

"The law of war is the law of the sacrifice. In sacrifice, there is either blood on your throat or on your hands."

"Why?" you ask naively.

Mirza Qadir tosses his cigarette butt away. In the same soft tone, he adds, "Brother, the logic of war is the logic of sacrifice. There's no 'why' about it. What matters is the act alone, not the cause or the effect."

He falls silent. He reads your eyes for the impact of his words. You nod your head as if you have understood. You wonder what the logic of war could possibly be. His words in themselves are well and good, but they're no cure for the troubles you and your son share. Murad is not a man who listens to advice or thinks about the law or logic of war. To him, blood is the only answer for blood. He'll take vengeance, even at the cost of his own neck. That's all there is to it. And he won't care too much if he has blood on his hands either.

"Old man, where are you? Come before your grandson drives me mad!"

The guard's shouts alarm you. You jump up, shouting, "Here I am, I'm coming!" as you run back to the hut.

Yassin is standing in front of the hut, tossing stones at it. The guard has taken shelter and is roaring with fury. You reach Yassin, slap him smartly on his small head, and take the stones out of his hands. The furious guard emerges.

"Your grandson's gone mad. He began throwing stones at the hut. It didn't matter what I said to him, he didn't pay a blind bit of notice . . ."

"I'm sorry, brother. The child is deaf. He can't hear a word . . ."

You take Yassin back toward the shop. Mirza Qadir comes out and makes his way toward the guard, laughing. You take up your place against the wooden post again and hug Yassin's head to your chest.

Yassin doesn't cry. As usual, he's bewildered.

"Have tanks come here too?" he asks.

"How should I know? Be quiet!"

You both fall silent. You both know that questions and answers are in vain. But then Yassin continues:

"They must've come and taken the voice of the shopkeeper and the voice of the guard . . . Grandfather, have the Russians come and taken away everyone's voice? What do they do with all the voices? Why did you let them take away your voice? If you hadn't, would they've killed you? Grandma didn't give them her voice and she's dead. If she were here, she'd tell me the story of Baba Kharkash . . . No, if she were here, she'd have no voice . . ."

. . .

He falls silent for a few moments, then he asks again, "Grandfather, do I have a voice?"

You answer involuntarily, "Yes."

He repeats the question. You look at him and nod "yes," making him understand. The child falls silent again. Then he asks, "So why am I alive?"

He buries his face under your clothes. As if he wants to put an ear to your chest to listen for some sound from within. He hears nothing and shuts his eyes. Inside himself everything must make a sound. If only you could enter inside him and tell him the story of Baba Kharkash . . .

Your wife's unsteady voice reaches your ears:

"Once upon a time there was a man named Baba Kharkash . . ."

You find yourself standing on the large branch of a jujube tree, stark naked. You've climbed up it to shake down jujubes for Yassin. At the base of the tree, Yassin is gathering the fruit. Without being able to help it, you start to urinate. Crying, Yassin moves away from the bottom of the tree and sits at the base of another. He empties the apples out of your scarf and replaces them with his jujubes, then ties up the bundle again. Digging into the ground with his small hands, he finds a door near the surface, secured with a big padlock. He opens the lock with a jujube stone and crawls underground.

"Yassin, where are you going? Wait! I'm coming down!"

Yassin doesn't hear your shouts and the door shuts behind him. You try to climb down from the tree, but the tree grows bigger and taller. You fall from the tree, but you don't hit the ground . . .

Your eyes are half-open. Your heart pounds in your rib cage. Yassin's head is still calmly buried under your clothes. Mirza Qadir is having a conversation with the guard beside the wooden hut. You try to open your eyes as wide as possible. You don't want to doze off again. You don't want to dream. But the heaviness of your eyes has crushed your will . . .

A woman's voice rings in your ears.

"Yassin! Yassin! Yassin!"

It's the voice of Zaynab, Yassin's mother. Her laughter echoes around your head. Her voice comes from somewhere far below. You step to the door that leads underground. It is closed. You call out for Zaynab, but your voice reverberates on the other side of the door. Then the door opens and you see Fateh, the guard. He laughs and says, "Welcome. Come in. I was waiting for you."

You walk down into the ground. Fateh closes the door on you from the outside. From the other side of the door, the sound of his laughter rings in your ears.

"You've been wanting desperately to leave," he says to you. "Since the morning you've been driving me mad. So, go on!"

Underground it's cold and damp. You take in the smell of clay. There's a large garden, an empty garden, without flowers or vegetation, a garden with narrow paths covered in mud and lined with bare oak trees.

Zaynab sits naked under a tree, next to a little girl. You call out to her. Your voice doesn't seem to reach her. She lifts the little girl from the ground, wraps her in the apple-blossom scarf, kisses her on the cheek, then carries her away. Yassin is naked in a jujube tree. He says that the little girl is his sister, that he gave his mother his grandmother's apple-blossom scarf, the one you knotted into a bundle, so that she could put it around his sister because it's cold. But Yassin doesn't have a sister! A few days ago, Zaynab was only four months pregnant. How quickly she's given birth! How quickly her daughter has grown!

Yassin is shivering with cold. He wants to climb down from the tree, but he can't. The tree keeps growing bigger and taller. Yassin weeps.

You feel snowflakes land on your skin. The garden paths fill with snow.

Zaynab runs from one tree to the next. You call out to her again. She doesn't hear. She runs across the snow naked, the little girl in her arms. She laughs. Her feet leave no prints in the snow, but the sound of her steps echoes through the garden.

Yassin calls for his mother. His voice has become high-pitched like hers . . . You look at his body. It's the body of a young girl. In place of his small penis, there is a girl's vulva. You are overcome with panic. Without thinking, you call for Murad. Your voice is stuck in your throat. It reverberates in your chest. Your voice has become Yassin's—weak, confused, questioning:

"Murad. Murad! Murad?"

Someone grips your shoulders from behind. You turn around in horror. Mirza Qadir, smiling his habitual smile, says, "Instead of the brains of our kids, Zohak's snakes are eating their pricks."

Terror seizes you. You want to free your shoulders from Mirza Qadir's grip. But you don't have the strength.

You open your eyes. Your body is covered in sweat. Your hands tremble.

In front of you are two kind eyes:

"Father, get up. Your lift is here."

Lift? For what? Where do you want to go? Where are you?

"Father, a vehicle headed to the mine."

You recognize Mirza Qadir's voice and come back to your senses. Yassin sleeps quietly in your arms. You want to wake him.

Mirza Qadir says, "Father, leave your grandson here. First, go there on your own, speak to your son in private. Then come back here. There's no room for both of you to spend the night at the mine. If your son sees his own child in this state, it'll be even worse . . ."

It's a good suggestion. Imagine what will happen when Yassin sees his father. He'll throw himself into his arms and, before you are able to say anything, he'll start shouting, "Uncle's dead, Mummy's gone . . . Qader's dead, Grandma's dead! Grandfather cries . . ."

Murad's heart will stop when he hears Yassin. How could you make Yassin understand that he shouldn't say anything?

You accept Mirza Qadir's offer, but a sense of foreboding settles within you. How can you abandon your grandson, the only son of your only son, to someone you don't know? You've known Mirza Qadir for no more than two hours. What will Murad say?

"Old man, are you coming or not?"

It's the guard's voice. You remain silently where you are with Mirza Qadir, your eyes full of questions. What should you do? Yassin or Murad? Dastaguir, this is not the time for questions. Surrender Yassin to God and go to Murad.

"Old man, your lift's leaving."

"I leave Yassin to you and God."

Mirza Qadir's look and smile quell all your doubts and fears.

You take your bundle and head for the hut. A big truck awaits you. You greet the driver and climb in. The guard, who's standing in front of the hut—slouched, dusty, drowsy, dressed in a makeshift uniform, with the same half-smoked cigarette between his lips—lifts the wooden beam blocking the road and waves the driver through.

The driver exchanges a few words with you. The guard yells angrily, "Shahmard! Are you going or not?"

Shahmard raises his hand in a gesture of apology and drives off.

The truck speeds onto the property of the mine. Through the rearview mirror, you watch the guard beside his hut disappear in a cloud of dust. You don't know why but his disappearance pleases you. Come on, the guard isn't a bad man. He's grief-stricken, that's all. You bless his father's soul. May he excuse you if you've thought ill of his son.

Your heart pounds in anticipation of visiting Murad. Your reunion is close now. This very road will take you to your son. Blessed be this road, a road that Murad has traveled many times. Would Shahmard stop the truck, so you could step down and prostrate yourself on this earth, before these stones, before these brambles that have kissed your son's feet? Blessed be the prints left by your feet, Murad!

· · ·

"Did you wait long?"

Shahmard's question prevents you from kissing Murad's footprints.

"Since nine this morning."

You both fall silent again.

Shahmard is a young man—about thirty years old, maybe even younger. But the blackened, smoked skin covering his bones and the lines and wrinkles on his face make him look older. An old astrakhan cap sits on his dirty hair. A black moustache covers his upper lip and yellow teeth. His head is pushed forward. His eyes, circled by black rings, dart about.

A partially smoked cigarette rests behind his right ear. Its scent fills your nostrils. You imagine it is the smell of coal, the smell of the mine, the smell of Murad—the sight of whom at any moment now will light up your eyes. You'll kiss his forehead. No, you'll kiss his feet. You'll kiss his eyes and his hands like a child reunited with his father. Yes, you will be Murad's son. He'll take you into his arms and console you. With his manly hands he'll hold your trembling ones and say, "Dastaguir, my child!"

If only you were his son—his Yassin. Deaf like Yassin. You'd see Murad but you wouldn't hear him. You wouldn't hear him say, "Why have you come?"

"Have you come to work in the mine?" Shahmard asks.
"No, I have come to see my son."

Your eyes drift over the rolling hills of the valley. You take a deep breath and continue.
"I come to drive a dagger into my son's heart."
Shahmard gives you a confused look, laughs, and says, "Dear God, I'm giving a ride to a swordsman."
With your gaze still lost in the valley, in its black stones, its dust and its scrub, you say, "No, brother, it's that I bear great sorrow and sorrow sometimes turns into a sword."
"You sound like Mirza Qadir."
"You know Mirza Qadir?"
"Who doesn't know him? In a way, he's a guide for us all."
"He's a man with a great heart. I didn't know him, but I just spent two hours in his company. I was won over. What he says is right. He understands sorrow. From his first glance, he instills trust. You can tell him

whatever lies in your heart . . . In our day, men like Mirza Qadir are rare. Where is he from? Why is he here?"

Shahmard takes the half-smoked cigarette from behind his ear, puts it between his dry lips and lights it. He inhales deeply and says, "Mirza Qadir is from the Shorbazar district of Kabul. He has only had a shop here for a short time. He doesn't like to talk about himself. He says little to those he doesn't trust. It took me a year to find out where he came from and what brought him here."

Shahmard falls silent again. But you want to know more about Mirza Qadir, the man to whom you've entrusted your grandson. Finally he continues:

"He had a shop in Shorbazar. In the daytime he'd work as a merchant and, in the evenings, as a storyteller. Each night a crowd would gather at the shop. He was a popular man who commanded great respect. One day his young son was called up to serve in the army. A year later he returned. He'd been made an officer and trained in Russia. This didn't please Mirza Qadir. He didn't want his son to have a military career. But the son liked the uniform, the money, and the guns. He ran away. Mirza disowned him. The sorrow killed his wife. Mirza left Kabul. His home and shop remained behind. He came to the coal mine, where he worked for two years. With his first savings he set up that shop. From morning to evening he sits there, writing or reading. He's beholden to no one. If he likes you, he'll respect you, but if he doesn't like you, best not to let even your dog pass his shop . . . Some nights I stay with him till dawn. The whole night he reads stories and poems. He knows the *Book of Kings* by heart . . ."

Mirza Qadir's words ring in your tired ears. He spoke about Rostam and Sohrab, and of the Sohrabs of our day . . . The Sohrabs of today don't die, they kill.

You think about Murad. Your Murad isn't a Sohrab who would kill his own father. But you . . .

You are a Rostam. You'll go and drive the dagger of grief into your son's heart.

No, you don't want to be Rostam. You're Dastaguir, an unknown father, not a hero burdened with regret. Murad's your son, not a martyred hero. Let Rostam rest in his bed of words; let Sohrab lie in his shroud of paper. Return to your Murad, to the moment when you will hold his black hands in your trembling hands

49

and your wet eyes will meet his exhausted eyes. When you will have to seek strength from Ali, asking for help in saying what you must say:

"Murad, your mother gave her life for you . . ."

No, why begin with his mother?

"Murad, your brother . . ."

No, why his brother?

But then with whom should you begin?

"Murad, my child, the house has been destroyed . . ."

"How?"

"Bombs . . ."

"Was anyone hurt?"

Silence.

"Where's Yassin?"

"He's alive."

"Where's Zaynab?"

"Zaynab? . . . Zaynab's . . . in the village."

"And mother?"

Then you should say, "Your mother gave her life for you . . ."

And Murad will start to weep.

"My son, be strong! These things happen to all men one day or another . . . If she was your mother, she was also my wife. She's gone. When Death comes, it makes no difference whether it is for a mother or a wife . . . My son, Death came to our village . . ."

And then tell him about his wife, tell him about his brother . . . And then tell him that Yassin's alive, and that you have left him with Mirza Qadir because he was tired. He was sleeping . . . Don't say anything about his condition.

The noise of a truck coming from the opposite direction disrupts your conversation with Murad. It passes at high speed, raising clouds of dust. Dust erases the lines of the valley. Shahmard brakes.

"Will you spend the night with your son?" he asks.

"I don't know if there will be a place for me."

"He'll find something."

"Anyway, I have to get back. I left my grandson with Mirza Qadir."

"Why didn't you take him with you?"

"I was afraid."

"Of what?"

"Why should I upset you with all this, brother."

"Don't worry about that. Tell me."

"All right, I'll tell you."

Shahmard stays silent. As if he doesn't want to goad you. Maybe he thinks you don't want to talk.

How could you not? When the village was destroyed, with whom could you sit and weep? With whom could you share your grief? With whom could you mourn? Everyone mourned their own dead. Your brother sat next to a pile of rubble, listening hopefully for a familiar voice to rise from beneath collapsed roofs and walls. Your maternal cousin, weeping, picked through the rubble for a piece of clothing or a scarf to use as a burial shroud. Your brother-in-law, lying next to a dead cow in the demolished barn, laughed as he suckled milk from its stiffened udder . . .

But you had Yassin. He couldn't hear your sobs, but he could see your grief. With whom did *you* sit? Whom did *you* comfort? You wanted to run from everybody. You were like an owl perched high on a ruin, or in an abandoned cemetery. If it weren't for Murad, if it weren't for Yassin, you would never have left that place. Thank God for Murad, for Yassin. You'd have stayed amid ruins till you turned to dust . . .

Dastaguir, where have you wandered off to this time? Shahmard wants you to explain why you didn't bring Yassin and you have drifted off into daydreams. Say something to him. Tell him about your people. Make an effort. They deserve some prayers. Who so far, apart from Mirza Qadir, has offered you their condolences? Who has prayed for the deliverance of their souls? Allow others to say the Fatiha prayer for your dead and to share your suffering. Say something!

And you speak. Speak of the ruins of your village, of your wife, your son, your two daughters-in-law, Yassin . . . And weep.

Shahmard is mute. His eyes dart, restlessly seeking appropriate words. He finds them. He whispers the Fatiha. He offers you his condolences and falls into silence again.

You continue. You speak of Murad. Of how to tell him about the death of his mother, his wife, and his brother. Still Shahmard remains silent. What should he say? All of his rage at hearing your story has gone to his legs. His feet are heavy. You can tell from the speed of the truck.

You also fall silent.

The bouncing of the truck and the drone of the engine make you feel sick. You want to close your eyes for a while.

A military jeep appears behind the truck. It overtakes you, throwing up dark dust.

. . .

Within a black billow of dust, you see Murad's wife running naked in front of the truck. Her damp hair streams behind her, parting the dust—as if she were sweeping away the dust with her hair. Her white breasts dance on her chest. Drops of water fall from her skin like dewdrops.

"Zaynab! Get out of the way of the truck!" you shout to her.

Your voice is confined to the truck. It doesn't reach outside. It reverberates endlessly around the cab. You want to roll down the window and free your voice so it can reach Zaynab. But you don't have the strength. You feel heavy. Your bundle weighs on your knees. You want to lift it up and put it beside you. But you don't have the strength. You untie it. Inside the apples have become black, they've turned to coal . . . Coalapples. You laugh to yourself. A bitter laugh. You want to ask Shahmard about the mystery of the coalapples. In place of Shahmard, Murad sits at the wheel. You can't prevent yourself from crying out. You don't know if it's from fear, surprise, or joy.

Murad doesn't look at you. He stares at the road, at Zaynab. You shout his name again. Still Murad doesn't hear. It's as if he too has gone deaf.

Zaynab continues to run in front of the truck. The dust gradually settles on her white, damp skin. A veil of black dust covers her body. She is no longer naked . . .

The jolts of the truck blur your view of Zaynab. She and the road disappear in a cloud of dark dust.

You take a deep breath and glance furtively toward the driver's seat. Murad isn't there. Thank God. You've woken up. You look around silently. Your bundle is at your side. An apple has rolled out onto the seat.

Nervously you look in front of the truck again. Zaynab is not there. Zaynab threw her naked body headlong into the fire. She was burned alive. She was burned naked. She left this world naked. She burned to death before your very eyes . . . How will you tell all this to Murad? Do you have to? No. Zaynab is simply dead. Like everyone else. There's nothing more to it. She died like all the others—in the house, beneath the bombs. She is bound for Paradise. We are the ones burning in the fires of Hell. The dead are more fortunate than the living.

What fine words you've learned, Dastaguir. But you know they're of no use. Murad's not the sort to ponder matters or withdraw calmly to a corner and cry. Murad is a man. He is Murad, son of Dastaguir. He's a mountain of fortitude, a vast land of pride. The smallest slight to his honor and he catches fire. Then he either burns himself or causes others to burn. The death of his own mother, wife and brother won't go unanswered. He'll seek vengeance. He has to take revenge . . .

On whom? What could he do alone? They'll kill him too. Dastaguir, have you lost your mind!

All you have left is a son, and you want to sacrifice him? Why? To bring back your wife and your other son? Swallow your anger. Leave Murad alone. Allow him to live. Let my tongue be still! Let my mouth fill with dust! Murad, sleep in peace.

After exploring your pockets, you pull out your box of naswar and offer some to Shahmard. You put a small amount into the palm of his hand and place some on your own palm before putting it under your tongue.

Silence.

You watch the rocks and scrub race past. It's not you who are passing them. No. It's as if they are passing you. You're not moving. It's the world that's moving. You've been condemned to exist and watch the world pass, to watch your wife pass, to watch your children pass . . .

Your hands tremble. Your heart flutters. Your sight goes dim. You roll down the window of the truck to refresh yourself. The air isn't refreshing. It has become thick, heavy, and black. It's not your sight that has gone dim, it's the air that has grown dark.

"Dastaguir, what have you done with my scarf?"

It's Murad's mother. You see your wife at the base of the hills, running at the same pace as the truck. You untie the bundle and let the coal-apples fall out. Then you let the scarf blow out of the window. The cloth dances through the air. Murad's mother runs after it, dancing as she goes.

"We've arrived."

The image of Murad's mother reflected in the pools of your pupils is lost to the ripples of Shahmard's voice.

You open your wet eyes. The truck is nearing the mine. You sense that Murad is close. Your chest tightens, your heart swells, your veins constrict, your blood freezes . . . Your tongue has become a piece of wood, a charred piece, half-burned, an ember, a silent piece of coal . . . Your throat is dry. Water! You swallow your naswar. The smell of ash fills your nostrils. You take a deep breath. You smell Murad. You fill your lungs to their utmost with his scent. For the first time, you realize how small your lungs are and how big your heart is—as big as your sorrow . . .

Shahmard slows the truck and turns to the left. He comes to a halt at the entrance to the mine. A guard appears from a wooden hut, just like the one at the start of the road. He asks for papers from Shahmard, looks them over, and begins a conversation. You sit silently. You don't move a muscle. Actually, you wouldn't have the strength to do so if you wanted to. You hold your breath. For a few moments, you're nothing but a hollow shell. Your lifeless gaze falls through the grille of the mine's large iron gate. You sense that Murad is waiting for you beyond the gate. Murad, don't ask Dastaguir why he has come.

The truck passes through the gate and enters the grounds of the mine. At the foot of a large hill lies a line of concrete workers' quarters. Which of them is Murad's? Men with blackened faces, wearing metal construction helmets, come down the hill as others climb up. You don't see Murad among them. The truck heads toward the small concrete buildings and stops in front of one. Shahmard suggests you get out and ask the mine's foreman about your son.

You experience a moment of confusion and don't react. There isn't enough strength in your hand to open the door. You are like a child who doesn't want to be separated from his father. You ask Shahmard, "Is my son here?"

"Of course, but you'll have to ask the foreman where."

"Where is the foreman?"

Shahmard points out a building to the right of the truck.

Your weak, trembling hand has difficulty opening the truck door. You put your feet on the ground. Your legs are of no use. They don't have the strength to hold you up. But your body is not heavy. It's the heaviness of the air that's pressing down on your body. The air is weighty and thick. You rest your hand on your waist. Shahmard passes your bundle through the window and says, "Father, I'm heading back to town between five and six. If you want to come, wait for me at the gate."

Bless you. You say this to yourself. To him you only nod. Your tongue doesn't have the strength to move. Words, like the air, have become heavy . . . The truck moves off. You remain nailed to the ground in a cloud of dust. A few black-faced miners walk by. Murad? No, Murad's not among them. Come on, go to the foreman and ask.

You try to move. Your legs are still tired and weak. It's as if they are sunk into the depths of the earth, all the way down to its molten center . . . Your feet burn inside your shoes. Wait a while. Take a deep breath. Calm down. Move your legs. You can walk. So walk.

You reach the foreman's building and stop outside the door. It's an imposing door. Like the entrance to a fortress. What might be on the other side? Probably a mineshaft. One that is long and deep, that goes right down to the depths of the earth, all the way down to furnaces of molten rock . . .

You place your hand on the doorknob. It is burning hot.

Dastaguir, what are you doing? Are you going to plunge a dagger into the chest of Murad, your only remaining child? Can't you keep your troubles to yourself? Leave Murad alone! One day he'll find out. It's better if he hears it from someone else's lips.

What should you do, then? Go and disappear from his life? No! What, then? You can't tell him today, you're exhausted, turn back! You'll come back tomorrow. Tomorrow? But tomorrow it'll be the same story, the same anguish. Knock on this door, then! Your hands have become heavy. You step back.

Where are you going, Dastaguir? Can't you decide? Don't abandon Murad. Take the hand of your son like a father and teach him about life.

You walk up to the door. You knock. The door creaks loudly. The shaven head of a young man peers out. He is blind in his right eye. A fine web of red blood vessels worms over the white of the eye. With a gesture of his head he asks you what you want. Gathering your resolve, you say, "Salaam. Murad, the son of Dastaguir, is my child. I have come to see him."

The man opens the door wider. The inquiring expression has left his face. Taken aback, he turns his head to a man who sits writing at a large desk at the far end of the room.

"Foreman sir, Murad's father is here."

On hearing these words, the foreman freezes. His pen drops onto his desk. His eyes bore into yours. A weighty silence fills the space between you. With all your strength, you draw yourself up and enter the room. But the silence and the strange expression of the foreman gradually burden your shoulders. Your legs tremble. Your body begins to stoop again. Dastaguir, what have you done? You have asked for Murad. You are going to kill Murad . . . No, may all be well. You won't speak to him. If he asks you why you've come, you'll say something else, an excuse. You'll say that his uncle visited the village, and you returned together by car to Pul-i-Khumri. Taking advantage of the opportunity, you came to the mine to get news of Murad. That's all. Afterward you're returning to the village . . . Stay well, Murad!

The foreman stands and limps toward you. He places his heavy hand on your tired shoulder. It's as if the mine, with its big hill, its coal, and its square cement buildings, rests there on your shoulders. Your body stoops even further. The foreman circles around you. He's very tall. It's his left leg that makes him limp. He is a mountain next to you. His mouth is open. As if he's about to devour you. His big black teeth are concealed under a dirty moustache. He smells of coal.

"Welcome, brother. You must be tired. Sit down."

He directs you toward the wooden chair in front of his desk and then limps back to his place on the other side of the table. You sit down, keeping your bundle pressed against you. On the wall in front of you, just above the foreman's chair, hangs a large framed portrait of him. He wears a military uniform and, under his black mustache, a victorious smile.

The foreman, sitting in his chair again, starts to speak, slowly and carefully.

"Murad is down the mine. It's his shift now. Would you like tea?"

In a quavering voice, you reply, "God protect you, sir."

The foreman calls to the man who led you inside and sends him for two cups of tea.

You are relieved that Murad isn't available right away. It'll give you some time to come up with coherent answers and words of comfort. Maybe the foreman can help you. You ask, "When will he be off work?"

"At about eight this evening."

Eight this evening? Shahmard will be returning at six. Where will you go till eight? What will you do? Could you spend the night here? And what about Yassin?

"Good brother, Murad is fine. He has received news of the incident that has stricken his family. May God absolve them and give their souls peace . . ."

You don't hear the rest of the foreman's words. Murad has received news? You repeat the words to yourself a few times. As if you don't understand what they mean. Or you didn't hear correctly. After all, at your age one grows hard of hearing and misunderstands.

You ask loudly, "He has received news?"

"Yes, brother, he knows."

Then why didn't he return to the village? No, it can't be your Murad. It must be another Murad. After all, your son's not the only one with that name. In this very mine there are probably ten men with his name. The foreman hasn't understood that you're looking for Murad, son of Dastaguir. He must also be hard of hearing. Start again.

"I'm talking about Murad, son of Dastaguir, from Abqul."

"That's right, brother, I'm referring to him too."

"My child Murad learned that his mother, his wife, and his brother have died and he . . ."

"Yes, brother. He even heard about you, that you . . . May God protect you."

"No, I'm alive. His own son's alive too . . ."

"Praise God . . ."

Why praise God? If only Yassin and Dastaguir had died as well! That way a father wouldn't have had to witness the frailty of his son, and a son the helplessness of his father. What has become of Murad?

Something must have happened to him. The mine has collapsed and he has been entombed in coal. Swear to God, foreman, tell the truth. What has happened to Murad?

Your eyes flit about. They seek an answer from every object: from the worm-eaten table; from the portrait in which the foreman is immortalized; from the pen lying lifelessly on the paper; from the ground that trembles under your feet; from the roof that is collapsing; from the window that will never be opened again; from the hill that has devoured your child; from the coal that has blackened his bones . . .

"What has happened to Murad?" you ask in a loud voice.

"Nothing, thank God, he's fine."

"Then why didn't he come to the village?"

"I didn't allow him to."

The bundle of apples falls from your knees to the ground. Once more, your eyes search the room before fixing on the dirty lines of the foreman's face. Once more, your mind fills with questions—and with hate.

Who does this foreman think he is? What does he take himself to be? You're Murad's father. Who is he?

He has taken Murad from you. There is no longer any Murad. Your Murad's gone . . .

The foreman's gruff voice echoes around the room: "He would have gone. But I didn't let him. Had I, he would have been killed as well . . ."

What of it? Death would have been better than dishonor!

The servant brings two cups of tea and gives one to you and the other to the foreman. They begin a conversation. You can't hear what they're saying.

With trembling hands you hold the cup on your knees. But your legs are trembling too. A few drops of tea spill onto your knees. They don't burn you. No, they do burn you, but you don't feel it. You're already burning within. Within, a fire burns that is more fierce than the tea. A fire stoked by the questions of friends and enemies, relatives and strangers:

"What happened?"

"Did you see Murad?"

"Did you speak to him?"

"What did you tell him?"

"What did he do?"

"What did he say?"

. . .

And how will you answer them? With silence.
You saw your son. Your son has heard about everything. But he didn't come for his dead mother, wife,
and brother. Murad has lost all his integrity, he has
become shameless . . .

Your hands tremble. You put the cup on the table.
You know that your sorrow has taken shape now. It
has become a bomb. It will explode and it will destroy
you too—like Fateh the guard. Mirza Qadir does indeed know all about sorrow. Your chest collapses like
an old house, an empty house . . . Murad has vacated
his place inside you. What does it matter if an abandoned house collapses?

"Your tea will get cold, brother."
"It's not important."

The foreman continues:
"Until two days ago Murad wasn't doing well. He
wouldn't go near bread or water. He withdrew to a
corner of his room. He didn't move. He didn't sleep.
One night he went out of his quarters completely
naked. He joined the group of miners who spend the

night beating their chests in repentance around a fire. At dawn he began to run around and around the fire and then he threw himself into the flames. His companions came to his aid and pulled him out . . ."

Slowly you open your clenched fists. Your shoulders, drawn up to your ears, relax. You know Murad. Murad isn't one to remain calm. He either burns or causes others to burn. He either destroys or is destroyed. He didn't set fire to others this time, he burned himself. He didn't cause destruction, he was destroyed . . . But why didn't he come back and burn together with his mother's corpse? If Murad were Dastaguir's Murad, he would have returned to the village, he would have beaten his chest beside his lost ones, not around a fire . . . They told him that you too were dead. The day when you do die—and you will die, you won't live eternally—what will he do? Will he see you have a proper burial? Will he lower your coffin into a grave? No, without shroud or coffin your body will fester under the sun . . . This Murad isn't your Murad. Murad has sacrificed his soul to the rocks, the fire, the coal, to this man sitting before you, whose hot breath stinks of soot.

"Murad is our best worker," the foreman says. "Next week we'll be sending him on a literacy course.

He'll learn to read and write. One day he'll hold an important post. We're sending him because he's a model mine worker who earns respect for being an enlightened, hard-working youth who's committed to the revolution . . ."

You don't hear the rest of the foreman's words. You think of Mirza Qadir. Like him you must choose whether to stay or leave. If you see Murad now, what will you say to him?
"Salaam."
"Salaam."
"You've heard?"
"I've heard."
"My condolences."
"Condolences to you too."
And after that? Nothing.
"Good-bye."
"Bye."
No, you have nothing else to share with each other. Not a word, not a tear, not a sigh.

You pick up the bundle resting on your knees. You no longer want to give it to Murad. The apple-blossom scarf smells of your wife. You stand and say to the foreman, "I am going. Please tell Murad that his father came, that he's alive, that Yassin, his son, is alive. With your permission . . ."

Good-bye, Murad. Head bowed, you walk out of the room. The air has grown thicker, heavier, and darker. You glance at the hilltop. It seems bigger and blacker . . . The men coming down the hillside have faces that are even more tired and even more black. You don't want to look at these faces, the way you did when you first arrived at the mine. What if Murad were among them?

You head toward the gate of the mine. You have only taken a few steps when a shout stops you:

"Father!"

The voice is unfamiliar, thank God. You recognize the foreman's servant hurrying stealthily to your side.

"Father! What I say stays between us. They told Murad that it was the mujahideen and the rebels who killed his family . . . in retaliation for his working here at the mine. They terrified him. Murad doesn't know you're alive."

You are now even more hopeless and forlorn. You glance back at the foreman's building and grab the servant by the arm.

"Take me to my child!"

"It's not possible, father! Your son is working at the bottom of the mine. If the foreman knew, he'd kill me. Go, father! I'll tell him that you came."

The servant wants you to release him. Confused, you place your bundle on the ground. You explore your pockets. You take out your box of naswar, hand it to the servant and request that he give it to Murad. He grabs the box and rushes away.

Murad will recognize your box of naswar. After all, he gave it to you himself, the first time he was paid. As soon as he sees the box, he'll know you're alive. If he comes after you, you'll know Murad is your Murad. If he doesn't, you will have no Murad anymore. Go, get Yassin and return to the village. Wait there a few days.

You quicken your step toward the exit of the mine. You reach the gate. Without waiting for Shahmard, you walk toward the hills. A sob constricts your throat. You close your eyes and weep quietly within. Dastaguir, be strong! A man doesn't weep. Why not?! Let your heart's sorrow overflow!

You wind around the side of the first hill. You want naswar. You have none. Maybe the box of naswar is already in Murad's hands.

. . .

You slow your pace. You stop. You bend down. You take a pinch of gray earth between your fingertips and place it under your tongue. Then you continue on . . . Your hands are clasped behind your back, holding tightly the bundle you tied from the apple-blossom scarf.

A Thousand Rooms of Dream and Fear

TRANSLATED FROM DARI BY

SARAH MAGUIRE AND YAMA YARI

To

MY MOTHER

and her abandoned dreams

Unless sleep is less restless than
wakefulness, do not rest!

—SHAMS-E TABRIZI

A
Thousand Rooms
of Dream and Fear

"Father?"

"Fuck your father!"

Have I got my eyes shut or is it dark? I can't tell. Maybe it's night and I'm dreaming. But then why would I be thinking like this?

No, I am awake, but my eyes are closed. I'm sure I've been asleep. I remember having a dream where a child cried out, "Father."

What child? I've got no idea. I didn't recognize his voice. Maybe it was me when I was a child, looking for my father.

"Father!"

The same voice! So it wasn't a dream. The voice seems to be coming from somewhere above my head. I must open my eyes.

"Who are you?"

. . .

Trying to speak is absolute agony. A violent pain shoots right through my temples. Darkness descends. Then total silence.

What has happened to that child? His voice is shaking with fear, and his breath is foul. It's as though he's calling to me from a cesspit or from the bottom of a dried-up well.

"Father!"

It sounds like he's fallen down a well and he's trying to get his father to save him . . . But what well? Aren't I at home? I must be at home. I'm home in bed, asleep. I'm asleep and I'm thirsty, so I've had this dream about a dried-up well.

"Father?"

But no, that voice isn't coming from the bottom of a well. I can't possibly be dreaming. That voice is coming from directly above my head.

. . .

I can actually feel it. I can feel its vibrations. I can feel the hot, anxious breath spilling its words on my frozen skin.

But why can't I see him?

"Father!"

"Be quiet! Go inside!"

And now whose is that other voice? Is it my mother?

"Mother!"

My own voice chokes in my throat. I am still in a dream. Not a dream, a nightmare. A nightmare where you scream but can't make a sound. A nightmare where you think you're awake but you're unable to open your eyes or move a muscle. Where you're completely paralyzed.

My grandfather used to say that, according to Da Mullah Saed Mustafa, when you're asleep your soul leaves your body and wanders around. And if you wake up before your soul has come back to your body, you get trapped in a terrible nightmare where you're paralyzed and totally powerless. Struck dumb. Petrified, abandoned. And you stay like that till your soul returns. My grandfather used to say that my grandmother had a heart attack because she tried to get up before her soul returned to her body.

I mustn't get up! I have to stay here in bed till my soul comes back. I mustn't open my eyes. I mustn't allow myself to think about anything other than this. The only thing you're supposed to do in bed is say your prayers. It's forbidden to think about anything else. In bed, Satan can take over your thoughts. That's what Da Mullah Saed Mustafa told grandfather, and grandfather told me. I will stop thinking. I'll do nothing but say the Kalima till my soul comes back home. In the Name of Allah . . .

I've collapsed. I've been kicked into a ditch by two jackbooted men.

They've cursed and sworn at me.

"Fuck your father!"

Before falling asleep, I must cross my arms over my heart and recite one of the ninety-nine names of God one hundred and one times. Al-Ba'ith, one. Al-Ba'ith, two. Al-Ba'ith, three . . . My grandfather used to say that Da Mullah Saed Mustafa told him that by reciting the ninety-nine names you can tame all the creatures in a nightmare. Al-Ba'ith, four. Al-Ba'ith, five. Al-Ba'ith, six . . .

I can smell stale shit and fresh blood.

"Father!"

But how can I possibly be having a nightmare? That child's voice is as real as the stench of shit and blood.

"Who are you?"

But the words die in my throat. I'm too weak to think straight. I must open my eyes . . . but I can't see a thing.

Darkness . . . nothing but darkness.

No, I can't be asleep. I've been taken over by the forces of darkness. The djinn have come, they are squatting on my chest. My grandfather used to say that, according to Da Mullah Saed Mustafa—who was more important than ten mullahs put together—the djinn live in those rooms that don't have a Koran. And when you're asleep at night and your soul has gone wandering about, they come and take over your body. They sit on your chest. They pin down your arms. They blindfold your eyes. They gag your mouth. Then they insult you and curse your family. But you must ignore them completely. Otherwise they'll have got you forever. Your only hope is to say your prayers. Call out the name of God! If you don't pray, the djinn will stay squatting on your chest, and your soul will never come back.

"Brother!"

That's not my mother. It's my sister, Parwaneh.

"Parwaneh, my love, is that you? Parwaneh, little sister, please get these djinn off my chest! Parwaneh, can you hear me?"

No, she can't hear me. The djinn have imprisoned my voice in my chest.

If only she could see them!

But how could Parwaneh see the djinn? She's not important enough. My grandfather used to say that only Da Mullah Saed Mustafa could see the djinn. He was so powerful he'd even cast a spell on them and they were at his command. The djinn were his informers. Everyone had to speak well of him, even behind his back, otherwise the djinn . . . Maybe these really are Da Mullah Saed Mustafa's djinn. The djinn my grandfather said were watching us all the time at home, so we'd get found out if we were naughty. But I used to curse the djinn. At night, when I was outdoors with my cousins, we used to find a big tree in a corner of an abandoned orchard behind a ruined wall, and we used to piss there, hoping we had pissed on Da Mullah Saed Mustafa's djinn. Tonight those djinn have come back to piss on my chest.

. . .

If Parwaneh sees the djinn she'll be possessed.

"Parwaneh, little one, please go away, don't stay here!"

The djinn have stolen my voice from my throat.

The officer shot me a look of pure hatred. He bawled at me:

"The commander's going to fuck your fucking sister hard!"

Then I felt the Kalashnikov butt thud into my guts. Everything went black. Vomit shot up my throat and sprayed out all over the officer's uniform, all over his gun, all over the photo of Hafizullah Amin dangling from the mirror of the jeep . . . The jeep stopped. Two jackbooted men hauled me out. They kicked and kicked me until I fell into the sewer by the side of the road.

They swore and shouted at me:

"Fuck your father!"

"Brother!"

Parwaneh is still here by my bed.

"Parwaneh, little one, is that you? If it's you, stay and say the Kalima with me. Recite a verse from the Koran and get these djinn off my chest. Dear Parwaneh, my soul got lost in the backstreets of the city and it was captured by these two men wearing jackboots and now the djinn have taken over my body. My soul has been kicked into the sewer. My soul is hurt, dear Parwaneh, please stay with your brother, please read me the Koran . . . Cast the djinn out so my battered soul can come home to my poor damaged body. Parwaneh?"

Parwaneh is gone. She has left me. She thinks I'm asleep. She has no idea the djinn have possessed me.

. . .

It's not that long till morning prayers. And then after prayers my mother will come and sit by my bed. Gently and quietly. As always, under her breath, she will whisper a prayer by my side. Tenderly. She will protect me with her prayers. Gentler than the breeze, the djinn will melt away. My eyes will open. And instead of grumbling, I will smile at my mother. I will kiss her hands. I will prostrate myself before her. Around my neck I will wear the talisman my grandfather got from Da Mullah Saed Mustafa. I will believe in heaven and in the heavenly host of angels, I will think continuously of my soul. Every night, before I go to sleep, I will wash and then I will pray. I will not masturbate in bed. I will cross my clean hands over my heart and I will repeat the name of God a hundred and one times, Al-Ba'ith, Al-Ba'ith, Al-Ba'ith . . .

"The commander's going to fuck your fucking mother."

The officer swore at me then told the two soldiers to dump me in the jeep. I was rammed in between them. The jeep pulled off. It lurched about so much I felt sick. I reached forward and gently tapped the officer on his shoulder.

"Excuse me, Commander . . ." I asked obsequiously.

The officer jerked round in fury screaming, "The commander's going to fuck your fucking sister, you scum."

I can feel cool water trickling over my face, gently cleansing the metallic taste of my blood from my lips and my nose and my eyes, cleaning away the powerful stench of shit, the heavy blackness of this long dark night. I feel movement coming back to my body, as though the djinn have fled and my soul has finally returned. I must try to open my eyes . . . but the excruciating pain in my temple is too much. I can feel my eyeballs moving behind my eyelids. Can I move my hands? I can. Am I awake? Perhaps.

In washing away these impurities, Parwaneh has scared off the djinn. My soul has survived the blows of those two jackbooted men, it has arisen from the filth. Now, slowly but surely, it is finding its way back to my body. My sore, wounded body. This is what they call the union of the body and soul. But now my body can feel the blows my soul has taken . . .

"Brother, are you feeling any better?"

"Parwaneh?"

But my broken voice is trapped in my throat.

"Can you get up?"

No, that doesn't sound like Parwaneh.

"Who are you?"

"What?"

She can't hear me. I must take a deep breath. Scorching air burns my battered lungs. My throat is raw with pain. I must open my eyes. In agony, I force my eyelids open.

Nothing but darkness. Am I still dreaming? Al-Ba'ith . . . how many? Dream within dream! Al-Ba'ith . . . Nightmare within nightmare! Al-Ba'ith . . . Blackness within blackness! Al-Ba'ith . . .

"Get up, Father!"

The child's voice is coming closer. I can see his small head looming toward me. He smiles, then he turns to someone behind him.

"Mother, did you see? I made Father wake up!"

Is it me he's calling "Father"? I try to lift my head. But my right cheek is stuck in blood and filth.

The smell of blood merges with the stench of shit, the child's face merges with the darkness. And the darkness wins.

A child called me "Father." What a beautiful ending to a nightmare. I wish my grandfather were alive. I would go and sit beside his prayer mat, which was always spread beneath him, and I'd tell him about my nightmare. Then, from under his embroidered cushion, he'd take out the book on the interpretation of dreams that was passed on to him by Da Mullah Saed Mustafa before he died. He'd undo the rubber band wrapped around the worn cover of the book, get out his magnifying glass, and recite a verse from the Koran. Next, he'd read to himself the sections related to my dream and, having compared them with each other, offer his interpretation:

"In a dream, a child represents an enemy. An unknown child is an enemy not yet encountered.

Mud and filth indicate how terrified you are of this enemy . . . and cold water is a sign of the weakness of your faith."

Then he'd take off the silver ring he always wore— engraved with one of the sacred names of Allah, "Al-Jabbar"—and he'd slip it onto one of my small fingers. He'd tell me that Da Mullah Saed Mustafa had once said that, if in the space of a single day, between sunrise and sunset, you recite this particular name of God two-thousand-two-hundred and sixty times, you'll always be protected against the wrath and mischief of your enemies and oppressors . . . Al-Jabbar, one. Al-Jabbar, two. Al-Jabbar, three . . .

"Father's saying something."

Al-Jabbar . . . what number? This strange child, this unknown enemy, won't let me recite. In fact this creature is not a child at all. It's a djinn. It's trying to stop me from counting the number of times I say Allah's name. It despises the holy name of God. Al-Jabbar, Al-Jabbar, Al-Jabbar . . . Didn't my grandfather used to say that the djinn are small, like children? Al-Jabbar . . .

"Yahya, come inside!"

Al-Jabbar. I can just make out the small djinn's body as it moves around in the dark. Al-Jabbar. It's going away. Al-Jabbar. It's going farther away.

Al-Jabbar. Now it's stopping. Al-Jabbar. I can see exactly where it's standing. It's standing by a door. A woman's face appears in front of my eyes. Al-Jabbar.

"Brother . . ."

Is this woman a djinn as well? Al-Jabbar. Perhaps it's a different kind of djinn. Al-Jabbar. I must lift up my head.

My head is exploding with pain. I think I'm beginning to see things a little more clearly, though I still can't move a muscle. Every single one of my bones feels as though it's broken, my veins have been severed, my brain turned to pulp, my muscles torn out . . . No, I'm not trapped in a nightmare. I've not been possessed by the djinn: I am dead.

"Name?"

"Can't you read? It's on my identity card!" I said to myself.

"Farhad," I said to the officer.

He scrutinized my face, then compared it with my ID-card photo.

"Father's name?"

"Mirdad."

"Age?"

"I was born in 1337 [1958]."

"I'm not blind. That's what it says here. I asked you how old you are."

"Let me see, I'll have to work it out because I get older every year . . ."

Silently the officer waited for me to finish my sums. Why did I start this stupid game? I have no idea. Childish arrogance. He blew cigarette smoke in my face. The sneer in his voice echoed all the way down the dark street:

"And what brings you here in the middle of the night when there's a curfew on?"

I brought my heels together sharply like a well-trained soldier, raised my right hand to my forehead in salute, and said:

"Sir, Commander, I'm not going anywhere, sir, I'm just on my way home to my mother."

"The commander's going to fuck your mother."

I am dead. This unbelievably foul smell tells me that I'm dead. After all, is it not said that, "God made man out of dirt before He breathed life into him"?

I'm dead. I've turned back into dirt. Maybe I was shot to pieces. The fact is, I'm neither dreaming nor possessed. I've died, and now I'm going through all those experiences in Imam Ghazali's Book of the Dead.

My grandfather used to say that Da Mullah Saed Mustafa told him that—according to Imam Ghazali— at the time of death, before leaving the body, the soul flies into the heart. At this precise moment, the heavy burden of the soul crushes the chest, stifling speech and paralyzing the tongue. Like when you've been thumped hard in the chest and can't speak.

. . .

Yes, I have died and I've been buried too. I've been buried in the family vault. Perhaps, who knows, I've been buried next to my grandfather. Or perhaps next to a child and his mother. Da Mullah Saed Mustafa used to say to my grandfather that when the deceased is interred in the grave, he first meets those people buried next to him, then the relatives who died shortly before him. Who knows? Maybe my grandfather will come to see me. He will come. He's bound to come and say, "So now you believe everything Da Mullah Saed Mustafa said! Didn't I warn you about the terrifying black-faced angels Da Mullah Saed Mustafa said descend upon the depraved alcoholic when he dies? And the words of the angel of death who commands the deceased: 'You cursed soul, leave this body and flee to your wrathful God!'? This angel then pierces the soul with a spear that, since the beginning of time, has been tempered in fire and brimstone, making the soul skitter about like a drop of mercury. But nothing can escape the angel of death. The other angels arrive to haul the soul up to heaven. God orders them to write the sinner's name in the list of the damned. Then He sends the soul back down to earth to rejoin its corpse. After that, the two interrogating angels, Nakir and

Munkar, visit the grave to question the sinner's soul: 'Tell us the name of your God. What is your religion? Who is Mohammed?' The corrupt soul replies 'I do not know' to each of these questions. So God tells his angels: 'My creature lies. Light the flames of hellfire beneath him and prop the gates of hell wide open so that the fearsome heat will burn him!' And then the gravestone he lies beneath begins to press down on his chest so his ribs are all crushed together . . ."

"Brother, quick, get up, come inside!"

Is that the angel of death or my sister? I can feel her warm hands stroking my face. My head shakes. My legs are trembling. I'm shivering inside. With pain. With cold. With the chill of the grave, with the ice of death . . .

The angel of death—or my sister—tries to lift me up. Her hair falls into my eyes. My head is spinning violently. I can feel my soul careering about inside me. Like water reaching boiling point, it surges up my throat and shoots right out of my mouth. I topple back into the filth.

The grave is even darker than the night.

As I knelt on the ground with my hands behind my head, the soldier went through my pockets. He found my ID card and my student card. He walked back to the jeep and handed them to the man in the front seat. They exchanged a few words, and then the soldier turned and shouted, "Come here!"

My legs turned to jelly. I felt as though my knees had sunk right through the tarmac. I couldn't get up.

"Are you deaf ? Get up! Come here!"

I managed to haul myself up off the ground. I even took a step toward them. But then I froze again, petrified.

"Hey! Don't you understand? Come here!"

The soldier bellowed at me. His voice was so loud it shook the alley walls. And me. I turned from being a rock into a trembling leaf. I must have floated through the air since that's the only way I could have found myself standing right next to the jeep. The officer sitting in the front seat was holding my documents. He shone his torch directly in my face. I screwed up my eyes against the light. But I opened them quickly at the sound of his voice.

"Name!"

I am dead. I died even before I was kicked and trampled on by men in jackboots. The gravestone crushed my ribs. My soul spewed from my mouth. The angels of death came to visit me in my grave with their blackened, twisted faces, their thick moustaches, and their heavy jackboots. Then they battered me with the butts of their Kalashnikovs.

I am dead. My next-door neighbor in the graveyard is a child who keeps on calling me.

"Father!"

I can feel his little hand smoothing my hair.

"Father, get up! This time I'm awake too. Like you!"

. . .

My grandfather used to say that Da Mullah Saed
Mustafa often cited the teachings of Saed Bin Zobair
who said that, when someone dies and goes to Barzakh, he sees his children who have died before him.
But they are complete strangers to each other. As if
the father had come from a distant universe.

I don't remember having a child.

Why does the angel of death keep pouring water on my face? Is this yet another punishment to be endured in the grave? It's never mentioned in the Book of the Dead! Maybe the angel of death is trying to keep me awake so I can experience the suffering of my soul all the more.

My eyes open. I can see the faces of the child and the angel. Behind them, there's a doorway. But there's no fire, nor any sign of hell, on the other side. Maybe this means I was never a real sinner. After all, I only drank alcohol. I never murdered anyone.

No, what you did isn't important. What's really important is what you didn't do. That was an-other of Da Mullah Saed Mustafa's lectures to my grandfather. You never prayed five times a day. You never made the Hajj. You never gave alms . . . You never fought jihad for God. You never became His martyr!

And all that means I'm not a true Muslim. That means I'm full of sin. Yet even so, it seems as though the angels haven't yet cast me into the seventh circle of hell. Perhaps my name isn't inscribed in the ledger of the damned, after all.

The angel of death tries to pour some water into my mouth. No. I mustn't drink this water! "If anyone offers you water when you're in the grave, do not drink of it," Da Mullah Saed Mustafa told my grandfather. On the day of my grandmother's burial, my grandfather recited this commandment so loudly his wife could hear it in her grave:

"Dearly departed! You burn with thirst in the grave. But beware! Satan will come to your grave with a pitcher of water. 'If you want to drink this water, just tell me you have no Creator!' he will whisper in your left ear. And if you keep silent, and if you refuse his water, he will stand on your right and whisper, 'Don't be afraid, I know you are thirsty—here, drink!' But beware, dearly departed! If you drink of Satan's water, you next will speak his words: 'Jesus is the son of God.' Dearly departed, shun Satan! Despise his speech! Cast his water to the ground!"

Satan's water is foul in my mouth. It burns my tongue. I spit it out. The gloom and stench of the grave make my head spin.

I can feel hands stroking my head. They are warm and tender. They are nervous; they tremble.

"Mother, is that you?"

A lock of my mother's hair caresses my face. So soft and gentle.

"Brother, are you awake?"

That's not my mother. Who is it?

Despite all the pain, I force my eyes open. I can't tell whether the blackness I see is her hair or the night. I move my head a fraction. Beneath the dark hair is a woman I do not know. To one side of her, I can make out the face of a child, who says, "Father!"

His hand is stroking my hair.

"Father! You woke up! You came back! Get up!"

Are these the same voices I heard before, the same faces? No, I'm still asleep. I'd better close my eyes again. I close them.

"Stop!"

I stopped. No, I didn't just stop, I froze to the spot. I froze at the sight of a soldier aiming his Kalashnikov right at my head. The soldier was standing in front of a jeep. Its headlights shone straight in my eyes. I put up my hand to stop myself being blinded.

"Stop! Hands behind your head!"

I froze to the spot while the soldier, the gun and the jeep spun around and around in front of my eyes. Then, at the sound of a gun being cocked, everything suddenly lurched to a halt and I turned to stone. Another soldier came around the side of the jeep. His Kalashnikov ready, he walked right up to me and said:

"Password?"

And I said:

"No idea."

"What's the password?" the soldier behind him shouted.

"But what time is it?" I asked, trying to catch a glimpse of my watch.

"Don't move!"

I felt the butt of a Kalashnikov ram into my guts. My mouth filled with blood and I spat out the words:

"The password for the curfew? Sorry, no, I've forgotten."

I tried to lean close to the soldier so I could tell him I'd been drinking, that I was too drunk to remember the password. But the terror of being picked up by the soldiers and then whacked in the stomach by a Kalashnikov was too much for me. Everything went black.

"Down on your knees!"

Those hands that stroked my forehead, that hair brushing against my face, that child who called me "Father," were they really real? Strange how, when you're dreaming, the dream-reality always seems to be more real than reality itself. This is what we are like: our dreams seem more plausible than our lives. But if they didn't, all those revolutions, those wars, those religions and ideologies, could never have been dreamed up . . .

"Brother, can you stand?"

Even though I'm terrified, I open my eyes. Nothing has changed. The same woman, the same child . . .

Morning never comes. Night is an eternity. That woman is here. I am dead. The woman—or angel—is dragging me away. Where is she taking me? To the abyss? How far to the bottom?

My breath stinks of booze, my mouth tastes disgusting. I have sinned. I can feel the wounds to my body that were given to me by Nakir and Munkar as punishment for my sins.

"Dear angel, pardon me! Oh God, have mercy! Save me!"

Which one of hell's doors are we going through? Why do the djinn close the door behind us?

"Let go of me, Angel . . ."

The angel lets go of me. I float in midair. I tumble to the ground. I hear nothing but silence.

"Brother, would you like some water?"

I shift my gaze from the face of the new moon to the face of the woman who haunts my nightmare. Here she is, standing above me, a glass of water in her outstretched hand. I lie flat out like a corpse. Wracked with agony. I move my head. I am outside on a terrace. The yellow light of an oil-lamp, shining through the window of a room indoors, illuminates this woman against the backcloth of the night.

No, I am not dreaming. I am not trapped in a nightmare. I am not lost in Barzakh. I am alive and I am awake! Look, I can take the glass from the woman and drink this water . . . I can feel the water coursing through my body. I can feel my burning throat, my aching bones . . . No. This is not a dream. I can clearly make out the slim face of this woman, the dark hair veiling her profile . . .

"Brother, would you like some more water?"

I can understand her too. And I can even reply to her question:

"Thank you!"

Yet the pain prevents me from asking where I am. Or how I got here . . .

The woman disappears down a dark corridor. Then the child emerges from the gloom with a big pillow in his arms.

"Here, Father, put it under your head!"

Why on earth does this child keep calling me "Father"?

The child props the pillow against the wall under the window of the room where the yellow light is shining. I heave myself onto it and collapse. A shadow crosses the terrace. I look behind me. In the lamplight I can make out someone shuffling across the room. He holds his arms away from his sides stiffly, as though they were two withered branches. Then he vanishes into the darkness beyond the door.

Anxiously, I examine the child sitting in front of me who, in turn, is staring at me with a tender smile on his lips. I lie back on the pillow. I close my eyes. I no longer want to think about all these ghosts and dreams.

I succumb to the nightmare.

"Father!"

No, I will never open my eyes again. I believe in my nightmare. I am a prisoner of dreams. I have recited the names of God to no avail.

The nightmare has proved stronger than my faith. My soul is now lost to me.

My grandfather used to say that, according to Da Mullah Saed Mustafa, if your soul ever ventures beyond your control, you should say the name Al-Mumit and then cross your hands on your chest.

I can feel the child's small hand on my forehead.

Al-Mumit. Al-Mumit . . .

· · ·

"Father, are you better?"

I am tired of all these nightmares. Let me have peace. Peace, are you listening?

The child strokes my forehead. I can see him. He's smiling at me. And suddenly, I want to laugh too—laugh at how helpless I am, laugh at the angels . . . at the djinn . . .

"Yahya, come inside!"

That's Yahya's mother, calling him from down the dark corridor.

"Mother, Father is better; he's smiling."

"I said come inside! It's time for bed!"

The child comes close, and with a look full of tenderness, gives me a kiss on my forehead. Then he scampers off down the corridor in the direction of his mother's voice.

What is going on? What could possibly explain this confusion? Why does this night never come to an end? Who were those soldiers and why did they stop and question me? How did I end up here, with this woman and child? Why does she call me "Brother" and he call me "Father"?

Why haven't they taken me home to my mother?

"Father, drink some juice!"

The child has come back with a glass of juice. With an unsteady hand and a mind brimming with questions, I take the glass from the child and bring it to my lips. The juice stings my mouth, burning my tongue and gums; I feel it swill down my gullet. I can't drink any more; I hand back the glass to the child. I try to move my bruised and battered bones a little, and I ask Yahya to come here. The child, excitedly, sits down next to me. Where do I start? With asking where I am? Or how I got here? Or why he calls me "Father"?

"Father, where have you been?"

But the child's own question throws me completely. Where on earth have I been?

"Yahya, I said go to bed!"

At the sound of his mother's voice, the child jumps up and runs down the corridor, heading for the light.

Where have I been? Perhaps I've lost my memory! It's not unknown for someone to suffer from amnesia after an accident and to have no idea of who he is or where he comes from. To completely forget his wife, his children, and his home . . . his mind a blank sheet, wiped clean of any familiar names or identifying details . . .

. . .

But, no, I do know who I am! My name is Farhad.
Mirdad's son. Born in 1337 [1958] . . . My grandfather was a devotee of Da Mullah Saed Mustafa. No
one else apart from him was ever allowed to visit Da
Mullah Saed Mustafa. Not my grandmother, not my
mother. Only my grandfather knew him. Every Friday, after returning from the mosque, my grandfather
would call his grandchildren around him, and from
under his embroidered cushion he would bring out
the Book of the Dead by Imam Ghazali, and then he
would begin to read us stories about the afterlife that
awaits us when we die. These tales would scare us so
much that we'd cry with fear, prostrating ourselves
before him, begging to be saved . . .

But these are the very things I was thinking about
when I was having that nightmare! And that means,
I'm simply repeating my dreams. My mind has gone
completely blank and I am taking my nightmare for
reality . . .

Ah, but in fact, there are other things I can remember! My mother's name is Humaira. She has three
children. My sister, Parwaneh, and I, and my brother,

Farid. Two years ago my father took a second wife, younger than my mother. Then, after the coup, he fled to Pakistan. He never divorced my mother, he simply abandoned her . . . Today's date is 24 Mirzan 1358 [October 16, 1979]. Not long ago, Hafizullah Amin, that faithful student of Taraki, murdered his own dear teacher and put himself in power . . . What else?

No, my memory is intact! I've never been married, nor had any children. So far—other than in my intense fantasies when I masturbate—I've yet to experience the delight of a woman's tender embrace . . .

So, I've got no reason to think I've lost my memory! Nor to question my identity or doubt my history. No. Something has happened. Probably a mistake. Well, we'll see. Maybe I drank too much again—so much that it's poisoned my mind and made everything seem like a very vivid nightmare.

"Brother, you must be hungry. Would you like something to eat?"

The woman stands in the doorway holding an oil lamp. The lamplight throws the pleats of her skirt into sharp relief, but her face is concealed by the darkness of the corridor.

Yes, I am hungry. But I can't face eating any food. I'm hungry to know where I am and how I got here.

"No, thank you, Sister . . . but . . ."

Suddenly, the ghost whose shadow I saw a few minutes ago, walking across the room, emerges from the darkness behind her, moaning. At the sight of his two bowed arms, like withered branches attached to his body, my question dies in my mouth. The woman, unmoved by his arrival, takes the strange phantom's hand and leads him back down the corridor.

Once again I'm left alone with a hundred-and-one unanswered questions, helpless in the house of a stranger.

My best friend, Enayat, and I decided to pay a visit to Moalem's shop. There, as always, we found the old man with his misshapen figure and his long, flowing hair wedged behind a counter laden with potatoes and chickpeas. And, as always, he winked at us, shooing off the two children who were haggling over a sack of beans. Then his smile broadened into a grin, his eyes twinkled with mischief and he announced in a quavering voice that echoed all around his humble little shop, "The Daughters of the Vine await your command!"

Tottering gingerly to the back of the shop on his unsteady legs, he tugged back a black-and-white curtain and invited us into his den.

"Always drink in secret, for those they find they punish cruelly!"

He laughed loudly, closing the curtain behind us to hide us from sight, then plumped himself down in front of two clay pitchers.

"Do you fancy the blonde or the redhead?" he asked, turning to me.

"The redhead."

"Well chosen!"

He poured red wine from the pitcher into a cheap metal cup and, taking the first mouthful himself, shook his old head and said, "Oh, if only Hafez were here, he'd dedicate a poem to me! Drink deeply and see what miracles can be found in the world."

He refilled the cup with red wine and handed it to me. Then he turned to Enayat.

"Redhead or blonde?"

"The blonde."

"Another excellent choice."

He poured out white wine from the other pitcher, drank it himself, as before, and shaking his head again said, "Oh, if only I'd lived in the time of Babur, he would have planted half of Kabul with vines just for me!"

Then he refilled the cup with white wine and handed it to Enayat. We drank until nightfall, then we took Moalem home, holding him up between us. His sleepy wife opened the door and swore at her husband,

and us. She told us to dump him on the terrace, grumbling, "I can never tell whether you go around there to buy drink from him or just to get him drunk."

Moalem's laughter floated over his small backyard.

"There was a man . . . a rotten drunk . . . who traded wine . . ."

"Like Shams," his wife shouted back at him, "God will never let you rest on this earth!"

But Moalem continued his slurred performance:

"Someone asked . . . That's strange . . . If you're selling wine . . . what could you want in return?"

Moalem's wife threw us out of the house and we fetched up near Enayat's place, in the middle of the garden belonging to the Party headquarters. It was pitch dark. Enayat decided we should piss on the roots of this big cherry tree, so our piss would find its way into the red cherries. So we pissed at the tree, and pissed ourselves laughing.

But the night watchman spoiled our fun and, waving his gun at us, chucked us out of the garden. I parted with Enayat by the gate and he vanished off into the night. The curfew went clean out of my head. Halfway home, a soldier's command froze me to the spot.

"Stop!"

I'm running. I'm running through the night. Quick as a breeze. Carbonized trees bearing desiccated cherries line both sides of the road, leading me on. The road is endless. I run. A soldier runs after me, pounding the ground with his big, heavy boots, bellowing, "STOP! STOP!"

But I do not stop. I run. Faster than an arrow. I grow bigger with each stride. Bigger and bigger. I'm taller than the trees. The soldier dwindles away. He gets smaller and smaller. I stop to piss on the soldier. But, as I piss, the soldier starts getting bigger. Bigger and bigger! I can't piss anymore. The soldier is laughing at me. I am crying. My sniveling sounds as though it's coming from somewhere small inside my chest. The soldier's laughter booms through the night.

He claps his big hand on my shoulder. My shoulder feels paralyzed. He shakes me like a doll.

"Brother!"

The night is even darker than when my eyes are closed. I move my head in the direction of the sound. Then, out of the dark, suddenly lamplight illuminates strands of hair that have fallen in front of my face. I pull back my head. And, once again, I see the same woman whose child calls me "Father." I look around. I'm where I was before. On a small terrace under a window.

The woman tucks her hair behind her ear. The lamplight reveals her face.

"Brother, get up! Quick!"

"What . . ."

What should I say? The woman wants to tell me something.

"Quick, get inside! The soldiers have come back!"

A sudden cacophony of slammed jeep doors, barked military orders, and jackboots hitting the cobblestones ricochets around the street below. The mother of the child whose name I still don't know extinguishes the lamp. Crouching down beside me, she goes completely still. In the dark, in agony, I try to heave myself onto my feet.

She rises up next to me and, gingerly, silently, glides toward the entrance to the house, beckoning me with the two fingers that had scooped back the hair from her eyes. I stagger to my feet and drag my broken body along after her, into the absolute darkness of the corridor. She closes the door behind us and is lost in the dark.

"Come in here!"

Blindly, I follow the rustle of her skirts. The sound moves into a room. And stops. A struck match flares up, canceling the dark. She lights an old candle whose wax has spilt an extravagant fringe all over the windowsill. It is a small room with a black-and-red carpet and two big floor cushions, one by the door, the other under the window. I kick off my shit-caked shoes and lower myself onto the cushion by the door as the woman goes back to the corridor.

"Stay here a minute."

"Sorry to . . ."

Why did I say that? The woman has vanished.

I feel as feeble as the faltering candle.

Night has finished the candle. In the pitch-black room, my anxiety grows so extreme that, eventually, shaking with fear, I force myself to raise the curtain a tiny bit to see if the soldiers are down in the court-yard. But it's dark, silent, utterly deserted. Where has the woman gone? What made the soldiers come here? Are they looking for me? But what am I supposed to have done?

I must get out of here. My mother hasn't the faint-est clue what's happened to me. Right this very minute she's sitting behind our front door in the hope of hearing my footsteps coming up the street. But she doesn't hear me. Now and then she peers around the door, straining this way and that, desperate to see me emerge from the gloom. But she doesn't see me. She wrings her hands. She recites verses from the Koran under her breath. She frowns. She bites her lip. She solemnly promises to make offerings at the Shah-Do-Shamshira Mosque if I turn up safe and sound. I must go.

I feel my way to the door. I know where my discarded shoes are from their terrible stench and, holding them in one hand, I creep on tiptoe into the corridor.

"Where are you going?"

I drop the shoes in shock. The woman is standing behind the glass door of the corridor.

"I must get out of here!"

"Where are you going?"

"Home."

"Now? The street is full of soldiers!"

The woman walks past me toward a half-opened door from which pale yellow lamplight spills out into the gloom of the corridor. Before going through it, she looks back for an instant through her disheveled hair; then she speaks to me softly, in a way that suddenly makes me long to hear my mother's voice:

"Put your shoes on."

In the time that it takes me to put on my shoes, she goes into the room and returns with the oil lamp in one hand. With the other, she leads the phantom I saw earlier, his arms still strangely arched from his sides. Now I can see his face. His hair and his beard are pure white. But he's not old. He's very young. Maybe even younger than I am.

"Come on, follow me."

At the sound of her voice I stop staring at his prematurely whitened hair, and instead try to make out the far end of the corridor from where I can hear her skirts rustle. She opens a little door that leads to the back of the house. We climb down a narrow flight of stairs. At the bottom of the staircase she sweeps straw and earth with her bare hands from a secret trapdoor. Easing it open, she asks me to go down first.

I descend without a moment's hesitation, without even asking myself—or her—what I'm doing.

I enter a rectangular-shaped hole, closely followed by the ghost, who squeezes in next to me. The woman closes the door above us and we hear the scratching sound of straw being scattered over our heads. Or maybe no one else hears this but me.

Who is this ghost? Her husband? Or just an unknown passerby like me, whom she has sheltered and cared for? Maybe I'll stay here too, like him and, like his, my hair will also turn white. What can she want from us?

They're banging on the front door. The ghost's breath comes faster, heavier. The smell of the shit on my shoes cuts through the dank, underground aroma of the hole. The sound of jackboots echoes faintly from the courtyard. The ghost whimpers quietly to himself, very quietly. Beads of cold sweat break out on my forehead and slide down my nose, one by one. I feel liquid lap around my feet. The ghost whines more urgently. A current of warm, moist air rises from the ground, then the sharp tang of urine. The ghost has pissed himself. His moans get louder.

Quite a cocktail: piss and shit; soft moans and sharp breaths; pain and pitch dark.

Buried alive, here in my grave.

My grandfather used to say that, according to Da Mullah Saed Mustafa, the evil deeds of sinners and infidels turn into blind and starving wolves that come to visit them in the grave. The wolves then ravage them until the day of judgment.

Or they turn into filthy, rancid pigs that rut and torture them . . .

Yes, I am a sinner. And to torture me now that I'm dead, they've sent down an angel who is blind and deaf so he can neither respond to my cries of agony nor witness the pain etched on my face.

Where is the winding-sheet inscribed with my sins?

"Brother?"

If I ever open my eyes again—I open them—there'll be nothing to see but the usual darkness . . . and here it is. Alongside the identical stink of shit and piss and sick, the changeless reek of the grave . . . the familiar moans of the white-haired ancient-young man . . . the blind ghost, the deaf ghost . . . and the woman who tells me, "Brother, come on, you can come out of there!"

Again I must move. But I can't. Again the woman must sprinkle my face with water; my eyes must open; I must raise myself out of the grave of this tight box-shaped earth burrow; I must climb stairs, tread the dark and endless passage, return to the tiny room that

isn't mine, collapse onto the floor . . . and I must hear
the woman tell me:

"Brother, the soldiers have gone . . ."

And then I must close my eyes, again.

I come around to the sound of pitiful whining. I open my eyes. Nothing to be seen. I put my hand on the floor: no shit, no dirt. The thick pile of a carpet. The moans are more urgent. A door shudders open; yellow light floods into the corridor; a shaft falls into this room. The light moves. Another door scrapes open and the light is gone. The plaintive cries come to a stop. A soft glow bathes the corridor.

I'm very thirsty. My throat is on fire, my head is pounding. The putrid smells of shit and piss and sick and blood and wine still cling to me. I need to drink some water. I get up. The gentle light from a half-open door leads me on, light that has abandoned this room full of pain and instead has banished night from the heart of the corridor. I reach the door. The oil lamp rests on the threshold. At the other end of the room the mother of the child who called me "Father" is sitting on the floor. She has taken her breast out of her blouse. Her nipple is in the mouth of the white-haired ghost, who is sucking like a baby.

I close my eyes. I take a breath. I open them. No, I'm not dreaming. The ghost is sucking on the woman's white breast. I want to move. I can't. My feet are fixed to the floor. The ghost closes his eyes. The woman tenderly lifts his white head from her breast and rests it on a cushion.

She mustn't see me. I have to go. But I'm transfixed. She tucks her exposed breast back inside her blouse. I'm frozen to the spot. She gets up and walks toward the door. I break out in a cold sweat. Picking up the lamp, she steps out into the corridor. The ordeal of the night sinks onto my shoulders. She stands in front of me. I am paralyzed. She says nothing.

"Where's the bathroom?" I ask.

The woman tucks her hair behind her ear. There's not a hint of nervousness, surprise, or shame about her. Holding the oil lamp aloft, she leads me to a small open door, goes in to put down the lamp then comes back into the corridor.

"I'll go and find you some clean clothes and a towel."

The mirror scares the life out of me. In its reflection I see a ghost whose hair has not yet gone white. Is that really me?

I toss my filthy clothes, covered in blood and vomit, into a corner, take the lamp, leave the bathroom, and go back to the room.

The woman is sitting on the cushion by the door. Neither the sudden light of the oil lamp nor my return stops her from staring at the carpet. Her head hanging down, her hair, as always, curtaining half her face. She is silent. I leave the lamp close to the door, within her reach, and moving very carefully so as not to disturb her, I go over to the cushion under the windowsill. From the corpse of the old candle, a new light burns. I sit down. My shadow trembles on the opposite wall, over the woman's body.

I gaze, transfixed, at the black lines on the carpet,

haunted by the desire to cast a quick glance at her. Is her breast still uncovered?

We sit in silence. Each of us waiting for the other to speak. Should I say something? But what? Who are you? Why have you mixed me up with somebody else? Why won't you let me go? All these questions, right on the tip of my tongue, make my heart pound, my stomach churn, my throat seize up.

I'm spellbound by the patterns on the carpet. I must say something.

"Sister, I can't begin to thank you for everything you've done for me. But the truth is, I have no idea what on earth has happened to me! Yesterday . . ."

"My son, Yahya, and I were sitting outside on the terrace when we heard a jeep pull up, and then soldiers cursing and shouting—followed by the sound of someone being kicked and punched. After they'd gone, I went into the street and found you passed out in the sewer."

My mesmerized gaze, now freed from the patterns on the carpet, falls instead on the flowers printed on the cushion beneath her. But it lacks the courage to travel any further up her body . . .

"Yes . . . I was out late. After curfew. I was on my

way home . . . I've caused you so much trouble . . . I really should be going now."

The woman's hand is hiding a flower on the cushion.

"You should stay here till morning; we can sort things out tomorrow. You're safe here—they've already searched the place thoroughly so they won't be coming back. I have a suspicion it was you they were after. They said a burglar had gone to ground around here. They've turned the whole area upside down."

My gaze, stricken with guilt, moves hesitantly upward, away from the woman's hand covering the flower pattern.

"They were looking for a burglar?"

Her blouse is done up.

"Well, they had to come up with something to convince us to go along with the search."

One half of her face is hidden by my shadow, the other by her hair.

"I have no idea why they arrested me and beat me up. All I did was forget the password!"

Releasing the crumpled flower on the cushion, her hand lifts her hair from one side of her face and tucks it behind her ear. And I shift my head away from the candle, lifting my shadow from the other side of her face.

"Not having the password or the Party member-ship card is a crime in itself."

"Oh no! My ID card and student card!"

Without thinking, I leap up and rush to the bath-room where I hurriedly search through my trousers and shirt pockets. Nothing. Dejected and exhausted, I return to the room. The woman is sitting on the cushion as calm as ever. Frantic with worry, I stay standing by the door.

"I have to go."

"Without your ID?"

"They've probably chucked my documents in the sewer; they wouldn't have hung on to them."

"Are you suggesting you go and look for them now? They're patrolling the streets."

Confused, I take a few steps back to the cushion under the window. In complete disarray, I cry out under my breath:

"Mother!"

"I'll fetch you something to eat," the woman says as if she hasn't noticed a thing.

She rises to her feet. Picking up the oil lamp, she unsettles the silence of the dark passageway.

Like the melting wax of the candle on the window-sill, I sink down onto the cushion once more.

Alone again, I'm haunted by the image of my mother's face, her worry hidden from my brother and sister because it's still night. They must sleep. They've got to go to school in the morning. My mother paces back and forth behind the door to the street, praying all the while. The courtyard is taut with her anxiety. I must go, otherwise my mother will stay up all night.

"I have to go!"

My voice rends the cavernous silence of the room. I get up. My shadow shatters all over the walls and ceiling. Yahya's mother comes in from the corridor, carrying a tray.

"I have to go!"

"Have something to eat first."

The woman kneels down to pour the tea. Her manner as unruffled as ever, just like her untroubled gaze, her steady speech.

"My mother won't be able to sleep."

"If you leave now and fall into the hands of the soldiers, your dear mother will never sleep again."

I am at her mercy. I feel like a child. Shaking as violently as my shadow, I sit down on the floor by the tray. The woman busies herself with the tea.

"Sister, I've caused you more than enough trouble already. You . . ."

The woman drops a sugar cube into a glass of tea and hands me some bread.

"Let me assure you, it's impossible to imagine anything worse than what I've been through these past few years. There's nothing darker than total darkness."

Her even gaze travels slowly across my trembling shadow.

"A year ago, my husband was thrown into jail. Then came the news that he'd been executed. I haven't told Yahya. He thinks his father has gone on a journey to a faraway city called Pul-e-Charkhi . . ."

"Why does he call me 'Father'? Do I look like his father?"

"No, you're nothing like him."

"Then why?" I want to ask. Has he forgotten what his father looks like? Aren't there any photos of his father in the house? What was going on when he announced, triumphantly, that he'd woken me out of my dreams?

Yahya's mother slumps back against the wall and disappears into her shadow. Her eyes track the movement of my hand. I put the bread down on the tray. Her gaze locks on the bread.

"The young man who was with you in that hole is my brother. He's not yet eighteen. He was in prison for three weeks. I don't know what on earth they did to him there. His mind is gone. His hair turned white overnight. Now, he never says a word. Every night he wakes up, moaning and sobbing like a newborn child . . ."

She falls silent, her eyes fixed on my trembling hand as it replaces the glass of tea on the tray. In my mind's eye I see her naked breast, as innocent as my mother's, fill with tears.

"Two times they've called him up to the army. They're convinced he's faking. Each time he's come back more damaged than before. All I can do now is try to hide him away."

She tucks her hair behind one ear. Silence. As though she is waiting for me to start asking all those unasked questions. But I too am silent.

Then, abruptly, she gets up, loading all my questions, my fears, and my feelings onto the tray with the bread and the tea, and she carries them off into the darkness of the corridor.

Yahya's mother comes back to say "Sleep well," then leaves me with my quaking shadow. I focus on the image of her fingertips gathering up her hair. Fingertips that, when I'm most afraid, seem to sweep my fear away with that lock of hair she tucks behind one ear.

What is it about this simple gesture that leaves me mesmerized and tongue-tied—and banishes all my doubts?

It moves me because, through this effortless movement, she reveals herself to me. When her face is hidden by her hair, I worry that she's anxious. But when she lifts it back, I can see she's not afraid.

"You should beware of two things about a woman: her hair and her tears."

God knows why my grandfather told my father that.

He muttered prayers to himself as he fingered three of his worry beads, then continued:

"Her hair will chain you and her tears will drown you!"

Another three beads, another three prayers, and then:

"That's why it's imperative they cover up their hair and their faces!"

He said this on the day my father decided to take a second wife. My mother wept—and then her face once again assumed its mask of fear.

My grandmother used to say that my mother was born with a terrified face, and it was the face I was used to. Whenever someone met her for the first time, they'd assume she was scared of them.

I couldn't understand what it was exactly that made her appear so frightened. Was it because her face looked so drawn and thin? Or because of the dark circles under her eyes? Or because her mouth turned down at the corners? If my mother ever smiled, she would smile between the two deep lines cut into her face like the brackets around a sentence; if she ever cried, she would cry between brackets. In fact she lived her whole life between brackets . . .

But, one day, the brackets vanished. The terrified mask dropped from her face. And then, a few months later, my father took a second wife. No one asked why, because even if someone had dared to ask, my father would never have answered.

My father had no interest whatsoever in why my mother always looked so frightened. He couldn't have, otherwise how could he have lived alongside a woman who always looked so terrified? Truth is, my father never loved my mother at all, he just fucked her. He'd get on top of her in the dark, close his eyes . . . and get on with it.

But what happened the day the fear vanished from my mother's face to make my father think about taking another wife? Probably my father needed a woman to be scared of him in order to get turned on. And the day my mother stopped being terrified of having sex, my father's desire vanished. So he had to get himself another wife. A younger wife who'd still be scared of sex.

And maybe the day my mother lost her fear of having sex was the first time she ever enjoyed it. The first and last time.

．．．

But it wasn't long before she put her frightened
mask back on. This time not because she was scared
of having sex, but because she was terrified he'd leave
her.

Tonight, lonelier than ever, my brave mother has
placed her frightened face behind the street door
while she waits for me to come home.

Her worn-out hands, free at night to be raised to
beg God's mercy, recite the prayer for safe return.

I must go.

"Where are you going?"

The woman's voice hits me just as I reach the far side of the terrace. I can't look at her face. I stare pathetically at the door in front of me, and weakly offer:

"I have to go home."

Under her gaze, once again, I feel like a child— small and pitiful.

"You want to go—go then! But take great care the soldiers never find out that I took you in."

I abandon my mother behind our door. I let her recite her prayers as many times as the stars she counts in the sky with her mouth enclosed in its brackets.

Like a naughty boy, my eyes fixed on the ground, I turn back to the terrace. I don't dare look at the fingers that gather the hair from the side of the woman's face to tuck it behind her ear.

I freeze at the door to the corridor.

"Sister . . ."

"Mahnaz. My name is Mahnaz. I hate being called 'Sister.' And you—what's your name?"

"Farhad . . . I just wanted to say that I have no desire to put your life in danger . . ."

"At the moment it's far more dangerous for me if you leave than if you stay. We will find a way tomorrow."

I walk back down the corridor. I take my shoes off. I enter the room I just left.

Night deals with the candle.

If mine doesn't stand up
If yours doesn't stand up
If his doesn't stand up
Then who will fuck the mothers of our nation?

Enayat condemned himself to exile with this variation on a favorite theme of the Communist Party. He'd written his little ditty on a scrap of paper that he folded in four and then tossed to me in class. Of course, it landed at the feet of a Communist-Party student who, of course, read it—and immediately recognized Enayat's handwriting.

Before the lecture had finished, Enayat was gone from the campus.

...

That night I went around to his house. My best friend had decided to flee the country.

We spent the next two nights together, saying farewell to Kabul. It was to be a very poetic farewell. We got drunk on both nights. We slept not a wink.

Enayat had wanted me to be at his side for his last Kabul sunrise. At the moment when night finally dies under the boots of the night-watchman, and dreams are interrupted by the mullah's call to prayer, Enayat and I were lost in the vineyards of Bagh-e-Bala. Waiting for sunup had made us thirsty, so Enayat drank dew from the leaves of each vine. Enayat was no poet, but he knew how to behave in true poetic fashion.

After the sun rose, we went back home and drank yet more wine. When our wine ran out, we returned to Moalem's shop, in search of the Daughters of the Vine.

The night has consumed all but the stub of the candle. Mechanically I move my hand toward the flame. If it burns me, I'll know I'm awake.

None of this really makes any sense. Maybe because I don't want it to make any sense. Maybe because I'd rather I were having a nightmare than living my life.

My little finger hurts.

I wish that Mahnaz—for all her extraordinary kindness and generosity—were merely a dream. I wish that when I opened my eyes, I'd find myself in my room at home, watching dawn break on my mother's lined face as she whispers a prayer above my head, while she wafts the fresh morning air over me . . . I wish she were holding me tight . . .

She holds us both in her arms, Farid and me. We're both very small. Farid cries out:

"Father! Father!"

Who's he calling "Father"? Me?

"No Farid, it's me! I'm your brother!"

Farid won't listen. He continues sobbing. My mother takes out her breasts and pushes a nipple into each of our mouths. Without saying a word. Farid begins to suck at my mother's breast, but then he pulls back. His mouth is filled with blood. I stare at my mother's breast. Instead of milk, blood spurts out. But I still suck her other breast. There is no smell of blood. Only the smell of milk. But it's milk that's gone off! I turn away from my mother's breast. Sour milk surges up my throat into my mouth.

"Mother, Father is being sick again!" Farid shouts.

The smell of vomit overwhelms me. Then I see Yahya standing in front of me. He jumps up and heads down the corridor calling to his mother.

"Mother, Father is throwing up!"

Mahnaz appears at the door with a cloth in her hand. She sits down next to me and puts the damp cloth on my forehead. After a huge effort—using all the power I no longer possess—I manage to move myself. Mahnaz helps me sit up. The shirt that must have belonged either to Mahnaz's mute, damaged brother or to her murdered husband is covered with vomit. She dabs my mouth and face clean. I avoid her eyes. I have the impression her breasts are uncovered. I fix my gaze on her hands, hands that with such tenderness gently wipe my face and neck.

"Do you feel a little better now?"

"Yes . . ."

Both of them are so sweet and kind! What do they want from me?

Yahya hands me a glass of water and sits down before me.

"Are you all right, Father?"

"Yahya, leave Farhad alone! Go into the other room!"

Mahnaz cleans up my vomit from the carpet. I should help her. But I can't. The child gets up and leaves the room. I want to say something. But my tongue is heavy. I am still staring at Mahnaz's hands. My heart beats more fiercely than ever. It pounds with utter exhaustion, it thumps with things unsaid . . . Mahnaz stands up.

"The curfew is over. I'll go and get you some medicine."

"Please don't go to any trouble . . . Really, I'll be fine . . ."

Mahnaz leaves the room.

Morning waits outside the window. It waits for the curtains to be drawn so it can slip into this room where I am waiting.

I will not draw back those curtains.

Daylight streams through the gap between the curtains, spilling onto the windowsill and down over the cushion that I'm sitting on, illuminating the black patterns woven into the deep red pile of the carpet. Mahnaz has gone out to get some bread for breakfast, and some medicine for me. Yahya sits on the cushion by the door. We both are silent. The child's trusting face mocks me. He doesn't look anything like me! Actually, he looks nothing like his mother, either. Which means he must take after his father. But, if that's the case, why would he mistake me for him?

I trawl the blank white walls of the room searching for a photograph of his father. On the windowsill, next to the candle stub, are two large books with gold inlaid covers. I take down both of them. One is *Haft*

Paikar and the other *Khosraw & Sheerin*. I put them back on the windowsill.

Why does Yahya call me "Father"? Mahnaz never answered my question. Maybe he's never seen his father.

I call him over to me. He springs up with excitement and sits down in front of me, right in the middle of the sunbeam that falls onto the carpet through the gap between the curtains. He looks at me intently, unquestioningly. Yet the mind of a child like Yahya should be full of questions, particularly for someone he calls "Father!" A father who's been missing for ages and has suddenly come back beaten to a pulp! Last night he asked me only one question—"Father, where have you been?"—and he did not wait for my answer. He left. It was a question without a question mark. He didn't even repeat it. But I'll be gone in a short while. He needs to understand that I'm not his father, that I'll be going away, that . . .

"Yahya, I . . ."

The child moves his right eye out of the sunbeam. A constant smile on his face. Nothing in the way he looks at me gives me any impression that he's eager for me to continue. On the contrary, he looks at me as though there's an entirely different conversation going on inside his head: "For heaven's sake, please leave me to my imagination. I know you're not my father. But can't we pretend for a while? Just as you want to imagine that everything that's happened here is nothing other than a terrible nightmare, I need to inhabit the dream that my father has returned. Please don't spoil it!"

"Father, I know where you've been!"

He says this like he's revealing an incredible secret, in a voice that matches the secretive look on his face.

"You do? Where have I been?"

He wriggles his little body closer to mine.

"You've been in the city of Pul-e-Charkhi."

"And what's it like there?"

He fingers the sunbeam, then traces the flower pattern on the cushion.

"It's a very big city with a huge bridge in the middle—and the bridge spins around and around all the time."

"Can you remember when I went away?"

"No, because I was fast asleep. The lamps had run out of oil. My mother said you'd gone out to get us some oil. Then you got lost and nobody recognized you there. You left your ID card at home so you got stuck and you couldn't come back. The bridge wouldn't stop spinning. When I asked Uncle Anwar when you'd be able to get off the bridge and leave Pul-e-Charkhi, he said: 'In a dream!'"

The child stops playing with the sunbeam and the flowers on the cushion.

"My mother cried. She thought you would never come back again. But just like Uncle Anwar said, at night you came back in my dreams, although you'd disappear before we woke up. So I promised my mother that one night when you came into my dream I'd catch you and I wouldn't let you go away again!"

The child has caught me in his dream. I am a dreamcreature. I am an imaginary father, an imaginary husband . . . So why bother going back to my life?

I leave Yahya in his silent dreams of a city with a huge bridge that spins around and around forever, and I close my eyes only to find myself in someone else's dream—in the feverish dreams of my mother.

My mother hasn't slept a wink. She's even forgotten her morning prayers. Now that the curfew is over, she ventures outdoors to wait at the end of the street. But I'm nowhere to be seen. She goes back indoors. Where else can she go? Who would know where I might have gone? She goes to Enayat's house. But I'm not there. Then what? Which department should she go to first—should she go to the Ministry?

"Over there, Mother, wait in the queue!"

She walks past another hundred mothers to find a place at the end of the queue. She smiles at the soldier for me. She calls him "Brother."

"Dear Brother, Farhad son of Mirdad did not come home last night . . ."

"Well, he's not here. He's gone, he's fled with the rest of them . . ."

"Gone. Fled." She repeats the words over and over between her bracketed lips. "Gone where? Fled where? Why didn't he say anything?"

How could I possibly leave my mother, Farid, and Parwaneh behind?

My mother has never forgotten how, when my father walked out on her and left her with three children, I cursed him—his cowardice and cruelty—to heaven and earth.

"No, he can't have left us! But where on earth can he have gone? Has the army got hold of him? Is he in prison?"

She swallows her fear, covering her mouth with both hands to stop herself crying out loud. She decides to wait it out in a corner, under the sympathetic gaze of all the other mothers . . .

I have to go! I get up. Yahya watches me with his penetrating gaze. I take a few steps toward the corridor.

"Father, Mother's coming back soon."

Right. I must leave before Mahnaz gets back. I don't want the look on her face to deflect my intentions. Where are my shoes? I look in the corridor.

They're nowhere to be seen. Have they hidden them away? I go back to the room. Yahya still sits there in silence, smiling to himself at my feeble attempt to escape.

"Where are my shoes?"

The child gets up calmly. With a tremulous look, full of longing for me to stay put, he walks past me down the corridor onto the terrace. He returns carrying my shoes.

"My mother cleaned them for you."

He puts my shoes down next to my feet and goes back to the room to sit on the cushion by the door and stare at my hesitant feet. The shoes are still damp. Never mind. My mother is waiting.

I hate having to walk out on Yahya. His plaintive stare is paralyzing. I move purposefully across the courtyard toward the door to the street. The door opens. It is Mahnaz.

"Where are you going?"

She hurriedly shuts the door behind her. The smell of fresh bread fills the courtyard.

"I have to go."

"Off you go then—go!"

She opens the door a little, just enough for me to see two soldiers lounging in the street. The sight of their jackboots makes my desire to leave vanish instantly. I jerk back. Mahnaz shuts the door. We walk back across the courtyard.

"I was under the impression that I've been sheltering an ordinary young man who's simply dodging the draft. But tell me, who are you?"

"Trust me, Mahnaz, I'm no one at all."

"So why are they still looking for you?"

"I have no idea! I keep asking myself that too. All night I've been thinking about everything I've done in the past couple of days—and nothing can explain it. I'm no rebel; I've got no connection to the resistance, to jihad, or to revolution . . . I was hanging out with a friend who was having to get out of Kabul. After we parted I was simply walking back home. Sure, it was late, well after curfew, and the night patrol caught me. But it was nothing, nothing serious . . . The only thing I can think of is that I made the mistake of calling an ordinary officer 'Commander'—and that he thought maybe I was making a fool of him . . ."

I walk close to Mahnaz. I want to look at her discreetly.

Whether or not she believes my story is hidden under her hair. I keep quiet.

. . .

We reach the corridor. Mahnaz and Yahya go to
the kitchen. I return to the room I was in. I take off
my damp shoes and sit down once more on the cushion under the windowsill.

What am I frightened of? Why do I always give
in to this woman? Is her disapproval more important
than my mother's anxiety? No! Then what? What's
stopping me from leaving? I'm out of here.

I get up from the cushion. My heart is pounding.

I am nobody. All I have to do is go to the Party's district office and give them an explanation of what happened last night. I'll tell them it's all a mistake. I had
no intention whatsoever of insulting an officer. I'd had
a bit too much to drink and I was out of control. If I've
caused any offense, I'm ready to offer a full apology.

I put my damp shoes on again in the corridor. My
heart thumps more than ever.

She steps out of the kitchen into the corridor carrying a plate on a tray that gives off the aroma of breakfast.

"Why don't you sit down in there?"

With one look into her eyes I am powerless. The decision to leave deflates into my sodden shoes. Why can't I just tell her I want to go? Why doesn't she understand that if anyone finds me here I am done for! And what about you? You're a widowed woman. Your husband was a political prisoner! Are we related? No. So what kind of relationship could I possibly be having with a woman who's not only a complete stranger but who's also a widow? If your family finds out I've been here, then how on earth will you explain why you've given shelter to a young man you know nothing about?

Mahnaz leaves me with a head full of questions and a paralyzed tongue. She has placed the tray beside the cushion under the window and has gone back to the corridor where she disappears into her brother's room. I return to this room and sit on the cushion. On the tray next to the cup of tea, Mahnaz has left some pills to calm nausea.

Yes, I do feel nauseous.

But not because of what I have eaten. I am sick with fear.

I'd gone to the university library to take out the *Book of Shams*, but the librarian told me someone else was reading it. So I borrowed another book and, having given it a quick glance, sat down. At the far end of the table was a young man wearing a pair of dark glasses. His head was buried in a book and he looked as though he wanted to devour every word. Since it happened to be the one I was after, I sidled up to him and coughed, so politely that even I could barely hear myself.

"Excuse me, but would you mind letting me know when you've finished with that book . . ." I whispered.

Lifting his intense gaze from the page he was scrutinizing, he shot me a look, loaded with the passion of the words he was consuming. He gave me a quick nod and once more buried his small head in the big book.

After a while he looked up again and wrote something in the margins of his book. Then he indicated to me with a gesture that he'd finished reading. We went up to the desk together so I could take the book out, and then I returned to the table. The first thing I did was look for the page that he'd written on. He'd underlined the words, "We cannot speak. But if only we could hear! Speech has no meaning without a listener. But ears are sealed, hearts are stopped, tongues are fettered . . ." And at the margin of the page, in pencil, he had written: "= annihilation."

The same day, in the university café, I found the scribe of the *Book of Shams*. We chatted together over a cup of tea. His name was Enayat.

What else can you call those moments of nameless terror other than "annihilation"? Those moments when
you begin to doubt your very existence. When you're
so paralyzed with fear that you turn to fantasies for
reassurance, to imaginary women, to djinn, to angels,
to life after death . . .

I'd managed to empty my head of those phantoms
a very long time ago. The djinn were nothing more
than children's games in a play directed by my grandfather, and the afterlife was a cover story dreamt up
by the human terror of nonexistence . . .

But the butts of those Kalashnikovs summoned
up my slumbering grandfather and the long-forgotten
djinn and set them center stage once more. I'd much

rather believe in the reality of their performance than in the utter abeyance of annihilation!

Yes, I do believe in the journey of my soul, in the existence of the djinn, in the finality of death—but I cannot believe what I'm going through right now . . .

"Farhad, have you got a phone at home?"

With the aid of a swig of tea, I manage to swallow the dry bread in my mouth, and without looking at Mahnaz's face framed by the doorway, I answer, "No! But . . ."

"Then give me your address!"

I get up and move toward the door.

"Please, my dear Mahnaz, really, you've done more than enough . . ."

"I want to know your address."

Reluctantly, I tell her.

"I won't be long."

She leaves. I remain fixed to the spot. Before opening the door out of the corridor, Mahnaz pauses to call Yahya. He comes running from his mother's bedroom.

"Yahya, don't open the door to anyone!"

She leaves the corridor. Takes a few steps on the terrace. And returns to the house. I move closer to the doorway.

. . .

"Is there anything you want me to tell your mother?"

"No . . . but . . ."

I cannot go on. I want to insist that I will go myself, that . . .

"You'll have to go before midday. Please don't leave the house until I get back. I don't want anyone to know you're here."

She turns to go on her way. I stand by the window. Mahnaz opens the street door and disappears. Yahya waits for me in the doorway to the room.

Perhaps I have landed in a city that spins forever around a giant bridge.

Mahnaz should have reached our street by now. She must have asked directions at the bakery:

"Can you tell me where Farhad's house is? His mother is a teacher, Humaira."

Safdar, known as "Long Fingers," has pulled his head out of the clay oven, wiped the sweat from his brow, and said, "First street on the left, second house, the wooden door with no paint."

At the mention of my name, as always, Safdar's brother stops kneading the dough, and his sweet voice calls from the far end of the bakery, *"Last night the sound of Farhad's chisel never reached us from Mount Beysitoun . . . It's into the dreams of Sheerin that Farhad now has gone . . ."*

· · ·

Mahnaz is standing outside our door. Without a moment's delay she presses the bell, but she can't hear it ring. She's forgotten that there's been no electricity in Kabul for some time now. After a minute, she rattles the chain on the door. And then she hears the voice of Parwaneh or Farid ask from behind the door, "Who is it?"

What should she say?

"I've got news from Farhad."

There's a brief silence and then Parwaneh or Farid opens the door halfway, and gives Mahnaz a curious look.

My mother's exhausted, hopeless voice calls from the courtyard, "Who is it?"

Parwaneh—or Farid—pushes the door nearly shut. No, why would they close the door? Their eyes fixed on Mahnaz, brimming with curiosity, they call back to my mother, "It's someone with news of Farhad."

My mother runs to the door. If she trips on the loose tile, for the first time ever she will forget to curse me for not having mended it. Her frightened face appears at the door. She doesn't open it completely. Peering around the half-opened door, she examines

Mahnaz from top to toe. She doesn't dare ask, "What has happened to him?"

"My name is Mahnaz. I've come on behalf of Farhad."

Who on earth is Mahnaz? Why have I never said anything about this girl? She sizes up Mahnaz. She is not short. So she's not a liar. She has a steady gaze. My mother opens the door to Mahnaz. She asks her in. Before shutting the door, she scans the street in both directions with an anxious look. She closes the door. She fixes her dark-ringed, sleepless eyes on those of Mahnaz. Mahnaz understands my mother's terrified, questioning look and immediately reassures her. She says that I'm fine, safe and sound, but I've had to hide in her house. What am I doing hiding in this woman's house? Is there anything going on between us? Mahnaz lifts her hair back from her face and tucks it behind her ear, and begins to recount the events of last night.

My mother hides her mouth behind her bony hands. What can she do? How can she help me? Which door should she knock upon? Should she go to her cousin who's become a high-ranking official?

No, never! How can she beg for help from someone she was once in love with when she was young— but whom she left for another man? Her cousin has never forgotten my father's jealousy. Every time my father set eyes on my mother's cousin, in his flashy military clothes, his blood would rise. He would say, "Fuck the mother and sister of Taraki and Hafizullah Amin!" He would pick petty political arguments, and my mother's old flame would get upset and walk out. Then my father would crow with joy in my mother's face. The very day my father took another wife and fled to Pakistan, my mother's cousin came to our house with a sheepish look on his face. My mother spat at him and threw him out.

What will my mother do?

She will ask Mahnaz to wait in the front room while she goes to put on her veil.
She will come to see me with Mahnaz.

"Look, Father, I'm drawing this for you."
Yahya's little hand moves a crayon across a black sheet of paper.
"What is it?"
"A moth."
"But where is it?"
"You can't see it because it's too dark."

Someone is banging on the door. It must be Mahnaz with my mother. Mahnaz? No, why would she be knocking on her own front door?

Yahya lifts his head out of the night and its creatures. The banging gets louder. Who on earth can it be? Another search party? Yahya's uncle's moaning can be heard along the corridor. Yahya leaves his invisible moth in its eternal night and heads for the corridor. I run after him. The banging gets even louder.

Yahya's uncle stands in the middle of his room, his strangely arched arms wrapped around his scrawny skeleton, his wails increasing in their intensity. Will we have to go back into that hole again? I take his hand. It's shaking. I'm shaking too. The banging still echoes around the courtyard. We reach the end of the corridor. Yahya's uncle continues to moan.

"Don't be scared, Uncle Moheb, it's all right."

But Uncle Moheb will not be reassured.

"Uncle Moheb, look, my father is here," says Yahya, taking his other hand. "There's no need to be frightened!"

Moheb wails even more bitterly. I drop his hand. The banging continues relentlessly.

"Uncle Moheb, it's only my mother. She's forgotten the key. I'll go and let her in."

Moheb calms down. His gaze, as always, set in the middle distance. Holding him by the hand, Yahya leads his distorted frame back into his room and sits him down on a cushion. And there we abandon him.

Once we're back in the corridor, the banging stops. Whoever it was has gone.

"I think it was my grandma . . ."

Yahya is tempted to go outside.

"No, Yahya! Your mother told you not to open the door to anyone."

"Not even to my granny?"

"But it might not have been your grandma."

Looking puzzled, Yahya goes back to his uncle, and I return to my place in the room.

. . .

Yahya's moth is completely invisible against paper that's the color of the night. I find a piece of white chalk in his pencil case and draw a moth for him.

But why should this moth be visible?
I scribble over the moth with a pencil the exact shade of the paper: night.

I got off the bus outside the university to find Enayat waiting for me in the entrance. He asked me if I'd like to go for a drink. We went off to the tomb of Sayed Jamaluddin. A few couples were declaring their love in the hidden depths of the shrubbery. Propped up against the marble tomb, we drank some wine and talked about our lives.

We'd only been there a while when Enayat's sister turned up—sobbing, utterly distraught—bearing the terrible news that their brother had committed suicide in prison. Enayat smashed the bottle of wine against Sayed Jamal-Udin's sepulchre and immediately ran off home. I made my way back to my class.

．．．

A few days before the Revolution Day celebrations, a decree was issued ordering everyone in Kabul to either paint their front door red or hang a red flag from the window. Enayat's brother and his friends went to the abattoir, anointed some sheets with sheep's blood, and then sold them to their neighbors. By Revolution Day, the blood had turned black. Enayat's brother and his friends were slung in jail.

I walk into the lecture theater. Above the huge blackboard they've rigged up a red banner on which a famous slogan has been written in white:

If I do not stand up,
If you do not stand up,
If he does not stand up,
Then who will light a torch in the midst of this darkness?

If Enayat's brother hadn't killed himself, maybe he'd have turned out like Yahya's uncle. A young man with no youth. With no soul. A body suspended between two arches. I do not want to see what Enayat's brother and Yahya's uncle have seen. No! I do not want my mother to put her breast in my dry mouth for me to suck her blood; or like Enayat's mother, to cry over her own son's empty grave . . . I want to stay alive.

"My mother's here!"

Yahya runs to the door. Once the door opens the house is filled with the smell of Mahnaz—and my mother too! I hurtle down the passageway. An old woman walks into the courtyard behind Mahnaz. But she is not my mother. Mahnaz doesn't close the street door. She stands completely still, as if she wants the old woman to finish what she has to say and leave as quickly as possible.

"Grandma!"

Yahya tries to run out to the courtyard, but I hold him back.

"Yahya, your granny mustn't see me!"

He stares at me with complete bewilderment. We fall silent. He drops his question, and his little head.

"One day grandmother said that you had died in Pul-e-Charkhi . . . but she can't say that anymore, can she, if she sees you're alive?"

"But, Yahya, I'm not really your . . ."

No, I can't bring myself to say it.

"When I told her that you came to see me in my dreams and one day I would catch you, she laughed in my face and got cross with me . . . But if she sees you now . . ."

"I'll go and tell her I'm back myself. Now, go and see how your uncle is doing . . ."

With a heavy heart, the child returns to Moheb's room. The old woman has come nearly as far as the terrace. Stealthily, on tiptoe, I creep back to the room. Through the open window I can hear Mahnaz's mother-in-law say, "You can do what you want, but

I'm taking Yahya with me. I'm not leaving my grandson in the care of a madwoman!"

I lift a corner of the curtain and peer cautiously outside. Mahnaz is still standing by the open street door. Her face is rigid. She's seething inside. I can't hear what she's saying, but I can guess. She pronounces the words very slowly, as if she were doling them out. Her mother-in-law sits on the steps up to the terrace. Her shaking voice echoes again:

". . . Anwar will show you we have not yet completely lost our honor!"

As she makes her reply, Mahnaz points toward the door. Silenced and exhausted, her mother-in-law drags herself up from the steps, adjusts her veil, and heads for the street. Her voice echoes through the front yard of her dead son:

"So now you're so important, you have the audacity to throw me out of my own son's house! Mark my words, you'll regret . . . "

Her voice follows her bent old body and disappears into the street. Mahnaz closes the door firmly behind her, and turns toward the house. I wait in the corridor. Yahya too.

The child opens the door to his mother. Like Yahya, I want to throw myself in Mahnaz's arms. She smells of my mother. My heart pounds. My hands shake. My tongue manages, "Hello . . . how are you?"

Mahnaz takes off her shoes that have kicked up the living-room carpet. This time she doesn't tuck away the hair that has fallen in front of her eyes. With lowered gaze she draws her little son's head into her arms.

Why won't she look at me?

"I found your house. They're all fine. I saw your mother. I told her everything. Thank God you didn't go there. At prayer time this morning, they searched the house. They were looking for pamphlets. They said you were out distributing leaflets last night . . ."

"That's not true! Believe me . . ."

"It's OK, I know . . ."

"How's my mother?"

"Everyone is fine. But anxious."

"Why didn't my mother come back with you?"

"She wanted to come, but I wouldn't let her."

Why not, I wonder. Mahnaz tells Yahya to go to his room. She answers my unspoken question:

"Your house may well be under surveillance. Your mother's coming here would be incredibly dangerous. Meanwhile, she's trying to come up with a plan to get you out of this mess. She wants you to leave Kabul as soon as you can. She'll come over later this afternoon. I've told her where we live."

Her eyes, hidden by her hair, still avoid mine.

What else is she hiding?

She leaves. In the privacy of her room, she lifts the weight of my questioning gaze from her worn-out body, and sits down.

All at once, the scent of my mother evaporates from the corridor.

If I didn't exist, I wouldn't be here.

If I wasn't here, Mahnaz would cry her eyes out; she would go wild with grief. Instead, she pens in her tears and her fury. Instead, she immolates her anguish in a pit at the bottom of her heart, until she's alone again.

Just like my mother. Only once did I ever see her cry—on the day my father took another wife. My mother appealed to my uncle—her brother—who was close to my father. My uncle laughed in her face. He sided with my father. My mother sobbed and wailed. And then my grandfather gave her a little talisman, something Da Mullah Saed Mustafa had given him a long time ago. From that day on, whenever my

mother felt her fury rise, she put the talisman between her teeth and bit down on it as hard as she
could. Clamped down on her gag, my mother's
twisted mouth would not let out a cry. Her eyes lit
up with fear, she'd make herself busy with menial
tasks in the kitchen. Sometimes, she'd even rewash
the dishes. After a while, she'd perform her ablutions
and say a prayer of atonement.

I never understood what it was exactly that she
needed to purge: anger or hate? Pride or humiliation?

My mother would say that all the water in the
world had sprung from her tears.

"Have some grapes, Father!"
Yahya, bearing a bunch of grapes, has slipped in
quietly; he crosses his legs and sits down next to me. I
pull myself up on the cushion.
"Where's your mother?"
"In the kitchen."

I take a grape from the bunch and drop it into my
mouth. Yahya holds the grapes up in front of me like
an offering.

...

I wonder whether Mahnaz told her mother-in-law
anything about me that could have made her angry
and fear for her honor.

I stand up.

"Honor": what an honorless word it is!

I must talk to Mahnaz. Why has she gone to so
much trouble, and fought with her mother-in-law, for
my sake? Why does she want to protect me, no matter
what the cost?
    Maybe she won't protect me. Maybe this is all a
trap. She wants something from me. But what? Am
I stuck here? Why would she want to keep a strange
man hidden in her house? So we can have an affair on
the sly? After all, she's certainly very intimate with
her brother. She puts her breast in his mouth . . .
    No. I can't stay here a minute longer! I move to-
ward the corridor. Clasping the bunch of grapes,
Yahya stares at my clumsiness.

How could I think of Mahnaz like that! Why can't
I believe that a woman could rescue a strange man

without any ulterior motive? Maybe rescuing me is an attempt to redress the balance since she couldn't save her husband. Maybe by helping me, she'll reclaim her dignity.

I sit down on the cushion again.

For the sake of Mahnaz and her secret, I've abandoned my mother—left her walled up alone with her fears all night long; I've condemned Parwaneh to stare from her window, hopelessly, for hours on end; I've left Farid, dejected, waiting outside my bedroom door . . .

I take the bunch of grapes from Yahya.

The mystery of Mahnaz is hidden in the lock of hair that she keeps having to tuck behind her ear.

I give myself up to the lifeless flowers on the cushion.

I've never felt this close to a woman before apart from my mother and Parwaneh. I've never been part of another woman's life. No other woman has ever entered my consciousness like this. In the space of

just one night, I have gone through a thousand different emotions with this woman, as though something momentous has happened between us. She
has given me shelter. My life is in her hands. It is
hers.

Yahya picks grapes off the bunch I hold in my
hands.

"Dear Mahnaz, why do you want to help me?"

She'll shrug her shoulders. She won't say a word. She'll give me a look that says, "What a stupid question! If you don't want to be here—leave! Go on—God be with you!"

"I'm asking you because I need to know what's going on—and I need to get to know you too . . ."

"Why?"

"In your eyes, in the things you say, there's a secret that I see in my mother's eyes . . . a secret I've never . . ."

With two fingers she'll lift the hair from the side of her face and she'll laugh at me! She'll smile at me and shake her head. She'll assume I'm trying to catch her out . . . that it's impossible for me to believe a woman can have integrity . . . that . . .

"Farhad, I'm so sorry to have left you on your own all this time!"

Her voice shocks me from my reverie. I try to sit up on the cushion, then I stand up, clutching the stripped bunch of grapes that I pass, stupidly, from one hand to another. I feel sure that Mahnaz has been waiting outside the door reading my mind, hearing every word of our imaginary conversation. I turn scarlet with shame.

"I'm making something to eat."

With unsteady steps, I cross the carpet toward her. Without having a clue of what I'm about to say to her, I hear myself speak:

"My mother . . . Please don't go to any more trouble . . . She'll come as . . . soon as possible . . ."

"Of course, but in the meantime, let's have something to eat."

She stares at the naked bunch of grapes I'm holding in my hands. I move a little closer to her. My heart pounds in my chest.

"I've caused you so much trouble . . . I hope that . . . Yahya's grandmother . . ."

A grim smile settles on her lips.

"Don't worry about that."

She looks away from the shriveled branch in my hands and peers down the corridor.

"As I told you last night, my husband was murdered when he was in prison . . ."

"Peace be with him . . ." I say, softly.

"And now my husband's family wants me to marry my brother-in-law . . . But that's not what I want . . . I keep telling them I don't feel as though I'm really a widow. No one has seen my husband's body . . . since, in prison, they bury the dead in unmarked, communal graves . . ."

A sudden shiver goes right through me. I don't know whether it's a tremor of fear, or hatred, or anger—or from thinking thoughts like these about Mahnaz. I look down, away from her face, and stare at the carpet.

"Now all of my husband's family is going to Pakistan . . . But I don't want to go . . ."

Mahnaz's delicate feet blend into the black patterns on the carpet. The patterns have neither ending nor beginning. These elaborate octagonal designs are infinitely intertwined and interwoven with endless other octagons. The octagons give birth to rectangles, the rectangles give birth to tiny dots . . .

I snap out of staring at the carpet when I catch sight of Mahnaz's feet moving a little to the left. The lock of hair hides the left side of her face. I look into her eyes. She is waiting for an answer to a question that I have not yet been asked.

The sudden loud hiss of the pressure cooker takes Mahnaz's questioning gaze out of the room.

I stay behind to keep company with her unspoken words.

Why on earth did I keep my mouth shut? Why didn't I say something helpful in response to Mahnaz's terrible story? Maybe this was the first time she'd confided this painful secret to anyone. And all I did was stand there, red-faced and dumbstruck, staring like an idiot at the carpet!

Mahnaz didn't just want to tell me about her suffering. Like any other woman, like my mother, she wanted someone to understand her pain. She wanted to share her distress with somebody else. The last thing she needs is another Moheb in her life—someone deaf to her cries and dead to the world!

I go back to my cushion under the window. Reaching one hand behind the colossus of candle wax, I open the curtains to let more light fall onto the carpet. Below me, the courtyard, alive with anxiety, awaits my mother's arrival.

I collapse with exhaustion onto the flower-patterned cushion.

In the clear light of day, the black lines on the carpet seem blacker than ever, and its deep red background glows with the quintessence of red. Suddenly I realize that these carpets are woven from hatred and anger. Black against red! As though the carpet weavers twisted the red weft of their anger with the black warp of their hatred . . . Women carpet weavers . . . children . . .

I'm sick to death of carpets!

I turn away from the black dots inside the rectangles of the carpet and lean back against the cushion's flowers.

Up on the ceiling, a spider has spun its web around the lampshade.

I lower my face into her hands. Her hands are frozen. They tremble. But they hold me so tenderly!

My mother. She got here an hour ago. In disguise, well concealed—underneath the local laundrywoman's veil. She couldn't risk anyone spotting how scared she was coming here.

At first even I didn't recognize her. There was a knock on the door. From behind the curtain I could see it was a heavily veiled woman. With her was an old porter with a large carpet balanced on one shoulder. They entered the room with Mahnaz. The porter deposited the carpet in the corner and went out. Then Mahnaz left too, closing the door behind her.

My mother took off her veil and examined her battered son with exhausted eyes, her troubled face lit up with a beautiful smile. But not a word escaped her lips, shut tight as always between those two tense brackets. And me, I shook. I shook deep down inside. I trembled in her arms. I could not speak. We stand together in silence. My head in her hands. I can hear her breath laboring in her chest. I can't open my eyes. I imagine she has loosened her blouse to take her worn-out breast and place it between my dry lips.

Her hand, shaking with anxiety, hovers over the gash on my temple.

"At three this afternoon, a trafficker is coming here to take you to Pakistan wrapped up in this carpet . . ."

That's all she says. I lift my head from her hands.

"Mother, but . . ."

"But what?"

Looking directly into her terrified eyes, I find that all that I wanted to say is reduced to a single word:

"Nothing."

She hands me an envelope. Inside is my father's address, together with a little money.

"Mother, where should I go?"

"Where else can you go?"

I put my father's unbearable pride back in the envelope.

"But what about you? And Parwaneh? What about Farid?"

She looks away, taking my hand in hers. She clears her throat. Trying not to cry.

"Things will get better soon."

I press her hand to get her to look at me. But she won't. She stares down at the carpet. Perhaps, for the very first time, my mother grasps the hatred and anger that has gone into weaving this carpet.

"Mother, let's both go!"

A bitter laugh shakes her tiny frame. Her eyes repeat her father's words:

"Faith is better than a roof!"

The door opens. It's Mahnaz.

"I've brought you some tea."

She puts the tray down next to my mother and pours out two cups of tea. The brackets round my mother's mouth relax, allowing a smile.

"I can't thank you enough for your kindness . . . I'm so sorry we've caused you such trouble . . ."

Mahnaz hands my mother a cup of tea.

"Here, please have some tea. These days it's important we all take care of each other."

She stands up and leaves the room.

My mother stops staring at the door through which
Mahnaz has just walked and turns to look straight
into my eyes.

"What a kind woman! After you've left, I'll give
her a present."

She soaks a sugar cube in her tea.

"Where is her husband?"

"He was executed."

My mother takes the sugar cube out of her tea and
drops it onto the saucer. It melts as quickly as her
heart. Her horrified gaze travels out of the room to
the corridor, where it alights on my battered shoes.

"May God be with him!"

She mutters something under her breath. Her
trembling hands bring the sugarless tea to her anxious lips. She downs it in one gulp. As if she wants to
wash the shame from her throat with hot tea. If she
were at home, she'd get up and leave the room, she'd
hold her hands under the cold tap, then she'd rewash
the washed dishes, or rescrub Parwaneh's immaculate
school veil . . .

. . .

Yahya peeps his head around the door to stare at me and my mother.

"Yahya, come in."

At the sound of my voice, the child steps into the room. But at the sound of his mother, he quickly goes back to Moheb's room.

"She has a child?"

"Yes."

My mother's troubled eyes, looking more lost than ever before, scan the empty corridor anxiously. I dare not tell her that Yahya calls me "Father."

"Mother, how did you find the trafficker?"

"Your uncle found him," she says, her gaze still lost in the corridor.

"How much money does he want?"

"His payment is that carpet. We don't have the money, so it's the only thing I could think of."

"Mother . . ."

She puts the cup back on the tray, drained of tea, filled with sadness.

The way she looks at me makes me lose track of what I want to say. She lifts her sky-blue skirt from the flower-patterned cushion, and stands up.

"I have to go. The laundry woman is waiting for her veil."

"No, Mother, I can't go without you."

"You must go. I'll bring Parwaneh and Farid with me once I sell the house."

I can hear the doubt in her voice.

She takes up the veil from a corner of the room.

"I've forgotten how to put it on!"

She laughs a small, bitter laugh. A laugh that makes me shiver. She adjusts the veil over her hair. The brackets around her mouth shake.

"Mother, I'm coming with you."

She covers her face, as though she hasn't heard what I said.

"Mother, I can't just leave without seeing Farid and Parwaneh . . ."

She brings her grief-stricken hands out from under her veil and presses them against my heart. My voice fails. My eyes fill with tears. I put my face in her hands. My mother's broken voice emerges from behind the folds of her veil:

"May God watch over you . . ."

Why does she move away? Isn't she going to kiss me goodbye? I need to look into her eyes again, I need to see the brackets that muffle her cries. I stumble toward her. I reach out to touch the veil that is covering her eyes but I cannot feel the exhausted face it hides. The veil is wet. My mother is crying. Crying without a sound. She is crying between those two brackets. She is crying under her veil. My mother is rinsing the laundrywoman's veil with her tears.

She takes another step away. Her whole body is shaking under her veil. She moves into the corridor. She searches for her shoes. I stand there, lost, like a button dropped on the black and red patterns of the carpet. Yahya and Mahnaz come out of Moheb's room. My legs won't move. Without a look, without a smile, my mother says to Mahnaz, "God be with you . . . May God reward . . ."

Her words are swallowed by her veil. My feet have been sewn to the carpet by the threads of hatred and anger that were woven together by all those nameless women and children. My mother is gone.

My feet are sewn to the carpet.

My heart breaks at the sound of the door to the terrace closing behind her.

"Mother . . ."

My voice breaks.

. . .

The carpet is sewn to my feet.

"Mother . . ."

I am nothing but a pattern in a carpet.

"Father!"

 . . . ?!

"Father!"

Everything has gone black.

I have passed out on the carpet. When I come to,
Yahya is sitting down next to me.

My mother is gone. She has left with my last sight
of her hidden away under her veil.

Yahya hands me a glass of water. I disentangle
myself from the patterns on the carpet and answer
Yahya's kind look with a smile. In agony, I haul myself up again onto the cushion under the windowsill. I
drink the water that Yahya has brought for me.

"Where's your mother?"

"In the kitchen."

I get up. The smell of onions leads me to the kitchen. With her back to the door, Mahnaz is busy slicing them into rings. For a moment, standing by the door, I watch her in silence. What am I doing here? Why am I shaking?

Mahnaz senses my presence. She turns toward me. With the end of her sleeve she wipes the onion-tears from her eyes, and smiles at me. This is the very first time I've seen her smile. She smiles to make me understand that her tears have been caused by onions, not by grief. I try to smile back. I manage a hopeless parody of a smile.

Mahnaz slides the onions into a saucepan. As always, the smell of frying onions makes me hungry. The kitchen fills with the aroma of my mother's cooking. As always, my heart beats faster. I want to take a piece of bread and steal some of the fried onions from the pan. I want to put my hands on Mahnaz's shoulders. I want to tuck that lock of hair behind her ear myself.

"You must be hungry."

"The smell of frying onions always makes me hungry."

I lean against the door. I find myself imagining I've lived in this house for years, that I've known Mahnaz for years, that Yahya has called me "Father" for years, that my mother has visited us here for years. For years I've wanted to go away, but I haven't been able to. For years I've been asking her the same question:

"Why don't you come away with me?"

Mahnaz stops stirring the onions. My heart thumps. She turns to smile at me. A bitter smile.

"Dear Farhad, life is not that simple!"

She turns back to the pan. The smell of frying onions makes the house seem more homely.

"If I go to Pakistan, I'll have to marry my brother-in-law."

I stop leaning on the door and move over to the wall.

"But where is *your* family?" I ask her.

She pours boiling water into the pan, and her voice comes from the middle of a cloud of steam.

"Only my brother Moheb is left with me. The rest have gone to Germany."

She stirs the onions with a wooden spoon.

"I've not been in touch with them for years."

She takes a deep breath.

"When I was born . . ."

She places the lid on the pan.

". . . I didn't scream, I didn't smile, I didn't cry . . ."

She takes a few chicken wings out of a bag.

". . . They all thought I'd been born deaf and dumb. So when I was a little girl they arranged for me to be married to my cousin. He was deaf and dumb too. When I got older, though, it turned out that I was neither deaf nor dumb. But by then it made no difference to them . . ."

She washes the chicken wings under the tap.

". . . My father died when I was young. I was never close to my mother. When I grew up, I had no choice but to marry my cousin. So I ran away and married Yahya's father."

She lifts the lid and pours some more water in the pan.

"The night when all of my family fled to Pakistan, my mother came and left Moheb behind on our doorstep."

With my back to the wall I slide down slowly until I'm crouching on the floor. Once again, the story of

Mahnaz's life reduces me to silence. Once again, anything I could say seems completely pointless.

I forget the smell of frying onions. For some time, I stare at the black locks of her hair falling down her back.

"Is there anything I can do to help you?" I ask her without thinking.

She gives me a painful smile.

"Nothing!"

Even her throwaway "Nothing" bears the weight of a history that demands to be known.

"Why don't we go to Iran?. Your husband's family couldn't find you there."

She remains silent for a moment. Tipping the chicken wings into the pan, without turning around to look at me, she says, "Farhad my dear, my husband's family are very strange people. The type for whom blood and family honor are one and the same. Don't get yourself mixed up with us. I'll be fine here."

She puts the lid back on the saucepan.

In a corner of the kitchen, my heart fills with love.

All of us sit around the tablecloth spread on the floor of Moheb's room. All of us eat in silence. Chicken wings have taken the place of words. As if we had already said all there is to be said. No more questions to be put, no more answers to be heard. We are all waiting for the trafficker to bang on the door.

A knock. Yahya gets up and runs down the corridor, a chicken wing in his hand. The sound of his small feet echoes from the courtyard. He reaches the street door. Having answered the door, he rushes back out of breath.

"It's a man who says he's come to buy a carpet."

I jump to my feet without thinking. My heart plummets. My legs go weak.

"It's the trafficker," I tell Mahnaz, "I can't go with him!"

Mahnaz gets up and tucks her hair behind her ear.

"Put on your shoes," she says in her usual even tone.

I stare deep into her eyes. But she turns her head away. I want to put my life in her hands. Mahnaz leaves the room. Moheb starts to moan. I begin to cry inside, in silence.

Mahnaz takes the trafficker to the room where I spent the night.

"Father, will you come back soon?" Yahya asks, grasping my hand, greasy with chicken.

I follow the trafficker into the room without even washing my hands. He has spread our carpet across the floor. From it rises the sound of all the guests who've ever walked across it. Our best carpet. Its color seems even redder than before, its "elephant-foot" patterns even bigger and blacker.

"Hey, Brother, let's give it a go."

Mahnaz is standing by the door. Yahya leans his little head against the green flowers patterning his mother's skirt. My unsteady frame collapses into the middle of the carpet under Mahnaz's inscrutable gaze. The trafficker swiftly rolls me up into the carpet saying "Ya Ali!" as he heaves us both up onto his strong, broad shoulders and takes a first step. From the sound of his feet I can work out when we leave the room and when we reach the courtyard. Where is he going? Where is he taking me? No, first I have to say goodbye to Mahnaz! The street door is opening. No!

"Mahnaz!"

My cry is smothered in the patterns of our carpet. I try to struggle free.

"Brother, be quiet! We're outside in the street."

"I don't want to go! Hey, do you hear me? Mahnaz! Yahya!"

My cries are cut off by the sound of a car door opening. The trafficker brings the carpet down from his shoulders and slides it inside. He shuts the door. I want to move, I want to get free of these carpet patterns.

"Father! Father!"

Yahya's cries chase the sounds of our guests from this carpet forever.

I have no idea anymore whether the patterns on our carpet have gotten bigger, or whether I've gotten smaller. I'm running along the black lines of the patterns. My father stands over me. He is big. Immense. He won't allow my feet to slip off the black patterns onto the red background of the carpet. I'm running. I'm spinning. As if I am trapped in a labyrinth. The black patterns have neither beginning nor end. All the lines turn back on themselves. Octagons and rectangles. I am crying and running.

"Run! Run!" my father shouts. "Shut up and stop crying! You unbeliever!"

I'm trying to work out how to escape from these octagons and rectangles without stepping onto the red background. The only possible way is to get through to the other side, to run and run till the carpet wears out under my feet. I run. I'm getting smaller and smaller with every turn. I run and I run. The patterns get bigger and bigger. As though I'm a part of the carpet's design. I can feel the texture of the threads.

I only know I'm in the carpet because of its smell. I can't see a thing. Just blackness. I can't breathe. I can't move.

"Tell him to keep still . . ."

I make out the sound of the trafficker's voice over the monotonous thrum of the engine.

"Brother, keep still," I hear a woman say. "We're coming up to a checkpoint."

I hold in my breath and my fear under the weight of the two bodies that sit on top of the carpet.

My head spins in the red-and-black labyrinth of the carpet.

As usual he sits with his hands laced across his bloated stomach, a look of complete indifference on his face.

"Hello, Father!"

No, I will not call him Father.

"Hello."

"Hello."

What next?

"So, what brings you here, then?"

Hiding his contempt with a laugh.

"You left your mother, your sister, and your brother behind to come and visit me?"

His arrogant sneer brings back the memory of the last thing I said to him before he walked out on us with his second wife in tow—a phrase that unfortunately escapes my mind as two people shift about on the carpet wrapped around me. The car comes to a halt. I leave my father with his disdain, his fat stomach, and his second wife. The back door of the car opens.

"Where are you going?" booms a voice.

The voice of the trafficker replies to the soldier: "Moosa-e-Logar."

"Who are these people?"

"My two wives."

I can feel the bayonet of a gun poking the carpet.

"Where are you taking this carpet?"

"It's a wedding present for my brother."

The door slams shut. The car moves off. The two people get off the carpet. A cold sweat films my entire body. They loosen the two pieces of cloth tucked into the ends of the carpet. I gasp for air.

My sweating face trapped inside the carpet heightens its smell. Such a familiar smell. The smell of our front room. Parwaneh used to play marbles on the black patterns of this carpet. Farid used to race his matchbox cars along its black lines . . . It was the best carpet in the house—my mother's dowry, given by her father to take to her new husband's house.

. . .

No. I will never go to see my father. I can't possibly stay in Peshawar. I'll go to Islamabad. But I don't really like it there either. I'll have to go somewhere else. Karachi or Lahore. I'll get through this somehow or other. Soon I'll be able to send for my mother, Parwaneh, and Farid.

I scratch my face on my mother's dowry.

The car stops. The carpet with me wrapped up inside it is hauled out of the car and put on the ground. I roll over as it's unrolled. The half-light of dusk hurts my eyes. I fill my chest with fresh air and the smell of the countryside. The trafficker drags my stiff frame free of the black patterns of the carpet. The car has pulled over by the side of a dirt track on top of a hill covered with thorn bushes.

"We're taking a shortcut. We'll be in the village in under an hour."

The trafficker takes a packet of cigarettes from his waistcoat pocket and offers me one.

"Thanks, but I don't smoke."

Putting a cigarette between his lips, he lights up. Then he squats down on the carpet. Covered by their veils, his two wives leave the car to sit on the opposite corner of the carpet, turning their backs to us. I stand up.

The cigarette smoke and the trafficker's voice steal over the golden slope of the hill.

"All being well, we'll set off for Pakistan at dawn the day after tomorrow, by morning prayers. It'll take two days. You . . ."

The low laughter of his two wives rises above his words.

"What are you laughing about?"

Both women immediately fall silent.

"You'll stay in the village mosque," the trafficker goes on. "But you mustn't talk to a soul. By the way, do you have a student card?"

"No."

"An ID card?"

"No, the soldiers took them off me."

"Never mind. Do you have any papers at all?"

I go through my pockets mechanically. Other than two thousand Afghanis and a folded paper with my father's address written on it, there's nothing else.

My heart gives a sudden leap. Of happiness. Happiness about what? Mahnaz must have looked for my ID card and student card in the sewer . . . and found them . . . and my clothes . . . Will she hang on to them?

"Hey, Brother, snap out of it!"

I come back to the hill and our carpet, which is spread over the ground. On one corner sits the trafficker wearing his astrakhan hat. On the other, the two women with their blue and yellow veils . . . The setting sun merges their shadows with the carpet's black patterns.

"Sorry, what did you say?"

"Do you know how to pray?"

"I think so, roughly . . ."

"Some nights the religious students get together and sleep in the mosque. They ask lots of questions of students like you from Kabul. But don't worry. You'll be all right unless you get into any kind of political discussions with them . . . It's not a good idea to let on that you've been to university . . . Tell them instead that you left school after sixth grade and then got a job."

I wonder if Mahnaz has washed my clothes? Will she give them to Moheb? No.

"Do you know anyone in Pakistan?"

"No."

He says nothing. His narrow eyes, hidden under his thick eyebrows, follow the smoke curling from his cigarette into the fading light.

"Don't you even have an address?"

"Is it important?"

"Yes. If anyone asks you, tell them you've already sent your wife and child to Pakistan and that they're all there waiting for you."

"My father is in Pakistan."

"Then why did you say you didn't know anyone there?"

"I don't want to have anything to do with my father."

"OK, that's up to you. But it's a good idea to have an address."

No. I have no desire whatsoever to be beholden to my father.

"Why didn't you bring your wife and child along with you?"

"My wife and child?"

Mahnaz and Yahya!

"It would be much easier if you were with your family."

He throws away his cigarette butt. His voice is clear in the still evening air.

"Ya, Allah! Let's go."

The two women get off the carpet and head toward the car. The trafficker rolls up the carpet, empty of me, and tosses it into the back of the car. I get in too. The backseats of the car have been taken out. I sit on the rolled-up carpet. The women settle themselves in the front seat next to their husband.

Traveling downhill, the car kicks up a thick cloud of dust as it speeds around the bends in the road. The last red seconds of the day burnish the shoulders of the trafficker as he drives.

I ease myself off the carpet onto the metal floor of the car. I put my head on the carpet and kiss my mother's footprints.

Once she'd left Mahnaz's house, safely hidden under her veil, my mother went to the Shah-Do-Shamsira Mosque. There she tied a ribbon to the grill of the shrine and made a prayer for her son to get to Pakistan safely. My mother wept. But no one saw her tears. No one asked, "Mother, why are you crying?"

My mother wept to herself, lonelier than ever before. Walking back home from the shrine, she concealed her terrified face beneath her veil. More anonymous than ever before. More insignificant than ever before. Unable to confide to a soul, "My oldest son, the man of my house, has become a fugitive!"

And no one replied, "Mother, may his absence be filled with patience and grace."

．．．

Shrouded in her veil, crazy with grief, my mother shed her tears in the backstreets of the ignorant city before finally reaching our home. She wrapped up her distress in the veil and gave it back to the laundrywoman. She squirreled herself away in the safety of her kitchen to rewash the clean dishes. When the laundrywoman left, she took all the clean linen off the clothesline and washed it all again.

She hasn't said a word to Parwaneh or Farid about my escape. She'll tell them tomorrow. My mother always hangs on to bad news. She lives with it for a while, she weeps, she curses . . . and then, the next day, during breakfast, she'll announce, "Children, Farhad has gone to Pakistan."

Parwaneh rushes next door to take out her fury by sinking her teeth into her pristine school veil. Farid, with tears in his eyes, stays close to my mother. His childhood is over. His chest swells. Now he is the man of the house. He takes the worn-out hands of my mother in his own small grasp and presses them tenderly. Tomorrow they will move the green kilim from my room and lay it on the floor of the front room.

. . .

The car comes to a halt next to a small mud compound. The trafficker unloads the atmosphere of our house, rolled up in our carpet, and, along with his two wives, takes it into the compound.

I stay behind with two earless dogs that appear from nowhere to sniff around the car, a car that is emptied of memories and filled with fear.

In a corner of the mosque a man lies asleep next to me, his head resting on a brick for a pillow. A dervish. A long white beard covers his face. A cloak is spread out over his curled-up body. He's sound asleep. So soundly even the call to prayer hasn't broken into his dreams. He's been left in peace, as if he didn't exist.

Four groups of men sit around four oil lamps: young and old, faces concealed by lengthy beards. Here, everyone is armed. Alone and unarmed in my corner, I sit with my back propped against the wall of the mosque.

Yahya has sprinkled water on the floor of the terrace, and the smell of dust and worn Hessian matting drifts across the small front yard. Mahnaz has brought Moheb out onto the terrace. Seated around the lantern, the three of them eat together. They eat in silence. What are they thinking about? Are they thinking about me?

"Has Father gone back to the city of Pul-e-Charkhi?" Yahya will ask.

Will Mahnaz tell him that I'm not his father? Perhaps, like me, she won't want to shatter his dreams.

She has hung my freshly washed clothes out to dry on the washing line by the terrace. Mahnaz is thinking of me.

Clouds of hashish smoke permeate the mosque with their pungent smell.

No, Mahnaz won't be thinking of me. She'll do everything in her power to forget all about me. She'll expunge from her life every last sign of me. Once she's washed my clothes, she'll donate them to the poor. I only wish that Mahnaz could know that someone is thinking about her at this very minute—someone who's fallen hopelessly in love with the troublesome lock of hair that insists on hiding one side of her face; someone who's in love with the persistence of her two slim fingers that repeatedly grant asylum to that

strand of hair as, once again, they carefully rescue it
and tuck it behind her ear . . .

The five bearded young men sitting in the circle
closest to me pass their spliff from hand to hand. One
of them offers me a drag. But the guy sitting next to
him says, without looking at me, "He's from Kabul.
He drinks vodka."

The scornful laughter of the little group echoes
through the smoke-filled mosque.

I've never once smoked a cigarette in my life, let
alone had a spliff.

But what will they think of me if I don't smoke
with them? Perhaps they're just testing me. No one's
allowed to smoke in a mosque in the first place!

"Just ignore us," says the guy with the black beard
who offered me the spliff. "We merely smoke the humble herb of the ignorant poor!"

Hash fumes and mocking laughter spiral above my
head. Someone in another group calls out, *"From the
ranks encircled of noble men: he who resists . . ."*

The others cry together:

"Cannot persist!"

The cacophony in the mosque wakes up the old
man who's been sleeping on a brick. Perhaps he's
been awake the whole time with his eyes shut. He

casts a glance at me. Light from a lantern hanging on a wooden pillar shines in his eyes. He smiles at me— why, I have no idea. Without thinking, I stretch my hand out to take the spliff and put it between my chapped lips. I try to inhale as much smoke as I can. An agonizing fit of coughing tears my chest apart.

"Vodka has mashed up your liver. Hash will mash up your lungs!"

My head rings with their sneering laughter. My limbs feel heavy. My mouth is dry. The mosque is thick with smoke.

What on earth made me smoke hash? Am I mad? I feel as though the blood has drained from my veins. My heart is pounding! I need to sit up.

Another group passes their spliff over to me: "This is a Shah-Jahani, try it!"

I take the proffered spliff. Once more I draw the smoke deep into my lungs. Once more I'm wracked with a coughing fit, making my ribs feel as though they're being dislocated one by one with every explosion.

The dervish raises his head. His eyes are blood-shot. His eyebrows look like two arches tacked to his wrinkled forehead. His jowls have caved in, as though he's sucked his cheeks behind his teeth. He looks both stern and kindly. He moves his lips. He murmurs something under his breath that only he can understand. He throws back the cloak that has covered his wizened frame.

The door of the mosque swings wide open. A man with a white beard appears; he strides inside, bringing with him the absolute silence and weight of the night. Everyone stands up at once and salutes him.

I'm in no fit state to stand up. My head is spinning. I force myself to sit upright by levering my back against the wall.

The man's right eye is hidden under a fold of his black turban. He stands at the front of the mosque. A few of the young men go over to sit by him. The man pulls out an old book from under his arm. He first recites a verse from the Koran himself and then he orders a young man to recite the sura of Joseph.

الرتلک آیات اللکتاب المبین... اد قال یوسف لابیه...

Is it me shaking or the wall of the mosque? I shut my eyes.

"... *Joseph said to his father: O Father, I dreamt that the sun, the moon, and eleven stars prostrated themselves before me.*"

"Praise be to Allah!"

My head is spinning wildly. I finally manage to stand up by hanging on to one of the wooden pillars that's holding up the roof. I leave Joseph with his father and walk toward the door of the mosque.

"... *In the tale of Joseph and his brothers can be found many signs of divine wisdom to aid those in search of truth . . .*"

Where have my shoes gone? I step outside in bare feet. It's freezing. The poisonous envy of Joseph's brothers echoes from the mosque and is taken up by the wind. I find myself standing by a stream. The gentle babbling of the water washes the clamor of Jacob's flock from my mind. The sky is clouded over. The moon and the stars lie prostrated at Joseph's feet. I plunge my face into the starless water. The stream cleanses the thick fumes of hash from my lungs and my brain. I drink some water, then walk over to a big tree to have a piss.

． ． ．

Joseph's cries resound inside the mosque. His
envious brothers have thrown him into a well. My
grandfather's sobs emerge from the darkness. He
would weep like Jacob every time he heard that
verse.

I aim my piss at the roots of the tree. A bullet whiz-
zes right past me.

"You atheist infidel!"

The bullet has lodged in the tree. My piss has come
to an immediate halt. The man crashes toward me
through the darkness of the night.

"Damn your father! Infidel! What do you think
you're doing pissing there like a donkey?"

He waves the barrel of the gun in the direction of
the mosque, so I turn and walk back. When we reach
the door he shouts, "Stay out! You'll defile the mosque
with your filth!"

He goes inside. The trials of Joseph stream
through the opened door of the mosque accompanied
by a dazzling shaft of lamplight. A passing caravan
rescues Joseph from the well, then sells him as a slave
to a minister of the Pharaoh.

· · ·

The man reappears and gestures with his gun for me to follow him. We walk back down to the stream.

"Make your ablutions!"

Mechanically I sit down by the water and begin to wash my hands, then my feet. I repeat the ritual prayer of ablution in silence to myself. My mind is fixed on the barrel of his gun.

"You atheist pig! Infidel! Aren't you going to wash your private parts?"

I am shaking. I don't know whether it's from cold or fear. I pull down my trousers. Just as I begin to wash myself, the man lunges at my balls. I spin backwards.

"Don't you dare move! Why haven't you shaved yourself ?"

He grabs at my pubic hair, ripping out a tuft. My yelp skims across the stream.

"You filthy infidel!"

I finish my ablutions and pull up my sopping trousers. I am speechless with fear and humiliation.

He forces me to bend over the stream and begin my ablutions again. Then, in bare feet, under pain of death, I follow the man back to the mosque. I wonder where Joseph has gotten to?

. . .

"... *Zulaikha, Potiphar's wife, desired Joseph. She invited him into her chamber and, locking the door demanded, 'Come close to me!'* "

The mosque is alive with the devilish temptations of Zulaikha.

"... *With Joseph intent on escape and Zulaikha intent on holding him fast, they both ran toward the door when suddenly Zulaikha's husband appeared. She cried out to Potiphar: Tell me how you will punish one who wishes to bring harm to your household? Does this crime not merit imprisonment or torture?*"

At the very moment I walk into the mosque, Joseph is thrown into jail. The man sitting at the front signals to the young student to stop reading, consigning Joseph's fate to the depths of the Koran.

The dervish is still in the same place, his eyes glued to a lantern hanging on the wall. The man who has brought me back to the mosque orders me over to the corner. I go to sit near the dervish.

. . .

The cleric's voice sounds out from the front of the mosque:

"Consider the plight of Joseph. Consider how Satan set many traps in his path. Never forget that women are the temptation of the devil!"

The man who stopped me from pissing goes over to the cleric and whispers something in his ear. The cleric fixes me with a horrified look and gets to his feet. The crowd of students begin to chant, "Praise be to Allah! Mohammed is our savior!"

But all I can hear is the voice of the dervish:

"Why can't you find in yourself the strength you attribute to Mohammed? In the end, only you can save yourself . . ."

Why don't they finish the story of Joseph? Is my fate really more important than his?

After a brief discussion with two or three of his students, the cleric walks toward me.

"This man is an infidel!" he informs the young bearded man, his eyes burning with hatred. "He must never be allowed to leave for Pakistan to spread his filth."

He turns his back and leaves the mosque.
The dervish settles his head back onto his brick.

The mosque, now emptied of hash fumes, is feverish with Joseph's anxiety.

Joseph lies in chains in a dungeon. In his grief-filled house, Jacob has gone blind. And Joseph's mother? Where is she? Surely her suffering is much worse than Jacob's. And Zulaikha's anguish is even more intense. If Jacob has shut himself away in his room to grieve, these two women have turned themselves into rooms of grief. Not rooms built of bricks and mortar, but rooms carved from the heart! Why does no one ever think about these two stricken women? It is his mother who most needs the healing sight of Joseph's coat of many colors, not his father!

The mosque slumbers in the stupor of hashish. While I take my rest in the strength of Zulaikha's love.

. . .

"Unless sleep is less restless than wakefulness, do not rest!"
It's the dervish standing right above my head. He gives me his hand and leads me out of the mosque.

The mosque, mute and immobile, is soon lost in the mists of the night. We find ourselves, the dervish and I, by the side of the stream. The dervish splashes a little water on my face.

"Who are you?" I ask.

He answers with a smile.

"That's a difficult question. Let me think about it for a while . . ."

He gulps down some water. I am waiting for his answer. He chuckles at my impatience.

"They call me 'the bird.'"

Not another word.

We walk together along the banks of the stream. By his side, all my fears and anxieties have gone. After a few meters, the dervish stops.

"You must always keep moving," he says.

He sits down by the stream and plunges his hand into the water.

"Once water stops flowing, it stagnates. Once water stagnates, it poisons the ground. Be like this stream, always in flux!"

"I want to go back."

"We'll all go back one day."

His hand caresses the water.

"No, I want to go back home, to Kabul."

"Here, they want to murder your body. There, they'll murder your soul!"

He takes the brick out from under his cloak and dips it in the stream.

"One day all of us will be like the mud of this brick."

With a smile on his face, he stands up and leaps to the other side of the stream. We walk beside the water. After a few paces the stream disappears underground.

I don't want to go back to the mosque. I want to stay with this man till dawn. Tomorrow I'll ask the trafficker to take me back to Kabul . . .

"Once you find yourself, always keep moving!"

The dervish's words pull me back from the journey to Kabul in my head. His voice becomes indistinguishable from the gurgling of the stream. We have arrived at its source.

"If you meet someone on your journey, grab him by the scruff of the neck and hang on!"

The dervish is getting fainter. The sound of his voice roots me to the spot.

"And if you never meet anyone . . . then hang on to yourself!"

He's going.

"Where?"

He can't hear me. Or he doesn't want to answer. I can't move.

I'm completely paralyzed. The dervish disappears into the night.

"Don't leave me!"

The despair in my voice settles on the water.

The dervish's voice emerges from the darkness.

"Hang on to yourself!"

A halo of smoke marks the place where the dervish was standing a minute ago. The oil lamps give off a weak light. Even weaker than I am. Everyone is asleep. I want to get up. I feel too heavy. I lean against the wall of the mosque.

"What are you doing?"

The sleepy voice of the man on the mat next to mine makes me freeze. Without knowing why, I hear myself asking, "Where is the dervish?"

I find myself pointing toward the place where the dervish used to be. The man lowers his head to his mat, covering his eyes with a corner of his turban. His murmuring voice disappears into the folds of cloth.

"What dervish?"

Another voice comes from across the room:

"That weed has really messed his head up!"

"No, he's just talking in his sleep."

They laugh a drowsy, nasty little laugh together. I make a move. The mosque trembles in sympathy. My throat aches with thirst. Water!

I reach the door of the mosque. In the hallway, a young man, his diminutive frame swamped in a huge quilt, opens his sleepy eyes.

"Where are you off to?" he asks.

"I need some water!"

"There's water in that jug."

"It's empty."

"Then go and fill it."

He turns his head away and buries himself in his quilt.

Where's the jug? My body feels entirely drained of both blood and water. I am utterly dry. Dry as the mat under my feet. As though my feet have been sewn to the mat. I can't move my feet. I need some fresh air. The mosque is stifling. There is no air.

"Are you going to say your Nafil prayer?" says the voice under the quilt.

My desiccated body shakes like a leaf. My right foot takes a step. Then stops. Another step. Heavier. Then another. I am outside. With no jug. With no shoes.

• • •

Dawn is breaking. The stream babbles loudly. The water invites me toward it. I run. The cold, stony ground shakes beneath my feet. I make it to the stream. Where is the dervish?

I sit down by the side of the stream.

Dawn will reveal where the dervish has gone.

Then the stream goes silent and dries up. I want to get up. My foot slips. I fall into the stream. The stream is a bottomless, dried-up well.

"God Is Great!"

The sound of the call to prayer drags me from the well.

The wolf and the lamb prowl above me in the sky. From the open door of the mosque, yawning voices drift down toward the stream.

I must go back.

Where is the morning star?

. . .

I stand up. I move my legs. I must run. I run. On water. On earth.

"STOP!"

Al-Ba'ith!

The voice nails me against the red dawn of the city. Where on earth am I?

My legs shake. I fall to the ground. The metallic taste of blood fills my mouth.

Al-Ba'ith!

A soldier's jackboots, there, right in front of my eyes. Darkness descends.

Is it nighttime?

So soon!

Translator's Note and Glossary

❧

A Thousand Rooms of Dream and Fear is set at a time of
acute political upheaval in Afghanistan. In 1973 Mohammed Daoud Khan engineered a coup that over-
threw the constitutional monarchy and inaugurated
the short-lived Republic of Afghanistan (1973–1978).
However, Daoud Khan's rule was marked by corrup-
tion and instability and, when the formerly faction-
ridden leftist parties overcame their differences to
oppose his regime, political chaos and violent state
repression ensued.

On April 27, 1978, Hafizullah Amin, the strong-
man of the Marxist People's Party, organized a coup
that toppled Daoud Khan's regime. Amin's mentor,
Nur Mohammed Taraki, was installed as party leader,
president, and prime minister of the Democratic

Republic of Afghanistan, with Amin as his deputy prime minister (until Amin decided he wanted more power and took over the role of prime minister just under a year later). After the April coup many Afghans fled the country. In this novel, Farhad's father is said to have left for Pakistan at that time.

The Soviet Union became increasingly concerned about Amin's burgeoning power and his anti-Islamic stance; the Soviets were convinced that Amin was exacerbating political unrest, particularly in the countryside, and they allegedly advised Taraki to get rid of him. But the attempt to have Amin assassinated was a failure, and instead Amin seized power on September 14, 1979. Taraki was killed in the violence (supposedly smothered to death with a pillow). Although his death was first announced in the *Kabul Times* on October 10, there were conflicting reports of the actual date he was murdered.

Unsurprisingly, Amin's attempts to improve relations with Pakistan and the United States were greeted with alarm by the Soviet Union. Unrest continued to escalate throughout the country, and then on December 24, 1979, Afghanistan was invaded by the Soviet Union. Amin was killed on December 27, and Babrak Karmal was handed the role of president by the invaders.

Though the narrator of *A Thousand Rooms of Dream and Fear* makes few overt references to the political situation in his country, it informs the whole novel. It is also assumed that the reader will understand the powerful social prohibitions that Farhad is breaking by being alone with a woman who no longer has a husband, and that Mahnaz is challenging by allowing her hair to be seen uncovered.

THE TITLE The phrase "a thousand rooms" is a direct translation of a Dari expression that can also mean "labyrinth."

THE EPIGRAPH Shams-e Tabrizi was a thirteenth-century Sufi mystic who was the close companion of the great Persian poet Mawlana Jalal ad-Din Muhammad Rumi (1207–1273), usually known as Rumi in the West. Shams was responsible for initiating Rumi into Islamic mysticism. After Shams's sudden disappearance in 1248, Rumi's grief and deep devotion to his friend found expression in his *Diwan-e Shams-e Tabrizi* (*The Book of Shams of Tabriz*) in which, as a sign of his love, Rumi attributed his own words to Shams. Poetry, especially that written by Rumi, has the highest possible status and importance for the people of Afghanistan.

BABUR   The descendant of Timur (Tamerlane the Great), founder of the Timurid dynasty, Zahiruddin Mohammed Babur (1483–1530) made Kabul the capital of his empire. He was famous for the beautiful gardens and vineyards he planted throughout Kabul, many of which remained until the city descended into chaos during the civil war. After capturing much of present-day Afghanistan, Babur turned his attention to India, where he established the Mughal dynasty. But he never lost his affection for Kabul, and his body is buried there, in Babur's Gardens.

BAGH-E-BALA   The summer palace of Abdur Rahman Khan (amir of Afghanistan from 1880 to 1901) was set on a hill to the north of the city, with a magnificent view over Kabul. In 1979 it was a place where young people would go to drink and hang out.

BARZAKH   The period between death and final judgment when the fate of the soul remains undecided.

BOOK OF THE DEAD   Abu Hamid Muhammad ibn Muhammad al-Ghazali (1058–1111) was one of the greatest Islamic theologians and philosophers of the Middle Ages. He was known in the West as Algazel. A Sufi mystic, his great work, *The Revival of the Religious Sciences*, made Sufism an acceptable part of orthodox Islam. Published in forty volumes, the final part, *On the Remembrance of Death and the Afterlife*, is commonly known as the "Book of the Dead."

DERVISH   A Sufi ascetic and mystic. Traditionally, dervishes practice austerity and live a life of poverty and prayer, much like Christian mendicant monks. Like monks, some live in orders and others are solitary. The great Sufi mystic poet Rumi was the founder of the most famous order of dervishes, the Mevlavi, well known for their "whirling" dance, through which they attain ecstasy and spiritual insight.

HAFIZ   Mohammed Shams al-Din Hafiz, or Hafiz of Shiraz (1325/6–1389/90) was one of the greatest lyric poets of Persia. A Sufi mystic, he had a profound influence on poetry in Persian and Arabic, especially for his mastery of the *ghazal*. Goethe was very affected by Hafiz's poetry. Hafiz was famous for his poems extolling alcohol as a means of attaining spiritual insight.

HAFT PAIKAR   A book written by Nazemi Ghan-
javi (c. 1141–1209), who is widely regarded as the
greatest romantic epic poet in Persian literature,
who introduced colloquial language and a degree
of realism to the Persian epic, and whose works
form an integral part of the culture of Iran and Afghanistan. *Haft Paikar* (*Seven Portraits*) is the story
of the Sassanid king, Bahram-e Gur, who discovers a mysterious room in his palace that contains
the portraits of seven beautiful princesses. He goes
in search of the princesses, each of whom represents one of the seven virtues.

KALIMA   The first verse of the Koran.

KHOSRAW & SHEERIN   (see *Haft Paikir*) A book by
Nizami Ganjavi. Sheerin (?–628) was the Christian wife of the Persian shah, Khosraw II. She was
first immortalized in Persian poetry by Firdausi
in his epic, the *Shahnama*. Around 1180, Nizami
retold the story, emphasizing Sheerin's love for the
master builder, Farhad. Khosraw was so jealous of
their love that he tricked Farhad into constructing
a tunnel under Mount Beysitoun; he then lied to
Farhad, telling him Sheerin was dead, a lie that
caused Farhad to fall from the mountain to his

death. As a result of Nizami's work, Sheerin and Farhad became symbols of pure, unrequited love. Their plight is recounted in many poems, including Goethe's *West-oestlicher Divan*.

Munkar   One of the two angels who are assigned to interrogate the dead before judgment day.

Nafil   Practicing Muslims are obliged to pray five times a day. These prayers are called: *Fajr* (at dawn); *Dhuhr* (at midday); *Asr* (in the afternoon); *Maghrib* (at sunset); *Isha* (at night). *Nafil* is the name for an additional, nonobligatory prayer, which can take place at any time.

Nakir   One of the two angels who are assigned to interrogate the dead before judgment day.

Ninety-nine names of God   Also known as the ninety-nine attributes of God (Asma' Allah al-Husná). According to Islamic tradition, Allah has ninety-nine names, each one representing one of his divine qualities. Repeating the names of God is a sacred practice, much as Roman Catholics will recite a litany of the names of saints. In this novel, Farhad recites the names Al-Ba'ith, meaning "the

resurrector," Al-Jabbar, meaning "the irresist-
ible, the powerful," and Al-Mumit, meaning "the
bringer of death, the destroyer."

PUL-E-CHARKHI Literally, "the bridge that spins
around." A large pentagon-shaped prison near
Kabul with a fearsome reputation for torture and
murder. It was built in the 1970s during the regime of Mohammed Daoud Khan and is still in
use today.

SHAH-DO-SHAMSHIRA MOSQUE One of the most
important shrines in Kabul, marking the burial
sight of an Islamic commander who was said to
have fallen in battle against Hindu forces, even
though he had continued fighting with a sword in
each hand after his head had been cut off.

TOMB OF SAYED JAMALUDDIN A striking land-
mark on the grounds of Kabul University with
huge black marble columns. The campus of Kabul
University was built in 1964 with the assistance of
the United States under Mohammed Daoud Khan.

Sarah Maguire

The Patience Stone

{Sang-e Saboor}

TRANSLATED FROM THE DARI BY

Polly McLean

WITH AN INTRODUCTION BY

Khaled Hosseini

This tale, written in memory of

N. A.

—an Afghan poet savagely murdered by

her husband—is dedicated to M. D.

From the body by the body with the body
Since the body and until the body.

—ANTONIN ARTAUD

Introduction

BY KHALED HOSSEINI

✣

It is a vexing fact that women are the most belea-
guered members of Afghan society. Long before the
arrival of the Taliban, Afghan women struggled for
basic rights. Outside of a few urban pockets, the iron-
clad rule of patriarchal, tribal law has long denied
women their right to work, education, adequate health
care, and personal independence—all of this made infinitely worse by three decades of war, displacement,
and anarchy. Though there have been some improve-
ments in recent years, far too many women continue
to languish under the unquestioned, absolute domina-
tion of tribal customs that deprive them of meaningful
participation in societal life. For far too long, Afghan
women have been faceless and voiceless.

Until now. With *The Patience Stone*, Atiq Rahimi gives face and voice to one unforgettable woman—and, one could argue, offers her as a proxy for the grievances of millions. The plot could not be simpler. The entire story unfolds in one room, where an unnamed woman nurses her badly injured husband, who lies motionless, wordless, and helpless. As warring factions plunder and pillage on the streets, the woman feeds her husband through a tube. She lubricates his eyes and changes him. And she speaks to him. Tentatively at first, until gradually, the dam ruptures, letting loose a flood of startling confessions. With increasing boldness, the woman reveals how she has resented her husband, her disappointments in him, her fiercely guarded secrets, her desires and hopes, the pains and sorrows she has suffered at his hands. As her husband lies before her like a stone—indeed like the legendary titular stone, which absorbs the anguish of all who confess to it—the woman suddenly finds herself free from all restraint and her monologues reach a fevered pitch. What pours out of her is not only a brave and shocking confession, but a savage indictment of war, the brutality of men, and the religious, marital, and cultural norms that continually assault Afghan women, leaving them with no recourse but to absorb without complaint, like a patience stone.

It is to Atiq Rahimi's credit that his heroine is no saint suffering quietly in purdah. Nor is she much of a heroine. As the woman's one-way discourse with her presumably unconscious husband goes on, the layers are peeled back, revelations come forth, and what emerges is the portrait of a complex and nuanced human being. Rahimi's heroine is brave, resilient, a devout mother, but she is also flawed in fundamentally human ways, a woman capable of lying, manipulating, of being spiteful, a creature that, pushed hard enough, bares her teeth. And her body. Here, Rahimi has broached a great Afghan taboo, the notion of a woman as a sexual being. A pair of passages in this novel may very well generate protest from the more conservative sectors of the Afghan community, but Rahimi is to be applauded for not shying away from the subject. He is to be commended for not turning his heroine into the archetype of the saintly, asexual, maternal figure. Perhaps, writing this novel in French, and not in Dari, made it easier for him. He has been quoted as saying, ". . . a kind of involuntary self-censorship has come into play when I've written in Persian. My acquired language, the one I have chosen, gives me a kind of freedom to express myself, away from this self-censorship and an unconscious shame that dwells in us from childhood." Whatever the reason, the reader benefits from his unflinching approach.

It is also a testament to Rahimi's considerable literary skills how vividly the war on the streets is depicted, even though the entire tale unfolds within the confines of a single bedroom. The specter of the unnamed conflict, fought between never-named factions, is the third character in the room. Rahimi chooses to not take us to the streets. Instead, we experience war as most helpless civilians do. We hear the sudden bursts of gunfire, the screams, the terrifying silences. We feel the impact of mortar fire when the room shakes and plaster flakes rain down. Despite never taking us to the streets—or perhaps because of it—Rahimi succeeds in making us experience the chaos, the helplessness, the senseless brutality committed with impunity, the random and sudden outbursts of violence that take unsuspecting lives. The years of factional infighting were some of the darkest of the last thirty years in Afghanistan, and in Rahimi's spare prose, the era comes to life to devastating effect.

The Patience Stone, winner of the prestigious Goncourt Prize in France, is a deceptively simple book, written in a spare, poetic style. But it is a rich read, part allegory, part a tale of retribution, part an exploration of honor, love, sex, marriage, war. It is without doubt an important and courageous book. In this reader's view, though, this novel's greatest achievement is in giving voice. Giving voice to those who, as the fable goes, suffer the most and cry out the least. Rahimi's nameless heroine is a conduit, a living vessel for the grievances of millions of women like her, women who have been objectified, marginalized, scorned, beaten, ridiculed, silenced. In *The Patience Stone*, they have their say at last.

The Patience Stone

⚜

Somewhere in Afghanistan or elsewhere

The room is small. Rectangular. Stifling, despite the paleness of the turquoise walls, and the two curtains patterned with migrating birds frozen midflight against a yellow and blue sky. Holes in the curtains allow the rays of the sun to reach the faded stripes of a kilim. At the far end of the room is another curtain. Green. Unpatterned. Concealing a disused door. Or an alcove.

The room is bare. Bare of decoration. Except between the two windows where someone has hung a small khanjar dagger on the wall, and above the khanjar a photo of a man with a mustache. He is about thirty years old. Curly hair. Square face, bracketed by a pair of neatly tended sideburns. His black eyes sparkle. They are small, separated by a hawklike nose. The man is not laughing, yet seems as if he is holding back a laugh. This gives him a strange expression, that of a man inwardly mocking those who look at him. The photo is in black and white, hand-colored in drab tones.

Facing this photo, at the foot of a wall, the same man—older now—is lying on a red mattress on the floor. He has a beard. Pepper and salt. He is thinner. Too thin. Nothing but skin and bones. Pale. Wrinkled. His nose more hawklike than ever. He still isn't laughing, and still looks strangely mocking. His mouth is half-open. His eyes, even smaller now, have retreated into their sockets. His gaze is fixed on the ceiling, on the exposed, blackened, rotting beams. His arms lie passive along his sides. Beneath his translucent skin, the veins twine around the jutting bones of his body like sleeping worms. On his left wrist he wears a wind-up watch, and on his ring finger a gold wedding band. A tube drips clear liquid into the crook of his arm from a plastic pouch attached to the wall just above his head. The rest of his body is covered by a long, blue shirt, embroidered at the collar and cuffs. His legs, stiff as two stakes, are buried under a white sheet. A dirty, white sheet.

．．．

A hand, a woman's hand, is resting on his chest, over his heart, rising and falling in time with his breath. The woman is seated. Knees pulled into her chest. Head sunk between them. Her dark hair—it is very dark, and long—covers her slumped shoulders, rising and falling with the regular movement of her arm.

In the other hand, the left, she holds a long string of black prayer beads. She moves them between her fingers, telling them. Silently. Slowly. In time with her shoulders. In time with the man's breath. Her body is swathed in a long dress. Crimson. Embroidered, at the cuffs and bottom hem, with a few discreet ears and flowers of wheat.

Within reach, open at the flyleaf and placed on a velvet pillow, is a book, the Koran.

A little girl is crying. She is not in this room. Perhaps she's next door. Or in the passage.

The woman's head moves. Wearily. Emerges from the crook of her knees.

The woman is beautiful. At the crease of her left eye, a small scar narrows the place where the eyelids meet, lending a strange wariness to her gaze. Her plump, dry, pale lips are softly and slowly repeating the same word of prayer.

A second little girl starts crying. She seems closer than the first, probably just behind the door.

The woman removes her hand from the man's chest. She stands up and leaves the room. Her absence doesn't change a thing. The man still does not move. He continues to breathe silently, slowly.

The sound of the woman's footsteps quiets the two children. She stays with them for some time, until the house and the world become mere shadows in their sleep; then she returns. In one hand, a small white bottle, in the other, the black prayer beads. She sits down next to the man, opens the bottle, leans over and administers two drops into his right eye, two into his left. Without letting go of her prayer beads. Without pausing in her telling of them.

The rays of the sun shine through the holes in the yellow and blue sky of the curtains, caressing the woman's back and her shoulders as they continue to rock to the rhythm of the prayer beads passing between her fingers.

Far away, somewhere in the city, a bomb explodes. The violence destroys a few houses perhaps, a few dreams. There's a counterattack. The retaliations tear through the heavy midday silence, shaking the window-panes but not waking the children. For a moment— just two prayer beads—the woman's shoulders stop moving. She puts the bottle of eyedrops in her pocket. Murmurs *"Al-Qahhar."* Repeats *"Al-Qahhar."* Repeats it each time the man takes a breath. And with every repetition, slips one of the prayer beads through her fingers.

One cycle of the prayer beads is complete. Ninety-nine beads. Ninety-nine times *"Al-Qahhar."*

She sits up and returns to her place on the mat-tress, next to the man's head, and puts her right hand back on his chest. Begins another cycle of the prayer beads.

As she again reaches the ninety-ninth *"Al-Qahhar,"* her hand leaves the man's chest and travels toward his neck. Her fingers wander into the bushy beard, rest-ing there for one or two breaths, emerging to pause a moment on the lips, stroke the nose, the eyes, the brow, and finally vanish again, into the thickness of the filthy hair. "Can you feel my hand?" She leans over him, straining, and stares into his eyes. No response.

She bends her ear to his lips. No sound. Just the same unsettling expression, mouth half-open, gaze lost in the dark beams of the ceiling.

She bends down again to whisper, "In the name of Allah, give me a sign to let me know that you feel my hand, that you're alive, that you'll come back to me, to us! Just a sign, a little sign to give me strength, and faith." Her lips tremble. They beg, "Just a word . . . ," as they brush lightly over the man's ear. "I hope you can hear me, at least." She lays her head on the pillow.

"They told me that after two weeks you'd be able to move, to respond . . . But this is the third week, or nearly. And still nothing!" Her body shifts so she is lying on her back. Her gaze wanders, joining his vacant gaze somewhere among the dark and rotting beams.

"Al-Qahhar, Al-Qahhar, Al-Qahhar . . ."

The woman sits up slowly. Stares desperately at the man. Puts her hand back on his chest. "If you can breathe, you must be able to hold your breath, surely? Hold it!" Pushing her hair back behind her shoulders, she repeats, "Hold it, just once!" and again bends her ear to his mouth. She listens. She hears him. He is breathing.

In despair, she mutters, "I can't take it anymore."

With an angry sigh, she suddenly stands up and repeats, shouting: "I can't take it anymore . . ." Then more dejected: "Reciting the names of God, over and over from dusk till dawn, I just can't take it!" She moves a few steps closer to the photo, without looking at it. "It's been sixteen days . . ." She hesitates. "No . . . ," counting on her fingers, unsure.

Confused, she turns around, returns to her spot, and glances at the open page of the Koran. Checks. "Sixteen days . . . so today it's the sixteenth name of God that I'm supposed to chant. *Al-Qahhar*, the Dominant. Yes, that's right, that is the sixteenth name . . ." Thoughtful: "Sixteen days!" She takes a step back. "Sixteen days that I've been existing in time with your breath." Hostile: "Sixteen days that I've been breathing with you!" She stares at the man. "Look, I breathe just like you!" She takes a deep breath in, exhales it laboriously. In time with him. "Even without my hand on your chest, I still breathe like you."

She bends over him. "And even when I'm not near you, I still breathe in time with you." She backs away from him. "Do you hear me?" She starts shouting *"Al-Qahhar,"* and telling the prayer beads again, still to the same rhythm. She walks out of the room. We hear her shouting, *"Al-Qahhar, Al-Qahhar . . ."* in the passage and beyond . . .

"Al-Qahhar . . ." moves away.
"Al-Qahhar . . ." becomes faint.
"Al . . ." Imperceptible.
Is gone.

A few moments drift by in silence. Then *"Al-Qahhar"* returns, audible through the window, from the passage, from behind the door. The woman comes back into the room and stops next to the man. Standing. Her left hand still telling the black prayer beads. "I can even inform you that while I've been away you have breathed thirty-three times." She crouches down. "And even now, at this moment, as I'm speaking, I can count your breaths." She lifts the string of prayer beads into what seems to be the man's field of vision. "And now, since my return, you have breathed seven times." She sits on the kilim and continues, "I no longer count my days in hours, or my hours in minutes, or my minutes in seconds . . . a day for me is ninety-nine prayer-bead cycles!" Her gaze comes to rest on the old watch-bracelet holding together the bones of the man's wrist. "I can even tell you that there are five cycles to go before the mullah makes the call to midday prayer and preaches the hadith." A moment. She is working it out. "At the twentieth cycle, the water bearer will knock on the neighbor's door. As usual, the old woman with the rasping cough will come out to open the door for him. At the thirtieth, a boy will cross the street on his bike, whistling the tune of "*Laïli, Laïli, Laïli, ∂jân, ∂jân, ∂jân, you have broken my heart,*" for our neighbor's daughter . . ." She laughs. A sad laugh. "And when I reach the seventy-second cycle, that cretinous mullah will come to visit you and, as always, will reproach me because, according to him, I can't have taken good care of you, can't have followed his instructions, must have neglected the prayers . . . Otherwise you'd be getting better!" She touches the man's arm. "But you are my witness. You know that I live only for you, at your side, by your breath! It's easy for him to say," she complains, "that I must recite one of the ninety-nine names of God ninety-nine times a day . . . for ninety-nine days! But that stupid mullah has no idea what it's like to be alone with a man who . . ." She can't find the right word, or doesn't dare say it, and just grumbles softly ". . . to be all alone with two little girls!"

A long silence. Almost five prayer-bead cycles. Five cycles during which the woman remains huddled against the wall, her eyes closed. It is the call to midday prayer that snatches her from her daze. She picks up the little rug, unfolds it, and lays it out on the ground. Makes a start on the prayer.

The prayer complete, she remains sitting on the rug to listen to the mullah preach the hadith for that day of the week: ". . . and today is a day of blood, for it was on a Tuesday that Eve, for the first time, lost tainted blood, that one of the sons of Adam killed his brother, that Gregory, Zachary, and Yahya—may peace be upon them—were killed, as well as Pharaoh's counselors, his wife Asiya Bint Muzahim, and the heifer of the Children of Israel . . ."

She looks around slowly. The room. Her man. This body in the emptiness. This empty body.

Her eyes fill with dread. She stands up, refolds the rug, puts it back in its place in the corner of the room, and leaves.

. . .

A few moments later, she returns to check the level
of solution in the drip bag. There isn't much left. She
stares at the tube, noting the intervals between the
drips. They are short, shorter than the intervals between the man's breaths. She adjusts the flow, waits
two drips, and turns around decisively. "I'm going
to the pharmacy for more solution." But before her
feet cross the threshold, they falter and she lets out a
plaintive sigh: "I hope they've managed to get hold of
some . . ." She leaves the room. We hear her waking
the children, "Come on, we're going out," and departing, followed by little footsteps running down the passage, through the courtyard . . .

After three cycles of the prayer beads—two hundred and ninety-seven breaths—they are back.

The woman takes the children into the next-door
room. One is crying, "I'm hungry, Mummy." The other
complaining, "Why didn't you get any bananas?" Their
mother comforts them: "I'll give you some bread."

Just as the sun withdraws its rays from the holes
in the yellow and blue sky of the curtains, the woman
reappears in the doorway to the room. She looks at

the man a while, then approaches and checks his breath. He is breathing. The drip bag is almost dry. "The pharmacy was shut," she says and, looking resigned, waits, as if for further instructions. Nothing. Nothing but breathing. She leaves again and returns with a glass of water. "I'll have to do what I did last time, and use sugar-salt solution . . ."

With a quick, practiced movement she pulls the tube out of his arm. Takes off the syringe. Cleans the tube, feeds it into his half-open mouth, and pushes it down until it reaches his esophagus. Then she pours the contents of the glass into the drip bag. Adjusts the flow, checking the gaps between drips. One drip per breath.

And leaves.

A dozen drips later, she is back, chador in hand. "I have to go and see my aunt." She waits again . . . for permission, perhaps. Her eyes wander. "I've lost my mind!" Agitated, she turns around and leaves the room. Behind the door, her voice comes and goes in the passageway: "I don't care," near, "what you think of her . . . ," far, "I love her," near, "she's all I have left . . . my sisters have abandoned me, and your brothers too . . . ," far, ". . . that I see her," near, "I need to . . . ," far, ". . . she doesn't give a damn about you . . . and neither do I!" She can be heard leaving with her two children.

Their absence lasts three thousand nine hundred and sixty breaths. Three thousand nine hundred and sixty breaths during which nothing happens except what the woman had predicted. The water bearer knocks at the neighbor's door. A woman with a rasping cough opens the door to him . . . A few breaths later, a boy crosses the street on his bike whistling the tune of *"Laïli, Laïli, Laïli, djân, djân, djân, you have broken my heart . . ."*

So they return, she and her two children. She leaves them in the passage. Opens the door, abruptly. Her man is still there. Same position. Same rhythm to his breath. As for her, she is very pale. Paler even than him. She leans against the wall. After a long silence, she moans, "My aunt . . . she has left the house . . . she's gone!" With her back against the wall she slips to the ground. "She's gone . . . but where? No one knows . . . I have no one left . . . no one!" Her voice trembles. Her throat tightens. The tears flow. "She doesn't know what's happened to me . . . she can't know! Otherwise she would have left me a message, or come to rescue me . . . She hates you, I know, but she loves me . . . she loves the children . . . but you . . ." The sobbing robs her of her voice. She moves away from the wall, shuts her eyes, takes a deep breath in an attempt to say something. But she can't say it; it must be heavy, heavy with meaning, voice-crushingly heavy. So she keeps it inside, and seeks something light, gentle, and easy to say: "And you, you knew that you had a wife and two daughters!" She punches herself in the belly. Once. Twice. As if to beat out the heavy word that has buried itself in her guts. She crouches down and cries, "Did you think about us for even a second, when you shouldered that fucking Kalashnikov? You son of a . . . ," the words suppressed again.

She remains still for a moment. Her eyes close. Her head hangs. She lets out a long, painful groan. Her shoulders are still moving to the rhythm of the breath. Seven breaths.

Seven breaths, and she looks up, wiping her eyes on the sleeve embroidered with ears and flowers of wheat. After looking at the man a while, she moves closer, bends over his face and whispers, "Forgive me," as she strokes his arm. "I'm tired. At breaking point. Don't abandon me, you're all I have left." She raises her voice: "Without you, I have nothing. Think of your daughters! What will I do with them? They're so young . . ." She stops stroking him.

Somewhere outside, not far away, a shot is fired. Another, closer, in retort. The first gunman shoots again. This time, no response.

"The mullah won't come today," she says with some relief. "He's scared of stray bullets. He's as much of a coward as your brothers." She stands up and moves a few steps away. "You men, you're all cowards!" She comes back. Stares darkly at the man. "Where are your brothers who were so proud to see you fight their enemies?" Two breaths and her silence fills with rage. "Cowards!" she spits. "They should be looking after your children, and me—honoring you, and themselves—isn't that right? Where is your mother, who always used to say she would sacrifice herself for a single hair on your head? She couldn't deal with the fact that her son, the hero, who fought on every front, against every foe, had managed to get shot in a pathetic quarrel because some guy—from his own side, would you believe—had said, *I spit in your mother's pussy!* Shot over an insult!" She takes a step closer. "It's so ridiculous, so stupid!" Her gaze wanders around the room and then settles, heavily, on the man who may or may not hear her. "Do you know what your family said to me, before leaving the city?" she continues. "That they wouldn't be able to take care of either your wife or your children . . . You might as well know: they've abandoned you. They don't give a fuck about your health, or your suffering, or your honor! . . . They've deserted us," she cries. "Us, me!" She raises her prayer-bead hand to the ceiling, begging, "Allah, help me! . . . *Al-Qahhar, Al-Qahhar . . .*" And weeps.

One cycle of the prayer beads.

Desolate, she stammers, "I'm going . . . I'm going . . . I am . . . mad." She throws her head back. "Why tell him all this? I'm going mad. Allah, cut off my tongue! May my mouth be filled with earth!" She covers her face. "Allah, protect me, guide me, I'm losing my way, show me the path!"

No reply.

No guide.

Her hand buries itself in her man's hair. Beseeching words emerge from her dry throat: "Come back, I beg you, before I lose my mind. Come back, for the sake of your children . . ." She looks up. Gazes through her tears in the same uncertain direction as the man. "Bring him back to life, God!" Her voice drops. "After all, he fought in your name for so long. For jihad!" She stops, then starts again: "And you're leaving him in this state? What about his children? And me? You can't, you can't, you've no right to leave us like this, without a man!" Her left hand, the one holding the prayer beads, pulls the Koran toward her. Her rage seeks expression in her voice. "Prove that you exist, bring him back to life!" She opens the Koran. Her finger moves down the names of God featured on the flyleaf. "I swear I won't ever let him go off to fight again like a bloody idiot. Not even in your name! He will be mine, here, with me." Her throat, knotted by sobs, lets through only the stifled cry *"Al-Qahhar."* She starts telling the prayer beads again. *"Al-Qahhar . . ."* Ninety-nine times, *"Al-Qahhar."*

The room grows dark.

"I'm scared, Mummy. It's all dark." One of the little girls is whimpering in the passage, behind the door. The woman stands up to leave the room.

"Don't be frightened, darling. I'm here."

"Why are you shouting? You're scaring me, Mummy," weeps the little girl. The mother reassures her: "I wasn't shouting. I was talking to your father."

They walk away from the door.

"Why are you calling my father *Al-Qahhar?* Is he cross?"

"No, but he will be if we disturb him."

The little girl falls silent.

It is now completely dark.

And, as the woman predicted, the mullah has not come.

She returns with a hurricane lamp. Puts it on the ground near the man's head, and takes the bottle of eyedrops out of her pocket. Gently, she administers the drops. One, two. One, two. Then leaves the room and comes back with a sheet and a small plastic basin. She removes the dirty sheet covering the man's legs. Washes his belly, his feet, his genitals. Once this is done she covers her man with a clean sheet, checks the gaps between the drips of sugar-salt solution and leaves, taking the lamp with her.

Everything is dark once more. For a long time.

At dawn, as the hoarse voice of the mullah calls the faithful to prayer, the sound of dragging feet can be heard in the passage. They approach the room, move away, then come back. The door opens. The woman enters. She looks at the man. Her man. He is still there, in the same position. But his eyes draw her attention. She takes a step forward. His eyes are closed. The woman moves nearer. Another step. Silently. Then two. She looks at him. Can't see clearly. She isn't sure. She backs out of the room. Less than five breaths later she is back with the hurricane lamp. His eyes are still closed. She collapses onto the floor. "Are you sleeping?!" Her trembling hand moves to the man's chest. He is breathing. "Yes . . . you're sleeping!" she shouts. Looks around the room for someone so she can say it again: "He's sleeping!"

No one. She is afraid.

She picks up the little rug, unfolds it, and stretches it out on the ground. The morning prayer done, she remains sitting, takes the Koran and opens it at the page marked with a peacock feather, which she removes and holds in her right hand. With her left, she tells the prayer beads.

After reading a few verses, she puts back the feather, closes the Koran, and sits thoughtfully for a moment, gazing at the feather peeking out of the sacred book. She strokes it, sadly at first, then anxiously.

. . .

She stands up, tidies away the rug, and walks toward the door. Before leaving, she stops. Turns around. Goes back to her place by the man. Hesitantly opens one of his eyes. Then the other. Waits. His eyes do not close again. The woman takes the bottle of eye-drops and measures a few drops into his eyes. One, two. One, two. Checks the drip bag. There's still some solution.

Before standing up, she pauses and looks nervously at the man, asking him, "Can you close your eyes again?" The man's vacant eyes do not respond. She persists, "You can, you can! Do it again!" And waits. In vain.

Concerned, she slips her hand gently under the man's neck. A sensation, a horror, makes her arm twitch. She shuts her eyes, clenches her teeth. Breathes in deeply, painfully. She is suffering. As she breathes out, she extracts her hand and examines the tips of her trembling fingers in the weak light of the lamp. They are dry. She stands up to roll the man onto his side. Brings the lamp closer to his neck so she can examine a small wound—still open, bruised, drained of blood but not yet healed.

The woman holds her breath, and presses the wound. The man still doesn't respond. She presses harder. No protest. Not in the eyes, or the breath. "Doesn't it even hurt?" She rolls the man onto his back again, and leans over him so she can look into his eyes. "You don't suffer! You've never suffered, never! I've never heard of a man surviving a bullet in the neck! You're not even bleeding, there's no pus, no pain, no suffering! *It's a miracle!* your mother used to say . . . Some bloody miracle!" She stands up. "Even injured, you've been spared suffering." Her voice rasps in her tightening throat. "And it's me who suffers! Me who cries!" Having said it, she moves to the door. Tears and fury in her eyes, she disappears into the darkness of the passage, leaving the hurricane lamp to project the trembling shadow of the man onto the wall until the full rise of dawn, until the rays of the sun make their way through the holes in the yellow and blue curtains, condemning the lamp to insignificance.

A hand hesitates to open the door to the room. Or is struggling to. "Daddy!" The voice of one of the children can be heard over the creaking of the door. "Where are you going?" At the woman's shout, the child pulls the door shut and moves away. "Don't bother your father, darling. He's sick. He's sleeping. Come with me!" The small footsteps run off down the passage. "But what about you, when you go in there, and shout, doesn't that bother him?" Her mother replies: "Yes, it does." Silence.

A fly sneaks into the heavy hush of the room. Lands on the man's forehead. Hesitant. Uncertain. Wanders over his wrinkles, licks his skin. No taste. Definitely no taste.

The fly makes its way down into the corner of his eye. Still hesitant. Still uncertain. It tastes the white of the eye, then moves off. It isn't chased away. It resumes its journey, getting lost in the beard, climbing the nose. Takes flight. Explores the body. Returns. Settles once more on the face. Clambers onto the tube stuffed into the half-open mouth. Licks it, moves right along it to the edge of the lips. No spit. No taste. The fly continues, enters the mouth. And is engulfed.

The hurricane lamp breathes its final breaths in vain. The flame goes out. The woman returns. She is filled with a deep weariness—of her being, and her body. After a few listless steps toward her man, she stops. Less decisive than the previous day. Her gaze lingers desperately on the motionless body. She sits down between the man and the Koran, which she opens at the flyleaf. She moves her finger over the names of God, one by one. Counts them. Stops at the seventeenth name. Murmurs *"Al-Wahhab*, the Bestower." A bitter smile puckers the edges of her lips. "I don't need a gift." She pulls at the peacock feather peeking out of the Koran. "I haven't the heart to go on reciting the names of God." She strokes her lips with the feather. "Praise be to God . . . He will save you. Without me. Without my prayers . . . He's got to."

The woman is silenced by a knocking at the door. "It must be the mullah." She hasn't the slightest desire to open. More knocking. She hesitates. The knocking continues. She leaves the room. Her footsteps can be heard moving toward the road. She is talking to someone. Her words are lost in the courtyard, behind the windows.

A hand timidly pushes open the door to the room. One of the little girls comes in. A sweet face beneath a mop of unruly hair. She is slender. Her little eyes stare at the man. "Daddy!" she cries, and shyly walks closer. "Are you sleeping, Daddy?" she asks. "What's that in your mouth?" pointing at the drip tube. She stops near her father, unsure whether to touch his cheek. "But you're not sleeping!" she cries. "Why does Mummy always say you're sleeping? Mummy says you're sick. She won't let me come in here and talk to you . . . but she's always talking to you." She is about to sit down next to him when she is stopped by a cry from her sister, squeezed into the half-open doorway. "Be quiet!" she shouts, mimicking her mother's voice, and runs up to the little one. "Come on!" She takes her by the hand and pulls her toward their father. After a moment's hesitation, the younger girl climbs onto her father's chest and starts yanking at his beard. The other shouts heartily, "Come on, Daddy, talk!" She leans toward his mouth and touches the tube. "Take out this thing. Talk!" She pulls away the tube, hoping to hear him say something. But no. Nothing but breathing. Slow, deep breaths. She stares at her father's half-open mouth. Her curious little hand dives in and pulls out the fly. "A fly!" she cries and, disgusted, throws it on the floor. The younger girl laughs, and rests her chapped cheek on her father's chest.

The mother comes in. "What are you doing?" she screams in horror. She rushes toward the children, grabbing them by the arms. "Get out! Come with me!"

"A fly! Daddy's eating a fly!" shriek the girls, almost in concert. "Be quiet!" orders their mother.

They leave the room.

The fly struggles on the kilim, drowning in saliva.

The woman comes back into the room. Before reinserting the tube into the man's mouth she looks around, anxious and intrigued. "What fly?" Noticing nothing, she replaces the tube and leaves.

Later, she comes back to pour sugar-salt solution into the drip bag, and eyedrops into the man's eyes.

Her tasks complete, she does not remain with her man.

She no longer puts her right hand on her man's chest.

She no longer tells the black prayer beads in time with her man's breathing.

She leaves.

She doesn't return until the call to midday prayer— and not to take out the little carpet, unfurl it, lay it on the ground, and say her prayers. Just to put new eye-drops into the man's eyes. One, two. One, two. And then leave again.

After the call to prayer, the mullah's hoarse voice beseeches God to lend his protection to the area's faithful on this, a Wednesday: "... because, as our Prophet says, *it's a day of misfortune during which the Pharaoh and his people were drowned, and the peoples of the Prophet Salih—the Ad and the Thamoud—were destroyed* ..." He stops and immediately starts again in a fearful voice. "Dear Faithful, as I have always told you, Wednesday is a day on which, according to our Prophet, the most noble, *it is right neither to practice bloodletting, nor to give, nor to receive.* However, one of the hadith, quoted by Ibn Younes, says that this practice is permitted during jihad. Today, your brother, our great Commander, is furnishing you with weapons that you may defend your honor, your blood, and your tribe!"

In the street, men are shouting themselves hoarse: *"Allah O Akbar!"* Running: *"Allah O Akbar!"* Their voices fading as they near the mosque: *"Allah O ..."*

A few ants prowl around the corpse of the fly on the kilim. Then grab hold of it and carry it off.

The woman arrives to gaze anxiously at the man. Perhaps she is afraid that the call to arms will have put him back on his feet.

She stays near the door. Her fingers stroke her lips and then, nervously, stray between her teeth, as if to extract words that don't dare express themselves. She leaves the room. She can be heard making something for lunch, talking and playing with the children.

Then it's time for a nap.

Darkness.

Silence.

The woman comes back. Less anxious. She sits down next to the man. "That was the mullah. He was here for our prayer session. I told him that since yesterday I have been impure, that I am menstruating, like Eve. He wasn't happy. I'm not sure why. Because I dared compare myself to Eve, or because I told him I was bleeding? He left, muttering into his beard. He wasn't like that before; you could have a joke with him. But since you people declared this new law for the country, he's changed too. He's afraid, poor man."

Her gaze settles on the Koran. Suddenly, she jumps: "Shit, the feather!" She looks for it inside the book. Not there. Under the pillow. Not there either. In her pockets. There it is. With a big sigh, she sits down. "That mullah is driving me out of my mind!" she says as she puts the feather back inside the Koran. "What was I talking about? . . . Oh yes, bleeding . . . I was lying to him, of course." She glances keenly at the man, more mischievous than submissive. "Just as I've lied to you . . . more than once!" She pulls her legs up to her chest and wedges her chin between her knees. "But there is something I'd better tell you . . ." She looks at him for a long time. Still with the same strange wariness in her gaze. "You know . . ." Her voice goes hoarse. She swallows to moisten her throat, and looks up. "When you and I went to bed for the first time— after three years of marriage, remember!—anyway, that night, I had my period." Her gaze flees the man to seek refuge in the creases of the sheet. She rests her left cheek on her knees. The look in her scarred eye loses some of its wariness. "I didn't tell you. And you, you thought that . . . the blood was proof of my virginity!" A muted laugh shakes her crouched, huddled body. "How thrilled you were to see the blood, how proud!" A moment. A look. And the dread of hearing a cry of rage, an insult. Nothing. And so, soft and serene, she allows herself to visit the intimate corners of her memory. "I shouldn't really have had my period then. It wasn't the right time, but I was a week early; it must have been nerves, fear about meeting you. I mean, can you imagine—being engaged for almost a year and then married for three years to an absent man; not so easy. I lived with your name. I had never seen, or heard, or touched you before that day. I was afraid, afraid of everything, of you, of going to bed, of the blood. But at the same time, it was a fear I enjoyed.

You know, the kind of fear that doesn't separate you from your desire, but instead arouses you, gives you wings, even though it may burn. That was the kind of fear I was feeling. And it was growing in me every day, invading my belly, my guts . . . On the night before you arrived, it came pouring out. It wasn't a blue fear. No. It was a red fear, blood red. When I mentioned it to my aunt, she advised me not to say anything . . . and so I kept quiet. That suited me fine. Although I was a virgin I was really scared. I kept wondering what would happen if by any chance I didn't bleed that night . . ." Her hand sweeps through the air as if batting away a fly. "It would have been a catastrophe. I'd heard so many stories about that. I could imagine the whole thing." Her voice becomes mocking. "Passing off impure blood as virginal blood, bit of a brainwave, don't you think?" She lies down right close to the man. "I have never understood why, for you men, pride is so much linked to blood." Her hand sweeps the air again. Her fingers are moving. As if gesturing to an invisible person to come closer. "And remember the night—it was when we were first living together—that you came home late. Dead drunk. You'd been smoking. I had fallen asleep. You pulled down my knickers without saying a word. I woke up. But I pretended to be deeply asleep. You . . . penetrated me . . . you had a great time . . . but when you stood up to go and wash yourself, you noticed blood on your dick. You were furious. You came back and beat me, in the middle of the night, just because I hadn't warned you that I was bleeding. I had defiled you!" She laughs, scornful. "I had made you unclean." Her hand snatches memories from the air, closes around them, descends to stroke her belly as it swells and slackens at a pace faster than the man's breathing.

Suddenly, she thrusts her hand downward, beneath her dress, between her legs. Closes her eyes. Takes a deep, ragged breath. Rams her fingers into herself, roughly, as if driving in a blade. Holding her breath, she pulls out her hand with a stifled cry. Opens her eyes and looks at the tips of her nails. They are wet. Wet with blood. Red with blood. She puts her hand in front of the man's vacant eyes. "Look! That's my blood too. Clean. What's the difference between menstrual blood and blood that is clean? What's so disgusting about this blood?" Her hand moves down to the man's nostrils. "You were born of this blood! It is cleaner than the blood of your own body!" She pushes her fingers roughly into his beard. As she brushes his lips she feels his breath. A shiver of fear runs across her skin. Her arm shudders. She pulls her hand away, clenches her fist, and, with her mouth against the pillow, cries out again. Just once. The cry is long. Heartrending. She doesn't move for a long time. A very long time. Until the water bearer knocks on the neighbor's door, and the old woman's rasping cough is heard through the walls, and the water bearer empties his skin into the neighbor's tank, and one of her daughters starts crying in the passage. Then, she stands up and leaves the room without daring to look at her man.

Later, much later, just as the ants carrying the fly's body reach the foot of the wall between the two windows, the woman comes back with a clean sheet and the small plastic basin. She pulls off the sheet covering the man's legs, washes his belly, feet, and penis . . . and covers him up again. "More repugnant than a corpse! He doesn't give off any smell at all!" She leaves.

Night, again.
The room in absolute darkness.

Suddenly, the blinding flash of an explosion. A deafening blast makes the earth tremble. Its breath shatters the windows.

Throats are torn apart by screaming.

A second explosion. This one closer. Therefore more violent.

The children are crying.

The woman is wailing.

The sound of their terrified footsteps rings out in the passage, and disappears into the cellar.

Outside, not far away, something catches fire—perhaps the neighbor's tree. The light rips through the dusk of the courtyard and the room.

Outside, some are yelling, some crying, and some firing their Kalashnikovs, who knows where from or toward whom . . . just firing, firing . . .

It all stops eventually, in the gray half-light of an undecided dawn.

Then a thick silence descends on the smoky street, on the courtyard now nothing but a dead garden, on the room where the man, covered in soot, is laid out as always. Motionless. Immune. Just breathing. Slowly breathing.

The hesitant creaking of an opening door and the sound of cautious footsteps proceeding along the passage do not shatter this deathly silence, but underline it.

The footsteps stop behind the door. After a long pause—four of the man's breaths—the door opens. It's the woman. She enters. Does not look at him straightaway. First, she examines the state of the room, the broken window panes, the soot now settled on the curtains' migrating birds, on the kilim's faded stripes, on the open Koran, on the drip bag emptying itself of its last salty-sweet drops . . . Then her gaze sweeps over the sheet covering the man's skeletal legs, takes in his beard, and finally reaches his eyes.

She takes a few fearful steps toward the man. Stops. Observes the movement of his chest. He is breathing. She walks closer, bends down so she can see his eyes more clearly. They are open, and covered in black dust. She wipes them with the end of her sleeve, takes out the bottle and administers drops to each eye. One, two. One, two.

She touches the man's face cautiously, to wipe off the soot, and then sits quite still, as still as he. Her shoulders weighed down with troubles, she breathes, as always, to the same rhythm as the man.

The neighbor's rasping cough travels through the silence of the gray dawn, turning the woman's head toward the yellow and blue sky of the curtains. She stands up and goes to the window, crushing shards of glass beneath her feet. She looks for the neighbor through the holes in the curtains. A shrill cry bursts from her chest. She rushes to the door, and out into the passage. But the deafening sound of a tank freezes her in her tracks. Bewildered, she comes back. "The door . . . our door onto the street has been destroyed. The neighbor's walls . . ." Her horrified voice is muffled by the roar of the tank. Her gaze travels once more around the room, stopping sharply at the window. She walks up to it, parts the curtains and gasps. "Not that! No, not that!"

The noise of the tank starts to fade; the neighbor's coughing is heard again.

The woman collapses on the shards of glass. Eyes closed, voice muffled, she begs, "God . . . merciful God, I belong to . . ." A shot rings out. She is silent. A second shot. Then a man's cry: *"Allah O Akbar!"* The tank fires. The explosion shakes the house and the woman. She hurls herself to the ground, slithers to the door, makes it into the passage, and hurtles down the cellar stairs to her terrified daughters.

The man remains motionless. Impassive.

When the shots cease—a lack of ammunition, perhaps—the tank drives away. The thick, smoky silence returns and settles.

In this dusty stillness, at the foot of the wall between the two windows, a spider is prowling around the carcass of the fly discarded by the ants. Examining it. Then it too abandons the fly, takes a tour of the room, returns to the window, attaches itself to the curtain, climbs it, and crawls over the migrating birds frozen in the yellow and blue sky. It leaves the sky and climbs onto the ceiling, to disappear among the rotting beams, where it will spin its web, no doubt.

The woman reappears. Once again carrying the plastic basin, a towel, and a sheet. She cleans up. The shards of glass, the soot that has spread all over the room, everything. Then she leaves. Comes back. Pours sugar-salt solution into the drip bag, returns to her spot at the man's side, and administers the bottle's remaining eyedrops. One. She waits. Two. She stops. The bottle is empty. She leaves.

On the ceiling, the spider reappears. Hanging from the end of its silken thread, it moves slowly downward. Lands on the man's chest. After a few moments' hesitation it follows the sinuous lines of the sheet up toward his beard. Suspicious, it turns away and slips between the folds of fabric.

The woman returns. "There is going to be more fighting!" she announces, and walks purposefully toward the man. "I'm going to have to take you down into the cellar." She pulls the tube out of his mouth, and wedges her hands under his armpits. Lifts him. Drags his scrawny body. Pulls him onto the kilim. Then stops. "I'm not strong enough . . ." She is desperate. "I'll never manage to get you down the stairs."

She drags him back onto the mattress. Reinserts the tube. Stands there for a moment, not moving. Upset and out of breath, she stares down at him. "It would be better if a stray bullet just finished you off, once and for all!" she says finally. She stands up abruptly to draw the curtains, and storms out of the room.

The neighbor's cough can be heard, ripping through the afternoon silence in the same way it racks her chest. She must be walking on the ruins of her home. Her slow, faltering steps wander through the garden, move closer to the house. Here is her broken shadow on the curtains' migrating birds. She coughs and murmurs an inaudible name. She coughs. She waits. In vain. She moves off, murmurs the name again, and coughs. No response. She calls, she coughs. She is no longer waiting. No longer murmuring. She is humming something. Names, perhaps. Then she walks away. Far away. And returns. Her hum can still be heard, over the sound of the street. Over the sound of boots. The boots of men carrying weapons. The boots are running. Scattering. In order to hide somewhere—presumably behind the walls, in the rubble . . . and wait for the night.

The water bearer doesn't come today. The boy doesn't cross the road on his bicycle whistling the tune of *"Laïli, Laïli, Laïli, ∂jân, ∂jân, ∂jân, you have broken my heart . . ."*
Everyone is lying low. They are silent. Waiting.

Now night falls on the city, and the city falls into the drowsiness of fear.
But nobody shoots.

The woman comes into the room to check on the sugar-salt solution in the drip bag, and leaves again. Without a word.

The old neighbor is still coughing, still humming to herself. She is neither near nor far. She must be among the ruins of the wall that, so recently, separated the two houses.

A heavy, ominous sleep steals over the house, over all the houses, over the whole street, with the old neighbor's hummed lament in the background, a lament that continues until she hears noise again, the noise of boots. She stops humming, but continues coughing. "They're coming back!" Her voice trembles in the vast blackness of the night.

The boots are near now. Arriving. They chase away the old lady, enter the courtyard of the house, and keep coming. They come right up to the window. The barrel of a gun pokes through one of the shattered panes, pushing aside the curtains patterned with migrating birds. The butt breaks open the whole window. Three yelling men hurl themselves into the room. "Nobody move!" And nothing does move. One of them switches on a torch and points it at the motionless man, barking, "Stay where you are, or I'll smash your head in!" He puts a booted foot on the man's chest. The faces and the heads of the three men are hidden by black turbans. They surround the man, who continues to breathe slowly and silently. One of the three bends over him. "Shit, he's got a tube in his mouth!" He pulls it out and yells, "Where's your weapon?" The recumbent man continues to stare blankly at the ceiling, his gaze lost in the darkness where the spider may already have spun its web. "We're talking to you!" screams the man holding the torch. "He's fucked!" concludes the second man, crouching down to pull off the watch and the gold wedding ring. The third man rifles through the whole room—under the mattress and pillows, behind the plain green curtain, under the kilim . . . "There's nothing here!" he complains. "Go and check the other rooms!" orders the other, the first man, the one with the torch in his hand and his boot on the man's chest. The other two obey. They disappear into the passage.

The one who is left lifts the sheet with the barrel of his gun, exposing the man's body. Perturbed by its lifelessness, its total silence, he grinds the heel of his boot into the man's chest. "What d'you think you're looking at?" He waits for a groan. Nothing. No protest. Flustered, he tries again. "Do you hear me?" He scans the vacant face. Exasperated, he scolds, "Cut your tongue out, did they?" then snorts, "Already dead, are you?" Finally, he falls silent.

After a deep, angry breath, he grabs the man by the collar and lifts him up. The man's pale and disturbing face scares him. He lets go and backs away, stopping in the doorway, unsettled. "Where are you, boys?" he grumbles from behind the strip of turban muffling his voice. He glances into the passage, dark as blackest night, and shouts, "Are you there?" His voice rings out in the emptiness. Like the man's, his breathing becomes slow and deep. He walks back over to the man, to stare at him again. Something intrigues him, and distresses him. His torch sweeps over the motionless body, returning once more to the wide open eyes. He kicks him gently on the shoulder with the tip of his boot. Still no reaction. Nothing. He swings his weapon into the man's field of vision, then rests the barrel on his forehead and presses down. Nothing. Still nothing. He takes another deep breath, and goes back to the doorway. At last, he hears the others sniggering in one of the rooms. "What the fuck are they doing?" he grumbles, afraid. His two comrades come back laughing.

"What did you find?"

"Look!" says one of them, brandishing a bra. "He's got a wife!"

"Yes, I know."

"You know?"

"You moron, you took off his wedding ring, didn't you?"

The second man drops the bra on the floor, joking with his mate: "She must have tiny tits!" But the man with the torch doesn't laugh. He is thinking. "I'm sure I know him," he mutters as he approaches the man. The other two follow.

"Who is it?"

"I don't know his name."

"Is he one of ours?"

"I think so."

They remain standing, faces still hidden behind the strips of black turban.

"Did he speak?"

"No, he doesn't say a word. He doesn't move."

One of the men kicks him.

"Hey, wake up!"

"Stop that, can't you see his eyes are already open?"

"Did you finish him off?"

The man holding the torch shakes his head, and asks, "Where is his wife?"

"There's no one in the house."

Silence, again. A long silence in which everything is pulled into sync with the man's breathing. Slow and heavy. At last one of the men cracks. "What shall we do, then? Get out of here?" No response.

They don't move.

The old neighbor's chant is heard again, interspersed with her rasping cough. "The madwoman's back," says one man. "Perhaps it's his mother," suggests the other. The third leaves the room via the window, and rushes up to the old woman. "Do you live here, Mother?" She hums, "I live here . . ." She coughs. "I live there . . ." She coughs. "I live wherever I like, with my daughter, with the king, wherever I like . . . with my daughter, with the king . . ." She coughs. Again the man chases her away from the rubble of her own house, and returns. "She's gone completely nuts!"

The coughing retreats and is lost in the distance.

The man with the torch notices the Koran on the ground, rushes up to it, grabs it, prostrates himself, and kisses the book as he prays behind the strip of his turban. "He's a good Muslim!" he cries.

They plunge back into their silent thoughts. Remain there, until one—the same one—becomes impatient. "Right, what the fuck are we doing? Let's patrol! Shit! We didn't bomb the area for nothing, right?"

They stand up.

The one holding the torch covers the prostrate man with the sheet, puts the tube back in his mouth, and gestures to the other two to leave.

Off they go. With the Koran.

Dawn, again.

The woman's footsteps, again.

She climbs the stairs from the cellar, walks down the passage and enters the room, not noticing that the door is open and the curtains too; not suspecting for a moment that visitors have forced their way in. She glances at her man. He is breathing. She leaves and comes back with two glasses of water. One for the drip bag, the other to moisten the man's eyes. Even now, she notices nothing. It must be because of the shadowy light. Day has not yet broken, the sun has not yet shone through the hole-studded sky of the curtains patterned with migrating birds. It is only later, when she comes back to change the man's sheet and shirt, that she finally notices his bare wrist and finger. "Where's your watch? Your ring?" She checks his hands, his pockets. She rummages around under the sheet. Unsettled, she takes a few steps toward the door, then comes back. "What's going on?" She is worried, then panicked. "Did someone come?" she asks herself, going to the window. "Yes, someone did come!" she exclaims, terrorized, as she sees how it has been smashed. "And yet . . . I didn't hear anything!" She backs away. "I was sleeping! My God, how can I have slept so deeply?" Horrified, she runs to the passage, leaving the man uncovered. Comes back. Picks up her bra from the doorway. "Did they search the house? But they didn't come down to the cellar?" She collapses next to the man, grabs his arm, and cries, "It was you . . . you moved! You're doing all this to terrify me! To drive me mad! It's you!" She shakes him roughly. Pulls out the tube. Waits.

Still no sign, no sound. Her head hunches into her shoulders. A sob tears through her chest, shaking her whole body. After a long burdened sigh, she stands up, wipes her eyes on the end of her sleeve, and, before leaving, reinserts the tube into the man's mouth.

She can be heard inspecting the other rooms. She stops when the neighbor's rasping cough comes near the house. She rushes into the courtyard and calls out to the old woman, "*Bibi* . . . Did someone come here last night?"

"Yes, my daughter, the king came . . ." She coughs. "He came to visit me . . . he caressed me . . ." She laughs, coughing. "Do you have any bread, daughter? I gave all mine to the king . . . he was hungry. How handsome he was! To die for! He asked me to sing." She starts singing. "*Oh, King of goodness/I weep in loneliness/Oh, King . . .*"

"Where are the others?" the woman asks. "Your husband, your son?" The old lady stops singing and continues her tale in a sad voice. "The king wept, as he listened to me! He even asked my husband and son to dance to my song. They danced. The king asked them to dance the dance of the dead . . . They didn't know it . . ." She smiles, before continuing: "So he taught them, by cutting off their heads and pouring boiling oil on their bodies . . . Well that made them dance!" She takes up her lament once more. *"Oh King, know that my heart can no longer bear your absence/It is time for you to come back . . ."* The woman stops her again. "But what . . . my God . . . your house! Your husband, your son , . . are they alive?" The old lady's voice becomes shrill, like a child's. "Yes, they are here, my husband and son are here, in the house . . ." She coughs. "With their heads under their arms." She coughs. "Because they are angry with me." The old woman coughs, and weeps. "They won't talk to me anymore! Because I gave the king all our bread. Do you want to see them?"

"But . . ."

"Come on! Talk to them!"

The women walk off across the rubble. They can no longer be heard.

Suddenly, a howl. From the woman. Horrified. Horrifying. Her footsteps stagger over the flagstones, stumble through the ruins, cross the garden, and enter the house. She is still screaming. She vomits. Weeps. Runs around the house. Like a madwoman. "I'm leaving this place. I'm going to find my aunt. Whatever the cost!" Her panicky voice fills the passage, the rooms, the cellar. Then she comes back up, with her children. They flee the house without stopping to check on the man. The sound of them leaving is accompanied by the old woman's coughing and chanting, which makes the children laugh.

Everything is absorbed into the man's silence and passivity.

And this continues.

For a long time.

Once in a while, flies' wings sweep through the silence. At first their flight is decisive, but after a tour of the room they become engrossed in the man's body. Then leave again.

Occasionally, a gust of wind lifts the curtains. It plays with the migrating birds frozen on the yellow and blue sky studded with holes.

Even a wasp, with its ominous buzzing, is not able to disturb the torpor of the room. It circles the man again and again, lands on his forehead—stings him or not, we shall never know—and flies off toward the ceiling, presumably to build itself a nest amid the rotting beams. Its dreams of nesting come to an abrupt end in the spider's trap.

It wriggles. And then nothing.

. . .

Nothing then.

Night falls.

Shots ring out.

The neighbor returns, with her singing and her lugubrious cough. And immediately goes off again.

The woman does not come back.

Dawn.

The mullah performs his call to prayer.

The weapons are asleep. But the smoke and smell of gunpowder maintain their presence.

It's when the first rays of sunlight pierce the holes in the yellow and blue sky of the curtains that the woman returns. Alone. She walks straight into the room, straight to her man. First she takes off her veil. Stands there a moment. Looking around, checking everything. Nothing has been moved. Nothing has been taken. The drip bag is empty, that's all.

Reassured, the woman comes to life. She walks unsteadily to the mattress on which the man is lying, half-naked, as she left him the previous night. Stares at him a long time, as if again counting his breaths. She starts to sit down but suddenly freezes, crying "The Koran!" Once more her eyes fill with dread. She searches every inch of the room. No sign of the word of God. "The prayer beads?" She finds them under the pillow. "Has someone been here again?" Again the doubt. Again the fear. "The Koran was here yesterday, wasn't it?" Unsure, she sinks to the floor. Then suddenly cries, "The feather!" and starts scrabbling around in a frenzy. "My God! The feather!"

From outside comes the sound of children's voices. Local kids, playing in the rubble.

"*Hajii mor'alé?*"

"*Balé?*"

"Who wants water? Who wants fire?"

The woman goes over to the window, parts the curtains and calls to the children: "Did you see anyone come into this house?" "No!" they all shout at once, and carry on with their game: "I want fire!"

She leaves the room, inspects the whole house.

Wearily she comes back and leans against the wall between the two windows. "But who is coming here? What do they do to you?" Worry and distress are visible in her eyes. "We can't stay here!" She falls silent suddenly, as if interrupted. Then, after a brief hesitation, continues: "But what can I do with you? Where can I take you in this state? I think . . ." Her gaze falls on the empty drip bag. "I've got to get water," she says to give herself time. She stands up, goes out, and comes back with the two glasses of water. Carries out her daily tasks. Sits down. Keeping vigil. Thinking. Which allows her, after a few breaths, to announce almost triumphantly, "I've managed to find my aunt. She's moved to the northern part of the city, to a safer area, to her cousin's house." A pause. The habitual pause, waiting for a reaction that doesn't come. So she continues: "I left the children with her." Again, she pauses. Then, overwhelmed, mutters, "I'm afraid, here," as if to justify her decision. Receiving no reaction at all, no word of agreement, she looks down as she lowers her voice. "I'm afraid of you!" She searches the floor for something. Words. But more importantly, courage. She finds them, grabs them, and hurls them at him: "I can't do anything for you. I think it's all over!" She falls silent again, then talks quickly, firmly. "It seems this neighborhood is going to be the next front line between the factions." She adds, furiously, "You knew, didn't you?" Another pause, just a breath to gather the strength to say, "Your brothers knew too. That's why they all left. They've abandoned us! The cowards! They didn't take me with them because you were alive. If . . ." She swallows her spit, and her rage as well. Continues, less fiercely, "If . . . if you had died, things would have been different . . ." She interrupts that thought. Hesitates. After a deep breath, decides: "One of them would have had to marry me!" Her voice shakes with a silent snigger. "Perhaps they would have been happier if you had died." She shudders. "That way, they could have . . . fucked me! With a clear conscience." Having said it, she stands up suddenly and leaves the room. Paces nervously up and down the passage. Searching for something. Calm. Serenity. But returns more febrile still. She rushes at the man and gabbles it all out in a rush: "Your brothers have always wanted to fuck me! They . . ." Walks away, and back again. "They spied on me . . . constantly, for the whole three years you were away . . . spied on me through the little window in the bathhouse while I was washing myself . . . and . . . jerked off. They spied on us too, at night . . ." Her lips tremble. Her hands move feverishly through the air, through her hair, through the folds of her dress. Her footsteps stumble on the faded stripes of the old kilim. "They jerk . . ." She breaks off, and again storms furiously out of the room, for a breath of fresh air and to purge herself of her rage. "The fuckers!" she yells in exasperation. "The bastards!" And can immediately be heard weeping and begging: "What am I saying? Why am I saying all this? Help me, God! I can't control myself. I don't know what I'm saying . . ."

She walls herself up in silence.

The children who were playing in the rubble can no longer be seen either. They have moved off at last.

The woman reappears. Her hair in a mess. A wild look in her eyes. After a little walk around, she sinks down by the man's head. "I don't know what's happening to me. My strength is deserting me, day by day. Just like my faith. I need you to understand." She strokes him. "I hope you are able to think, to hear, to see . . . to see me, and hear me . . ." She leans against the wall, and lets a long moment go by—a dozen cycles of the prayer beads, perhaps, as if she were still telling them to the rhythm of the man's breathing—enough time to think, to explore the nooks and crannies of her life, and return with memories. "You never listened to me, never heard me! We never spoke about any of this! We've been married for more than ten years, but lived together for only two or three. Isn't that right?" She counts. "Yes, ten and a half years of marriage, three years of conjugal life! It's only now that I'm counting. Only now that I'm realizing all this!" A smile. A short, false smile worth a thousand words of regret and remorse . . . but very soon, the memories take hold. "At the time, I didn't even question your absence. It seemed so normal! You were at the front. You were fighting for freedom, for Allah! And that made every-thing okay. It gave me hope, made me proud. In some way, you were with us. Inside each of us." She is look-ing back, seeing it all again . . . "Your mother, with her enormous bust, coming to our place to ask for the hand of my younger sister. It wasn't her turn to get married. It was my turn. So your mother simply said, *No prob-lem, we'll take her instead!* pointing her fleshy finger at me as I poured the tea. I panicked and knocked the pot over." She hides her face in her hands. In shame, or to dispel the image of a mocking mother-in-law. "As for you, you didn't even know this was happen-ing. My father, who wanted nothing more, accepted without the slightest hesitation. He didn't give a damn that you weren't around! Who were you, really? No one knew. To all of us, you were just a title: the Hero! And, like every hero, far away. Engagement to a hero was a lovely thing, for a seventeen-year-old girl. I said to myself, 'God is far away, too, and yet I love him, and believe in him . . .' Anyway, they celebrated our engagement without the fiancé. Your mother said, *Don't worry, victory is coming! It will soon be the end of the war, we will be free, and my son will return!* Nearly a year later, your mother came back. Victory was still a long way off. *It's dangerous to leave a young, engaged woman with her parents for such a long time!* she said. And so I had to be married, despite your absence. At the ceremony, you were present in the form of a photo, and that wretched khanjar, which they put next to me in place of you. And I had to wait another three years for you. Three years! For three years I wasn't allowed to see my friends, or my family . . . It was not considered proper for a young married virgin to spend time with other married women. Such rubbish! I had to sleep in the same room as your mother, who kept watch over me, or rather my chastity. And it all seemed so normal, so natural to everyone. To me too! I didn't even know how lonely I was. At night I slept with your mother, in the daytime I talked to your father. Thank God he was there. What a man! He was all I had. And your mother hated that. She would get all wound up whenever she saw me with him. She used to send me straight to the kitchen. Your father read me poems, and told me stories. He encouraged me to read, and write, and think. He loved me. Because he loved you. He was proud of you, when you were fighting for freedom. He told me so. It was after freedom came that he started to hate you—you, and also your brothers, now that you were all fighting for nothing but power."

Children's shouts ring out again on the rubble. The noise floods into the courtyard, and the house.

She falls silent. Listens to the children, who are playing the same game:

"*Hadji mor'alé?*"

"*Balé?*"

"Who wants the foot? Who wants the head?"

"I want the foot."

They run off into the street again.

She takes up her story. "Why was I talking about your father?" Rubs her head against the wall, seeming to think, to scour her memory . . . "Yes, that's right, I was talking about the two of us, our marriage, my loneliness . . . Three years of waiting, and then you come home. I remember it like it was yesterday. The day you came back, the day I saw you for the first time . . ." A sarcastic laugh bursts from her chest. "You were just like you are now, not a word, not a glance . . ." Her eyes come to rest on the photo of the man. "You sat down next to me. As if we already knew each other . . . as if you were seeing me after just a brief absence or I were some tawdry reward for your triumph! I was looking at you, but you were staring into thin air. I still don't know if it was modesty or pride. It doesn't matter. But I saw you, I watched you,

I kept glancing at you, observing you. Noticing the slightest movement of your body, the slightest expression in your face . . ." Her right hand plays with the man's filthy hair. "And you seemed so arrogant, so absent; you just weren't there. That saying is so true: *One should never rely on a man who has known the pleasure of weapons!*" She laughs again, but gently this time. "Weapons become everything to you men . . . You must know that story about the military camp where an officer tries to demonstrate the value of a gun to the new recruits. He asks a young soldier, Benam, *Do you know what you have on your shoulder?* Benam replies, *Yes, sir, it's my gun!* The officer yells back, *No, you moron! It's your mother, your sister, your honor!* Then he moves on to the next soldier and asks him the same question. The soldier responds, *Yes, sir! It's Benam's mother, and sister, and honor!*" She is still laughing. "That story is so true. You men! As soon as you have guns, you forget your women." She sinks back into silence, still stroking the man's hair. Tenderly. For a long time.

Then she continues, her voice sad. "When I got engaged, I knew nothing of men. Nothing of married life. I knew only my parents. And what an example! All my dad cared about was his quails, his fighting quails! I often saw him kissing those quails, but never my mother, nor us, his children. There were seven of us. Seven girls starved of affection." She stares at the frozen flight of the migrating birds on the curtains. Sees her father: "He always used to sit cross-legged. He would be wearing his tunic, holding the quail in his left hand and stroking it at just the level of his thing, with its little feet poking through his hand; with the other hand, he would caress its neck in the most obscene way. For hours and hours on end! Even when he had visitors he didn't stop performing his *gassaw*, as he called it. It was a kind of prayer for him. He was so proud of his quails. Once, when it was bitterly, freezing cold, I even saw him tucking one of the quails under his trousers, into his *kheshtak*. I was little. For a long time after that I thought that men had quails between their legs! Thinking about it used to make me laugh. Imagine my disappointment when I saw your balls for the first time." A smile interrupts her and she closes her eyes. Her left hand strays into her own loosened hair, caressing the roots. "I hated his quails." She opens her eyes. Her sad gaze loses itself once more in the hole-studded sky of the curtains. "Every Friday, he used to take them to the fight in the Qaf gardens. He would place bets. Sometimes he won, sometimes he lost. When he lost he would get upset, and nasty. He would come home in a rage and find any pretext to beat us . . . and also my mother." She stops herself. The pain stops her. A pain that spreads to the tips of her fingers and digs them more deeply into the roots of her black hair. She forces herself to carry on. "He must have won a lot of money in one of those fights . . . but then he put everything he had into buying a hugely expensive quail. He spent weeks and weeks getting it ready for a very important fight. And . . ." She laughs, a bitter laugh that contains both sarcasm and despair, and continues. "As fate would have it, he lost. He had no money left to honor his bet, so he gave my sister instead. At twelve years old, my sister was sent to live with a man of forty!" Her nails leave the roots of her hair, and move down her forehead to finger the scar at the edge of her left eye. "At the time, I was only ten . . . no . . ." She thinks about it. "Yes, ten years old. I was scared. Scared that I too would become the stakes of a bet. So, do you know what I did with the quail?" She pauses a moment. It is unclear whether this is to make her story more exciting, or because she is afraid to reveal the next part. Eventually, she continues. "One day . . . it was a Friday, while he was at the mosque for prayers before going to the Qaf gardens, I got the bird out of its cage, and set it free just as a stray cat—a ginger and white tabby—was keeping watch on the wall." She takes a deep breath. "And the cat caught it. He took it into a corner to eat it in peace. I followed. I stood there watching. I have never forgotten that moment. I even wished the cat '*bon appétit.*' I was happy, thrilled to watch that cat eat the quail. A moment of pure delight. But very soon, I started to feel jealous. I wanted to be the cat, this cat savoring my father's quail. I was jealous, and sad. The cat knew nothing of the quail's worth. It couldn't share my joy, my triumph. 'What a waste!' I thought to myself, and suddenly rushed over to grab what was left of the bird. The cat scratched my face and scurried off with the quail. I felt so frustrated and desperate that I started licking the floor like a fly, licking up those few drops of blood from my father's quail that had dripped onto the floor." Her lips grimace. As if still tasting the warm wetness of the blood. "When my father came home and found the cage empty, he went mad. Out of his mind. He was screaming. He beat up my mother, my sisters, and me, because we hadn't kept watch over his quail. His bloody quail! While he was beating me, I shouted that it was good riddance, because that bloody quail had sent my sister away! My father understood immediately. He shut me in the cellar. It was dark. I had to spend two days in there. He left a cat with me—another stray who must have been roaming around—and told me gleefully that if the animal got hungry it would eat me. But luckily, our house was full of rats. So the cat became my friend." She stops, shakes off her memories of the cellar, and comes back to the room, and her man. Unsettled, she gazes at him a while, and suddenly moves away from the wall. "But . . . but why am I telling him all this?" she murmurs. Overcome by her memories, she stands up heavily. "I never wanted anyone to know that. Never! Not even my sisters!" She leaves the room, upset. Her fears echo down the passage. "He's driving me mad. Sapping my strength. Forcing me to speak. To confess my sins, my mistakes. He's listening to me. Hearing me. I'm sure of it. He wants to get to me . . . to destroy me!"

She shuts herself in one of the other rooms, to calm her nerves with total solitude.

The children are still shouting among the ruins.

The sun moves over to the other side of the house, withdrawing its rays of light from the holes in the yellow and blue sky of the curtains.

Later, she comes back. Eyes solemn, hands shaking. She walks up to the man. Stops. Takes a deep breath. Grabs hold of the feeding tube, closes her eyes, and pulls it out of his mouth. Turns around, her eyes still closed. Takes an uncertain step. Sobs "Forgive me, God!" picks up her veil and disappears.

She runs. Through the garden. Down the street . . .

The sugar-salt solution drips, one drop at a time, from the hanging tube onto the man's forehead. It flows into the valleys of his wrinkles, then toward the base of his nose, into his eye sockets, across his chapped cheeks, and finally into his thick, bushy mustache.

The sun is setting.
The weapons awakening.
Tonight again they will destroy.
Tonight again they will kill.
Morning.
Rain.
Rain on the city and its rubble.
Rain on the bodies and their wounds.

A few breaths after the last drop of sugar-salt solution, the sound of wet footsteps slaps through the courtyard, and into the passage. The muddy shoes are not removed.

The door to the room creaks open. It's the woman. She doesn't dare enter. She observes the man with that strange, wary look in her eyes. Pushes the door a fraction wider. Waits some more. Nothing moves. She takes off her shoes and slips quietly in, remaining on the threshold. She lets her veil fall to the floor. She is shaking. With cold. Or fear. She walks forward, until her feet are touching the mattress on which the man is lying.

The breathing has its usual rhythm.

The mouth is still half-open.

The look is still mocking.

The eyes are still empty, soulless . . . but today they are wet with tears. She crouches down, terrified. "Are you . . . are you crying?" She sinks to the ground. But soon realizes that the tears come from the tube; they are sugar-salt tears.

Her throat is dry, her voice deadened. Blank. "But, who are you?" A moment goes by—two breaths. "Why doesn't God send Ezraeel, to finish you off once and for all?" she asks suddenly. "What does he want from you?" She looks up. "What does he want from me?" Her voice drops. "You would say, *He wants to punish you!*" She shakes her head. "Don't kid yourself!" Her voice is clearer now. "Perhaps it's you he wants to punish! He's keeping you alive so you can see what I'm capable of doing with you, to you. He is making me into a demon . . . a demon for you, against you! Yes, I am your demon! In flesh and blood!" She lies down on the mattress to avoid the man's glassy stare. Lies there a long moment, silent and thoughtful. Traveling far, far back into the past, to the day the demon was born in her.

"After everything I confessed yesterday, you would tell me that I was already a demon as a young child. A demon in my father's eyes." Her hand touches the man's arm tenderly. Strokes it. "But I was never a demon to you, was I?" She shakes her head. "Or maybe I was . . ." Her silence is full of doubt and uncertainty. "But everything I did was for you . . . in order to keep you." Her hand slips onto the man's chest. "Or actually, to tell you the truth, so that you would keep me. So that you wouldn't leave me! Yes, that's why I . . ." She stops herself. Draws in her knees and curls up on her side, next to the man. "I did everything I could to make you stay with me. Not just because I loved you, but so that you wouldn't abandon me. Without you, I didn't have anyone. They would all have sent me packing." She falls silent. Scratches her head. "I admit that to start with I wasn't very sure of myself. Wasn't sure I could love you. I didn't know how to love a hero. It seemed so out of reach somehow, like a dream. For three years, I had been trying to imagine what you were like . . . and then one day you came. You slipped into the bed. Climbed on top of me. Rubbed yourself against me . . . and couldn't do it! And you didn't even dare say a word to me. In total darkness, with our hearts beating furiously, our breathing all jerky, our bodies streaming with sweat . . ." Her eyes are closed. She is far away, far from this motionless body. Drowning in the darkness of that night of desire. Of that hunger. She remains there a moment. Totally silent. Totally still.

Then: "After that, I very quickly became used to you, to your clumsy body, your empty presence, which at that point I didn't know how to interpret . . . and gradually, I started to worry when you went away. To keep watch for your return. I used to get in a terrible state when you went away, even for a little while . . . I felt as if something was missing. Not in the house, but inside of me . . . I felt empty. So I started to stuff myself with food. And each time, your mother would come over to me, asking impatiently whether I didn't feel nauseous at all. She thought I was pregnant! When I told other people—my sisters—about this distress, about the state I got into when you were away, they said I was just in love, that was all. But all that didn't last long. After about five or six months, everything changed. Your mother had decided I was barren, and kept hassling me all the time. And you did too. But . . ." Her hand reaches up and swipes through the air above her head, as if to chase away the remaining words bent on attacking her.

A few moments later—five or six breaths—she continues: "And you took up your gun again. Left again for that crazy fratricidal war! You became conceited, arrogant, and violent! Like all your family, except your father. The others despised me, they all did. Your mother was dying to see you take a second wife. I soon realized what was in store for me. My fate. You know nothing . . . nothing of all I did, so that you would keep me." She rests her head on the man's arm. A timid smile, as if to beg for his mercy. "You will forgive me, one day, for all that I've done . . ." Her face closes. "But when I think about it now . . . if you had known, you would have killed me straightaway!" She leans right over the man and looks at him for a long time, staring into his vacant eyes. Then she rests her cheek tenderly on his chest. "How strange this all is! I've never felt as close to you as I do right now. We've been married ten years. Ten years! And it's only these last three weeks that I'm finally sharing something with you." Her hand strokes the man's hair. "I can touch you . . . You never let me touch you, never!" She moves toward the man's mouth. "I have never kissed you." She kisses him. "The first time I went to kiss you on the lips, you pushed me away. I wanted it to be like in those Indian films. Perhaps you were scared— is that it?" she asks, looking amused. "Yes. You were scared because you didn't know how to kiss a girl." Her lips brush against the bushy beard. "Now I can do anything I want with you!" She lifts her head, to get a better look at her vacant-eyed man. Stares at him a long time, close up. "I can talk to you about anything, without being interrupted, or blamed!" She nuzzles her head into his shoulder. "After I left, yesterday, I was filled with such a strange, indefinable feeling. I felt both sad and relieved, both happy and unhappy." She stares into the thickness of his beard. "Yes, a strange relief. I couldn't understand how, as well as feeling upset and horribly guilty, I could also feel relieved, as if a burden had been lifted. I wasn't sure if it was because of . . ." She stops. As always, it is difficult to know whether she is blocking out her thoughts, or groping for the right words.

She rests her head back on the man's chest, and continues. "Yes, I thought that maybe I felt relieved because I had finally been able to desert you . . . to leave you to die . . . to rid myself of you!" She huddles into the man's motionless body, as if cold. "Yes, rid myself of you . . . because yesterday, all of a sudden, I started thinking that you were still conscious, quite well in mind and body but determined to make me talk, to find out my secrets and possess me completely. So I was scared." She kisses his chest. "Can you forgive me?" She looks at him tenderly. "I left the house, hidden beneath my chador, and wandered the streets of this deaf, blind city in tears. Like a madwoman! When I went back to my aunt's house in the evening, everyone thought I was ill. I went straight to my room to collapse into my distress, my guilt. I didn't sleep all night. I was sure I was a monster, a proper demon! I was terrorized. Had I lost my mind, become a criminal?" She pulls away from her man's body. "Like you, like your cronies . . . like the men who beheaded the neighbor's whole family! Yes, I belonged to your camp. Coming to that conclusion was terrifying. I cried all night long." She moves closer to him. "Then, in the morning, at dawn, just before it started raining, the wind opened the window . . . I was cold . . . and afraid. I snuggled up to my girls . . . I felt a presence behind me. I didn't dare look. I felt a hand stroking me. I couldn't move. I heard my father's voice. I gathered every ounce of strength, and turned around. He was there. With his white beard. His little eyes blinking in the darkness. The worn-out shape of him. In his hands he was carrying the quail I had given to the cat. He claimed that everything I told you yesterday had brought his quail back to life! Then he embraced me. I stood up. He wasn't there. Gone, taken by the wind. The rain. Was it a dream? No . . . it was so real! His breath on my neck, his calloused palm against my skin . . ." She rests her chin on her hand, to keep her head upright. "I was thrilled by his visit, lit up. I finally realized that the cause of my relief was not my attempt to abandon you to death." She stretches. "Do you understand what I'm saying? . . . The thing that was actually releasing me was having talked about that business of the quail. The fact of having confessed it. Confessed all of it, to you. And then I realized that since you've been ill, since I've been talking to you, getting angry with you, insulting you, telling you everything that I've kept hidden in my heart, and you not being able to reply, or do anything at all . . . all of this has been soothing and comforting to me." She grasps the man by the shoulders. "So, if I feel relieved, set free—in spite of the terrible things that keep happening to us—it is thanks to my secrets, and to you. I am not a demon!" She lets go of his shoulders, and strokes his beard. "Because now your body is mine, and my secrets are yours. You are here for me. I don't know whether you can see or not, but one thing I am absolutely sure of is that you can hear me, that you can understand what I'm saying. And that is why you're still alive. Yes, you are alive for my sake, for the sake of my secrets." She shakes him. "You'll see. Just as my secrets were able to resuscitate my father's quail, they will bring you back to life! Look, it's been three weeks now that you've been living with a bullet in your neck. That's totally unheard of! No one can believe it, no one! You don't eat, you don't drink, yet you're still here! It's a miracle. A miracle for me, and thanks to me. Your breath hangs on the telling of my secrets." She gets to her feet with ease and then stands over him, full of grace, as if to say: "Don't worry, there is no end to my secrets." Her words can be heard through the door. "I no longer want to lose you!"

She returns to refill the drip bag. "Now I finally understand what your father was saying about that sacred stone. It was near the end of his life. You were away, you'd gone off to war again. It was a few months ago, just before you were hit by this bullet, your father was ill, and I was the only one looking after him. He was obsessed by a magic stone. A black stone. He talked about it the whole time . . . What did he call that stone?" She tries to think of the word. "He asked every friend who visited to bring him this stone . . . a precious, black stone . . ." She inserts the tube into the man's throat. "You know, that stone you put in front of you . . . and tell all your problems to, all your struggles, all your pain, all your woes . . . to which you confess everything in your heart, everything you don't dare tell anyone . . ." She checks the drip. "You talk to it, and talk to it. And the stone listens, absorbing all your words, all your secrets, until one fine day it explodes. Shatters into tiny pieces." She cleans and moistens the man's eyes. "And on that day you are set free from all your pain, all your suffering . . . What's that stone called?" She rearranges the sheet. "The day before he died, your father called for me, he wanted to see me alone. He was dying. He whispered to me, *Daughter, the angel of death has appeared to me, accompanied by the angel Gabriel, who revealed a secret that I am entrusting to you. I now know where this stone is to be found. It is in the Ka'bah, in Mecca! In the house of God! You know, that Black Stone around which millions of pilgrims circle during the big Eid celebrations. Well, that's the very stone I was telling you about . . . In heaven, this stone served as a throne for Adam . . . but after God banished Adam and Eve to earth, he sent it down too, so that Adam's children could tell it of their problems and sufferings . . . And it is this same stone that the angel Gabriel gave to Hagar and her son Ismael to use as a pillow when Abraham had banished the servant and her son into the desert . . . yes, it is a stone for all the world's unfortunates. Go there! Tell it your secrets until it bursts . . . until you are set free from your torments."* Her lips turn ash-gray with sadness. She sits a moment in the silence of mourning.

Her voice husky, she continues. "Pilgrims have been going to Mecca for centuries and centuries to circle around that stone, praying; so how come it hasn't exploded yet?" A sardonic laugh makes her voice ring out, and her lips regain their color. "It will explode one day, and that day will be the end of the world. Perhaps that's the nature of the Apocalypse."

Someone is walking through the courtyard. She falls silent. The steps move further away. She carries on. "Do you know what? . . . I think I have found that magic stone . . . my own magic stone." The voices emanating from the ruins of the neighboring house prevent her once more from pursuing her thoughts. She stands up nervously and goes to the window. Opens the curtains. She is petrified by what she sees. Her hand goes to her mouth. She doesn't make a sound. She closes the curtains and watches the scene through the holes in the yellow and blue sky. "They are burying the dead in their own garden," she exclaims. "Where is the old lady?" She stands quite still for a long moment. Overwhelmed, she turns back to her man. Lies down on the mattress, her head against his. Hides her eyes in the crook of her arm, breathing deeply and silently, as before. To the same rhythm as the man.

The voice of the mullah reciting burial verses from the Koran is drowned out by the rain. The mullah raises his voice and speeds up the prayer, to get it over with as quickly as possible.

The noise and whispering disperse across the sodden ruins.

Someone is walking toward the house. Now he is behind the door. Knocking. The woman doesn't move. More knocking. "Is anyone there? It's me, the mullah," he shouts impatiently. The woman, deaf to his cry, still doesn't move. The mullah mutters a few words and leaves. She sits back up and leans against the wall, keeping quite still until the mullah's wet footsteps have disappeared down the street.

"I have to go to my aunt's place. I need to be with the children!" She gets to her feet. Stands there a moment, just long enough to listen to a few of the man's breaths.

Before she has picked up her veil, these words burst from her mouth: *"Sang-e saboor!"* She jumps.

"That's the name of the stone, *sang-e saboor*, the patience stone! The magic stone!" She crouches down next to the man. "Yes, you, you are my *sang-e saboor*!" She strokes his face gently, as if actually touching a precious stone. "I'm going to tell you everything, my *sang-e saboor*. Everything. Until I set myself free from my pain, and my suffering, and until you, you . . ." She leaves the rest unsaid. Letting the man imagine it.

She leaves the room, the passage, the house . . .

Ten breaths later she is back, out of breath. She drops her wet veil on the floor and rushes up to the man. "They'll be patrolling again tonight— the other side this time, I think. Searching all the houses . . . They mustn't find you . . . They'll kill you!" She kneels down, stares at him close up. "I won't let them! I need you now, my *sang-e saboor*!" She walks to the door, says "I'm going to get the cellar ready," and leaves the room.

A door creaks. Her steps ring out on the stairs. Suddenly she cries desperately, "Oh no! Not this!" She comes back up, in a panic. "The cellar has flooded!" Paces up and down. Her hand to her forehead, as if rummaging through her memories for somewhere to hide her man. Nothing. So it will have to be here, in

this room. Determined, she snatches the green curtain and pulls it aside. It's a junk room, full of pillows,
blankets, and piled-up mattresses.

Having emptied the space, she lays out a mattress. Too big. She folds it over and scatters the cushions around it. Takes a step back to get a better sense
of her work—the nook for her precious stone. Satisfied, she walks back over to the man. With great
care, she pulls the tube out of his mouth, takes him
by the shoulders, lifts him up, drags the body over,
and slides it onto the mattress. She arranges him so
that he's almost sitting up, wedged in by cushions,
facing the entrance to the room. The man's expres-
sionless gaze is still frozen, somewhere on the kilim.
She reattaches the drip bag to the wall, inserts the
tube back into his mouth, closes the green curtain,
and conceals the hiding place with the other mattresses and blankets. You would never know there
was anyone there.

"I'll be back tomorrow," she whispers. She is in the
doorway, leaning down to pick up her veil, when a
sudden gunshot, not far away, rivets her to the floor,
freezing her midmovement. A second shot, even closer.
A third . . . and then shots ringing out from all directions, going in all directions.

・ ・ ・

Sitting on the floor, her wails of "my children . . .".
reach no one, drowned out by the dull rumblings of a
tank.

Bent double, she makes her way to the window.
Peeks outside, through the holes in the curtain, and is
filled with despair. A tear-soaked cry bursts from her
chest, "Protect us, God!"

She sits against the wall between the two windows, just beneath the khanjar and the photo of her
mocking man.

She is groaning, quietly.

Somebody shoots right next to the house. He is
probably inside the courtyard, posted behind the wall.
The woman chokes back her tears, her breath. She
lifts the bottom of the curtain. Seeing a shape shooting toward the street, she moves sharply back, and
cautiously makes her way to the door.

In the passage, the silhouette of an armed man
makes her freeze. "Get back in the room!" She goes
back into the room. "Sit down and don't move!" She
sits down where her man used to lie, and does not

move. The man emerges from the dark passage, wearing a turban, with a length of it concealing half his face. He fills the doorway, and dominates the room. Through the narrow gap in his turban his dark gaze sweeps the space. Without a word, he moves over to the window and glances out toward the street, where shots are still being fired. He turns back toward the woman to reassure her: "Don't be afraid, sister. I will protect you." Once again, he surveys his surroundings. She is not afraid, just desperate. And yet she manages to act serene, sure of herself.

Sitting between the two men, one hidden by a black turban, the other by a green curtain, her eyes flicker with nerves.

The armed man crouches on his heels, his finger on the trigger.

Still suspicious and on edge, he looks away from the curtains toward the woman, and asks her, "Are you alone?" In a calm voice—too calm—she replies, "No." Pauses a moment, then continues fervently, "Allah is with me," pauses again, and glances at the green curtain.

The man is silent. He is glaring at the woman.

. . .

Outside, the shooting has stopped. All that can be heard, in the distance, is the dull roar of the tank leaving.

The room, the courtyard, and the street sink into a heavy, smoky silence.

The sound of footsteps makes the man jump and he turns his gun on her, gesturing to her not to move. He peers through a hole in the curtain. His tensed shoulders relax. He is relieved. He lifts the curtain a fraction and hisses a code in a low voice. The steps pause. The man whispers, "Hey, it's me. Come in!"

The other man enters the room. He too is wearing a turban, with a part of it hiding his face. His thin, lanky body is wrapped in a *patou*—a long, heavy woolen shawl. Surprised by the woman's presence, he crouches down next to his companion, who asks him, "So?" The second man's eyes are fixed on the woman as he replies, "It's ok-ok-okay, th-the there's a c-cceasefire!" stammering, his voice a teenager's in the process of breaking.

"Until when?"

"I . . . I . . . d-d-d-don't know!" he replies, still distracted by the woman's presence.

"Okay, now get out of here and keep watch! We're staying here tonight."

The young man doesn't protest. Still staring at the woman, he asks for "a c-c-c-cigarette," which the first man chucks over to get rid of him as quickly as possible. Then, having completely uncovered his bearded face, he lights up himself.

The boy darts a final stunned glance at the woman from the doorway, and reluctantly disappears down the passage.

The woman stays where she is. She observes the man's every movement with a distrust she is still attempting to hide. "Are you not afraid of being all alone?" the man asks, exhaling smoke. She shrugs her shoulders. "Do I have any choice?" After another long drag, the man asks, "Don't you have anyone to look after you?" The woman glances at the green curtain. "No, I'm a widow!"

"Which side?"

"Yours, I presume."

The man doesn't push it. He takes another deep drag, and asks, "Have you any children?"

"Yes. Two . . . two girls."

"Where are they?"

"With my aunt."

"And you—why are you here?"

"To work. I need to earn my living, so I can feed my two kids."

"And what do you do for work?"

The woman looks him straight in the eye, and says it: "I earn my living by the sweat of my body."

"What?" he asks, confused.

The woman replies, her voice shameless: "I sell my body."

"What bullshit is this?"

"I sell my body, as you sell your blood."

"What are you on about?"

"I sell my body for the pleasure of men!"

Overcome with rage, the man spits, *"Allah, Al-Rahman! Al-Mu'min!* Protect me!"

"Against whom?"

The cigarette smoke spews out of the man's mouth as he continues to invoke his God, "In the name of Allah!" to drive away the devil, "Protect me from Satan!" then takes another huge drag to belch out alongside words of fury, "But aren't you ashamed to say this?!"

"To say it, or to do it?"

"Are you a Muslim, or aren't you?"

"I'm a Muslim."

"You will be stoned to death! You'll be burned alive in the flames of hell!"

He stands up and recites a long verse from the Koran. The woman is still sitting. Her gaze is scornful. Defiantly, she looks him up and down, from head to foot, and foot to head. He is spitting. The smoke of his cigarette veils the fury of his beard, the blackness of his eyes. He moves forward with a dark look. Pointing his gun at the woman, he bawls, "I'm going to kill you, whore!" The barrel sits on her belly. "I'm going to explode your filthy cunt! Dirty whore! Devil!" He spits on her face. The woman doesn't move. She scoffs at the man. Impassive, she seems to be daring him to shoot.

The man clenches his teeth, gives a great yell, and leaves the house.

The woman remains motionless until she hears the man reach the courtyard, and call out to the other, "Come on, we're getting out of here. This is an ungodly house!" Until she hears the flight of their footsteps down the muddy road.

She closes her eyes, sighs, breathes out the smoky air she has been holding in her lungs for a long time.

A triumphant smile flickers across her dry lips. After a long gaze at the green curtain, she unfolds her body and moves over to her man. "Forgive me!" she whispers. "I had to tell him that—otherwise, he would have raped me." She is shaken by a sarcastic laugh. "For men like him, to fuck or rape a whore is not an achievement. Putting his filth into a hole that has already served hundreds before him does not engender the slightest masculine pride. Isn't that right, my *sang-e saboor*? You should know. Men like him are afraid of whores. And do you know why? I'll tell you, my *sang-e saboor*: when you fuck a whore, you don't dominate her body. It's a matter of exchange. You give her money, and she gives you pleasure. And I can tell you that often she's the dominant one. It's she who is fucking you." The woman calms down. Her voice serene, she continues, "So, raping a whore is not rape. But raping a young girl's virginity, a woman's honor! Now that's your creed!" She stops, leaving a long moment of silence for her man—if he can, and she hopes he can—to think about her words.

"Don't you agree, my *sang-e saboor*?" she continues. She approaches the curtain, moving aside some of the mattresses concealing the hiding place. She looks deep into her man's glassy eyes, and says, "I

do hope you're managing to grasp and absorb everything I'm telling you, my *sang-e saboor*." Her head is
poking slightly through the curtain. "Perhaps you're
wondering where I could have picked all this up! Oh
my *sang-e saboor*, I've still so much to tell you . . ." She
moves back. "Things that have been stored up inside
me for a while now. We've never had the chance to
discuss them. Or—let's be honest—you've never given
me the chance." She pauses, for one breath, asking
herself where and how she should start. But the mullah's cry, calling the faithful to prostrate themselves
before their God at twilight, throws her into a panic
and drives her secrets back inside. She stands up suddenly: "May God cut off my tongue! It's about to get
dark! My children!" She rushes over to lift the curtain
patterned with migrating birds. Behind the gray veil
of the rain, everything has been plunged once more
into a gloomy darkness.

By the time she has checked the gaps between the
drops of sugar-salt solution one last time, picked up
her veil, closed the doors, and made it to the courtyard, it's already too late. Now that the call to prayer
is complete, the mullah announces the neighborhood
curfew and asks everyone to respect the ceasefire.

The woman's footsteps pause on the wet ground.

They hesitate.

They are lost.

They go back the way they came.

The woman comes back into the room.

Upset, she drops her veil on the floor and lets herself fall, wearily, onto the mattress previously occupied by the body of her man. "I leave my daughters in Allah's hands!" She recites a verse from the Koran, trying to persuade herself of God's power to protect her girls. Then she lies down, abandoning herself to the darkness of the room. Her eyes manage to see through the dark toward the mattresses. Behind the mattresses, the green curtain. Behind the curtain, her man, her *sang-e saboor*.

A gunshot, far away. Then another, close. And thus ceases the ceasefire.

The woman stands up, and walks toward the plain green curtain. She pushes the mattresses aside, but doesn't open the curtain. "So I'll have to stay here. I've got a whole night to myself, to talk to you, my *sang-e saboor*. Anyway, what was I saying before that stupid mullah started screeching?" She makes herself focus. "Oh yes, you were wondering where I could have gotten all these notions. That was it, wasn't it? I have had two teachers in my life—my aunt and your father. My aunt taught me how to live with men, and your father taught me why. My aunt . . ." she opens the curtain slightly. "You didn't know her at all. And thank God! You would have sent her packing straightaway. Now I can tell you everything. She is my father's only sister. What a woman! I grew up enveloped in her warmth. I loved her more than my own mother. She was generous. Beautiful. Very beautiful. Big hearted. She was the one who taught me how to read, how to live . . . but then her life took a tragic turn. They married her off to this terrible rich man. A total bastard. Stuffed with dirty cash. After two years of marriage, my aunt hadn't been able to bear a child for him. I say for him, because that's how you men see it. Anyway, my aunt was infertile. In other words, no good. So her husband sent her to his parents' place in the countryside, to be their servant. As she was both beautiful and infertile, her father-in-law used to fuck her, without a care in the world. Day and night. Eventually she cracked. Bashed his head in. They threw her out of her in-laws' house. Her husband sent her away too. She was abandoned by her own family—including my father. So, as the 'black sheep' of the family, she vanished, leaving a note saying she had put an end to her days. Sacrificed her body, reduced it to ashes! Leaving no trace. No grave. And of course, this suited everyone just fine. No funeral. No service for that 'witch'! I was the only one who cried. I was fourteen years old at the time. I used to think about her constantly." She stops, bows her head, closes her eyes as if dreaming of her.

After a few breaths, she starts up again, as if in a trance. "One day, more than seven years ago, just before you came back from the war, I was strolling around the market with your mother. I stopped at the underwear stall. Suddenly, a voice I know. I turned around. There was my aunt! For a moment I thought I was seeing things. But it really was her. I greeted her, but she acted as if she hadn't heard, as if she didn't know me. And yet I was absolutely, one hundred percent sure. I knew in my blood that it was her. So I managed to lose your mother in the crowd. Began trailing my aunt. I didn't let her out of my sight, all the way to her house. I stopped her at her front door. She burst into tears. Gave me a big hug, and asked me in. At the time she was living in a brothel." She falls silent, giving her man, behind the green curtain, the chance to take a few breaths. And herself too.

. . .

In the city, the shooting continues. Far away, nearby, sporadic.

In the room, everything is sunk in darkness.

Saying "I'm hungry," she stands up and feels her way into the passage, and then into the kitchen to find something to eat. First she kindles a lamp, which brightens part of the passage and sheds a little light into the room as well. Then, after the slamming of a few cupboard doors, she returns. A hard crust of several-day-old bread and an onion in one hand, the hurricane lamp in the other. She sits back down near her man, by the green curtain, which she pulls aside in the yellowish lamplight to check that her *sang-e saboor* has not exploded. No. It is still there. In one piece. Eyes open. Mocking expression, even with the tube thrust into the pathetically half-open mouth. The chest continues to, miraculously, rise and fall at the same pace as before.

"And now, it's that aunt who has taken me in. She likes my children. And the girls like her too. That's why I'm slightly more relaxed." She peels the onion.

"She tells them loads of stories . . . as she used to before. I grew up with her stories too." She puts a layer of onion on a bit of bread, and shoves the whole thing into her mouth. The cracking of the dry bread mingles with the softness of her voice. "The other night, she wanted to tell a particular story that her mother used to tell us. I begged her not to tell it to my girls. It's a very disturbing tale. Cruel. But full of power and magic! My girls are still too young to understand it." She takes a sip from the glass of water she had brought to moisten her man's eyes.

"As you know, in my family we were all girls. Seven girls! And no boy! Our parents hated that. It was also the reason our grandmother told my sisters and me that story. For a long time, I thought she had invented it especially for us. But then my aunt told me that she had first heard that story from her great-grandmother."

A second layer of onion on a second crust of bread.

"In any case, our grandmother warned us in advance, by telling us that the story was a magical tale that could bring us either happiness or misfortune in our actual lives. This warning frightened us, but it was also exciting. And so her lovely voice rang out to the frenetic beating of our hearts. *Once upon a time there was, or was not, a king. A charming king. A brave king. This* king, however, had one constraint in his life—just one, but of the utmost importance: he was never to have a daughter. On his wedding night, the astrologers told him that if ever his wife should give birth to a girl, she would bring disgrace upon the crown. As fate would have it, his wife gave birth to nothing but girls. And so, at each birth, the king would order his executioner to kill the newborn baby!"

Lost in her memories, the woman suddenly takes on the appearance of an old lady—her grandmother, no doubt—telling this story to her grandchildren.

"The executioner killed the first baby girl, and the second. With the third, he was stopped by a little voice emanating from the mouth of the newborn. It begged him to tell her mother that if she kept her alive, the queen would have her own kingdom! Troubled by these words, the executioner visited the queen in secret, and told her what he had seen and heard. The queen, not breathing a word to the king, immediately came to take a look at this newborn with the gift of speech. Full of wonder yet terrified, she asked the executioner to prepare a cart so they could flee the country. At exactly midnight, the queen, her daughter, and the executioner secretly left the city for distant lands."

Nothing distracts her from her tale, not even the shots fired not far from the house. "Furious at this sudden flight and determined to see his wife again, the king departed in conquest of foreign lands. Grandmother always used to pause at exactly this point in the story. She would always ask the same question: *But was it to see his wife again, or to track her down?"*

She smiles. In just the way her grandmother smiled, perhaps. And continues:

"The years went by. During one of these warmongering trips, the king was resisted by a small kingdom governed by a brave, fair, and peaceful queen. The people refused the interference of this foreign king. This arrogant king! So, the king decreed that the country be burned to the ground. The queen's advisors counseled her to meet the king and negotiate with him. But the queen was against this meeting. She said she would rather set fire to the country herself than attend the negotiation. And so her daughter—who was much loved by the court and the people, not only for her remarkable beauty but also for her outstanding intelligence and kindness—asked her mother if she could meet the king herself. On hearing her daughter's request, the queen seemed to lose her mind. She began screaming, cursing the entire world at the top of her voice. She no longer slept. She wandered the palace. She forbade her daughter to leave her bedroom, or to take any action. Nobody could understand her. With every day that passed, the kingdom sank a little deeper into catastrophe. Food and water became scarce. At this point the daughter, who could understand her mother no better than anyone else, decided to meet the king despite the prohibition. One night, with the help of her

confidant, she made her way to the king's tent. On seeing her heavenly beauty, the king fell madly in love with the princess. He made her the following offer: if she would marry him, he would renounce his claim to the kingdom. The princess accepted, somewhat entranced herself. They spent the night together. In the early hours, she made her triumphant way back to the palace, to tell her mother about this encounter with the king. Luckily, she didn't admit that she had also spent the night in his tent. When she heard her daughter had so much as seen the king, the queen succumbed to absolute despair. She was willing to face any ordeal life could throw at her, except this one! Overcome, she howled, 'Fate! Oh cursed fate!' and fainted. Still understanding nothing of what was going on inside her mother's head, the daughter spoke to the man who had been at her mother's side throughout her life, and asked him the cause of the queen's distress. And so he told her this story. 'Dear princess, as you know, I am not your father. The truth is that you are the daughter of this swaggering king! As for me, I was only his executioner.' He told her everything that had happened, finishing with this enigmatic conclusion: 'And this, my princess, is our fate. If we tell the king the truth, the law decrees that all three of us shall be sentenced to hang. And all the people of this kingdom shall become his slaves. If we oppose his intentions, our kingdom shall be burned down. And if you marry him, you shall be committing the unpardonable sin of incest! All of us shall be cursed and punished by God.'

Grandmother used to stop at this point in the story. We would ask her to tell us what happened next, and she would say: *Unfortunately, my little girls, I don't know how the story ends. To this day, nobody knows. They say that the man or woman who discovers the end of the story shall be protected from hardship for the rest of their life.* Not fully convinced, I would object that, if no one knew the end of the story, how could anyone tell if an ending was right? She used to laugh sadly and kiss me on the forehead. *That's what we call mystery, my dear. Any ending is possible, but to know which is the right ending, the fair ending . . . now that is the preserve of mystery.* At that point, I used to ask her if it was a true story. She would reply, *I told you, 'Once upon a time there was, or was not . . .'* My question was the same question she, as a young girl, used to ask her own grandmother, and to which her grandmother would reply, *And that is the mystery, my dear; that is the mystery.* That story haunted me for years. It used to keep me awake at night. Every night, in bed, I would plead with God to whisper the end of the story to me! A happy ending, so that I could have a happy life! I would make up all kinds of stuff in my head. As soon as I came up with an idea, I would rush to tell my grandmother. And she would shrug her shoulders and say, *It's possible, my dear. It's possible. Your life will reveal whether you are right or not. It's your life that will confirm it. But whatever you discover, never tell anyone. Never! Because, as in any magical tale, whatever you say may come to pass. So, make sure to keep this ending to yourself."*

She eats. A crust of bread, a layer of onion. "Once, I asked your father if he knew the story. He said no. So I told it to him. At the end, he paused a long while, then said these poignant words: *You know, my daughter, it's an illusion to think you can find a happy ending to this story. It's impossible. Incest has been committed, and so tragedy is inevitable."*

In the street, we hear someone shouting, "Halt!" And then a gunshot.

And footsteps, fleeing.

The woman continues. "So, your father disabused me of my illusions. But a few days later, when I brought him his breakfast early one morning, he asked me to sit down so we could talk about the story. Speaking very slowly and deliberately, he said, *My daughter, I have thought long and hard. And actually, there could be a happy ending.* I was so keen to hear this ending that I felt like throwing myself into his arms, kissing his hands and feet. Although, I restrained myself, of course. I forgot your mother and her breakfast, and sat down next to him. At that moment, my whole body was one giant ear, ignoring all other voices, all other sounds. There was only the wise, trembling voice of your father, who after a great slurp of tea said the following: *As in life, my daughter, for this story to have a happy ending there must be a sacrifice. In other words, somebody's misfortune. Never forget, every piece of happiness must be paid for by two misfortunes. 'But why?'* I asked with naive surprise. He replied in simple words: *My daughter, unfortunately, or perhaps fortunately, not everyone in the world can attain happiness, in real life or in a story. The happiness of some engenders the hardship of others. It's sad, but true. So, in this story, you need misfortune and sacrifice in order to arrive at a happy ending. But your self-regard, and your care for your loved ones, prevents you from considering this. The story requires a murder. But who must be killed? Before replying, before killing anyone, you must ask yourself another question: who do you wish to see happy, and alive? The father-king? The mother-queen? Or the daughter-princess? As soon as you ask yourself this question, my daughter, everything changes. In the story and in you. For this to happen you must rid yourself of three loves: love of yourself, love of the father, and love of the mother!* I asked him why. He looked at me quietly for a long time, his pale eyes shining behind his glasses. He must have been searching for words I would be able to understand. *If you are on the daughter's side, your love*

*for yourself prevents you from imagining the daughter's sui-
cide. In the same way, love for the father doesn't allow you to
imagine that the daughter could accept the marriage and then
kill her own father in the marital bed on the wedding night. Finally, love for the mother stops you from considering the murder of the queen in order that the daughter can live with the
king and conceal the truth from him.* He let me think for a
few moments. He took another long sip of tea and continued: *In the same way, if I, as a father, imagined an end to
this story, it would be the strict application of the law. I would
order the beheading of the queen, the princess, and the executioner, to ensure that the traitors were punished and the secret
of the incest buried forevermore.* 'And what would the mother
suggest?' I asked him. With a small private smile, he
replied, *My daughter, I know nothing of maternal love, so I
cannot give you her answer. You yourself are a mother now;
it's for you to tell me. But my experiences in life tell me that
a woman like the queen would rather have her kingdom destroyed and her people enslaved than reveal her secret. The
mother behaves in a moral way. She will not allow her daughter to marry her father.* My God, it was hard, listening
to those wise words. I was still desperately seeking
a merciful outcome, and I asked him if this was at
all possible. First of all he said yes—which comforted
me—but then he shouted, *My daughter, tell me, who in
this story has the power to forgive?* I replied naively, 'The

father.' Shaking his head, he said, *But, my daughter, the father—who has killed his own children, who during his warfaring has destroyed whole cities and populations, who has committed incest—the father is as guilty as the queen. As for her, she has betrayed the king and the law, certainly, but do not forget that she too was misled, by her newborn daughter and by the executioner.* Desperate, I concluded before I left, 'So there is no happy ending!' *There is*, he said. *But, as I told you, it involves accepting a sacrifice, and renouncing three things: self-regard, the law of the father, and the morality of the mother.* Stunned, I asked him if he thought that was feasible. His reply was very simple: *You must try, my daughter.* I was much affected by the discussion, and thought of little else for months. I came to realize that my distress came from one thing and one thing only—the truth of his words. Your father really knew something about life."

Another crust of bread and layer of onion, swallowed with difficulty.

"The more I think of your father, the more I hate your mother. She kept him shut up in a small, sweaty room, sleeping on a rush mat. Your brothers treated him like a madman. Just because he had acquired great wisdom. Nobody understood him. To start with, I was afraid of him too. Not because of what your mother and brothers kept saying about him, but because I remembered what my aunt had suffered at the hands of her father-in-law. And yet, bit by bit I became closer to him. With a great deal of fear. But at the same time a shadowy, indefinable curiosity. An almost erotic curiosity! Perhaps it was the part of me haunted by my aunt that drew me to him. A desire to live the same things she had lived. Frightening, isn't it?"

Full of thoughts and emotion, she finishes her onion and stale bread.
She blows out the lamp.
She lies down.
And sleeps.

As the guns grow weary and quiet, the dawn arrives. Gray and silent.

A few breaths after the call to prayer, hesitant footsteps can be heard on the muddy courtyard path. Someone reaches the house and knocks on the door to the passage. The woman opens her eyes. Waits. Again there is a knock. She stands up. Half-asleep. Goes to the window to see who this person is who doesn't dare enter without knocking.

In the leaden fog of dawn, she makes out an armed, turbaned shadow. The woman's "Yes?" draws the shape to the window. His face is hidden behind a length of turban; his voice, more fragile than his appearance, stammers, "C-c-can I . . . c-c-come in?" It's the breaking teenage voice, the same one as yesterday. The woman tries to make out his features. But in the weak gray light she cannot be sure. She consents with a nod of the head, adding, "The door is open." She herself stays where she is, next to the window, watching the shadow as it moves along the walls, down the passage, and into the doorway. The same clothing. The same way of hesitating on the threshold. The same timidity. It's him. No question. The same boy as the day before. She waits, quizzical. The boy is struggling to step into the room. Glued to the door frame, he tries to ask, "How . . . m-m-much?" The woman can't understand a word he's saying.

"What do you want?"

"How . . ." The voice breaks. It picks up speed— "How . . . m-m-much?"—but not clarity.

Holding her breath, the woman takes a step toward the boy. "Listen, I'm not what you think I am. I . . ." She is interrupted by a cry from the boy, fierce to start with, "Sh-sh-sh . . . shut up!" and then calm, "How . . . m-m-much?" She tries to move back, but is halted by the barrel of the gun against her belly. Waiting for the boy to calm down, she says gently, "I'm a mother . . ." But the boy's tense finger on the trigger prevents her from continuing. Resigned, she asks, "How much do you have on you?" Trembling, he pulls a few notes from his pocket and throws them at her feet. The woman takes a step backward and turns a little so she can cast a furtive glance at the hiding place. The green curtain is slightly open. But the darkness makes the man's presence imperceptible. She slips to the ground. Lying on her back, looking toward her man, she spreads her legs. And waits. The boy is paralyzed. She cries impatiently: "Come on, then, let's get this over with!"

He puts his gun down next to the door, then, hesitantly, walks over, and stands above her. Inner turmoil has made his breathing all jerky. The woman closes her eyes.

Abruptly, he throws himself on top of her. The woman, struggling to breathe, gasps, "Gently!" Overexcited, the boy awkwardly grabs hold of her legs. She is frozen, numb beneath the wild flapping of this clumsy young body as it tries vainly, head buried in her hair, to pull down her pants. She ends up doing it herself. Pulls his down too. As soon as his penis brushes her thighs, he groans dully in the woman's hair; very pale, she keeps her eyes closed.

...

He is no longer moving. She neither.

He is breathing heavily. She too.

There is a moment of total stillness before a light breeze lifts and pulls apart the curtains. The woman opens her eyes at last. Her voice—weak but forgiving—whispers, "Is it over?" The boy's wounded cry shocks her. "Sh-sh-shut . . . sh-sh-sh-shut your mouth!" He doesn't dare raise his head, still buried in the woman's black hair. His breathing becomes less and less intense.

The woman, silent, gazes with infinite sadness at the gap in the green curtain.

The two entwined bodies remain still, fixed to the ground, for a little while longer. Then a new breeze creates a slight movement in this mass of flesh. It's the woman's hand that is moving. Gently stroking the boy.

He does not protest. She continues stroking. Tender and maternal. "It doesn't matter," she assures him. No reaction at all from the boy. She perseveres: "It can happen to anyone." She is cautious. "Is . . . is this the first time?" After a long silence, lasting three slow breaths, he nods his head—still sunk deep in the woman's hair—in shy, desperate assent. The woman's hand moves up to the boy's head, and touches his turban. "You had to start somewhere." She glances around to locate the gun. It is far away. Looks back at the boy who is still in the same position. She moves her legs a little. No protest. "Right, shall we get up?" He doesn't reply. "I told you, it doesn't matter . . . I'll help you." Gently, she pushes up his right shoulder so she can shift onto her side and free herself of the boy's broken weight. Having done this, she attempts to pull up her knickers, first wiping her thighs with the hem of her dress. Then she sits up. The boy moves too, at last. Avoiding the woman's eyes, he pulls up his trousers and sits with his back to her, staring at his gun. His turban has come undone. His face is visible. He has large, pale eyes, outlined in smoky kohl. He is beautiful, his face thin and smooth. He has barely any facial hair. Or else he's very young. "Do you have family?" the woman asks in a neutral voice. The boy shakes his head no, and quickly winds his turban back up, hiding half his face. Then, abruptly, he gets to his feet, grabs his gun, and flees the house like lightning.

The woman is still sitting in the same place. She stays there a long time, without a glance at the green curtain. Her eyes fill with tears. Her body huddles up.

She wraps her arms around her knees, tucks in her head, and wails. A single, heartbreaking wail.

A breeze flutters, as if in response to her cry, lifting the curtains to let the gray fog flood the room.

The woman raises her head. Slowly. She does not stand. She still doesn't raise her eyes to the green curtain. She doesn't dare.

She stares down at the crumpled notes scattering in the breeze.

Cold or emotion, tears or terror makes her breath come in gasps. She is shaking.

Eventually she gets to her feet, and rushes into the passage, to the toilet. She washes, and changes her dress. Reappears. Dressed in green and white. Looking more serene.

She picks up the money and goes back to her spot by the hiding place. Pulls the curtain tight shut, without meeting the man's vacant eyes.

After a few silent breaths, a bitter laugh bursts from her guts, juddering her lips. "So there you go . . . it doesn't just happen to other people! Sooner or later, it had to happen to us too . . ."

She counts the notes, "poor thing," and puts them in her pocket. "Sometimes I think it must be hard to be a man. No?" She pauses for a moment. To think, or to wait for a reply. Starts again, with the same forced smile: "That boy made me think about our own first times . . . if you don't mind me saying so. You know me . . . my memories always hit me just when I'm not expecting them. Or no longer expecting them. They plague me, I just can't help it. The good ones and the bad. It leads to some laughable moments. Like just now, when that boy was all distraught, and our first, belated honeymoon nights suddenly flashed into my brain . . . I swear, I didn't mean to think of you, it just happened. You were clumsy too, like that boy. Of course, at the time, I didn't know any better. I thought that was how it was supposed to be—how you did it. Although it often seemed to me that you weren't satisfied. And then I would feel guilty. I told myself that it was my fault, that I didn't know how to do it right. After a year, I discovered that actually, it was all coming from you. You gave nothing. Nothing. Remember all those nights when you fucked me and left me all . . . all keyed up . . . My aunt is quite right when she says that those who don't know how to make love, make war." She won't let herself continue.

She pauses for a long time before saying, suddenly,
"Anyway, tell me, what is pleasure for you? Seeing
your filth spurt? Seeing the blood spurt as you tear
through the *virtuous veil*?"

She looks down, and bites her bottom lip. Furiously. The anger takes hold of her hand, grips it,
turns it into a fist, and crashes it against the wall. She
groans.

Falls silent.

"Sorry! . . . This . . . this is the first time I've spoken
to you like this . . . I'm ashamed of myself. I really don't
know where it's all coming from. I never used to think
about any of this before. I promise. Never!" A pause,
then she continues. "Even when I noticed you were the
only one whose pleasure peaked, it didn't bother me.
On the contrary, I was pleased. I told myself it was normal. That it was the difference between us. You men
take your pleasure, and we women derive ours from
yours. That was enough for me. And it was my job and
mine alone to give myself pleasure by . . . touching myself." Her lip is bleeding. She blots it with her ring finger, then her tongue. "One night, you caught me in the
act. You were asleep. I had my back to you and was

touching myself. Perhaps my panting woke you up. You jumped, and asked me what I was doing. I was hot, and shaking . . . so I told you I had a fever. You believed me. But you still sent me to sleep in the other room with the children. What a bastard." She falls silent, out of dread, or decency. A blush appears on her cheeks, and spreads slowly to her neck. Her gaze is concealed behind dreamily closing eyelids.

She stands up, buoyant. "Right, I must be going. My aunt and the children must be worried!"

Before leaving, she fills the drip bag with sugar-salt solution, covers her man, closes the doors, and disappears into her veil, into the street.

The room, the house, the garden, all of it, buried in fog, disappears beneath that sad gray mantle.

Nothing happens. Nothing moves, except the spider, which for a while now has been living in the rotting ceiling beams. It is slow. Slothful. After a brief tour of the wall, it returns to its web.

Outside:
They shoot a while.

Pray a while.

Are silent a while.

At dusk, someone knocks on the door to the passage.

No voice invites him in.

He knocks again.

No hand opens the door to him.

He leaves.

Night comes, and goes again. Taking the clouds and the fog with it.

The sun is back. Its rays of light return the woman to the room.

After glancing around the space she pulls a new drip bag and a new bottle of eyedrops from her bag. Goes straight over to the green curtain and draws it aside so she can see her man. His eyes are half-open. She pulls the tube out of his mouth, takes a cushion from under his head, and inserts the drops into his eyes. One, two; one, two. Then, she leaves the room and returns with the plastic basin full of water, a towel, and some clothes. She washes her man, changes his clothes, and settles him back into his spot.

. . .

Carefully she rolls up his sleeve and wipes the crook of his arm. Inserts the tube, fills the dropper correctly, and then leaves, carrying everything she must remove from the room.

We hear her doing the washing. She hangs it out in the sun. Returns with a broom. Brushes off the kilim, the mattresses . . .

She hasn't yet finished her task when someone knocks at the door. She walks to the window in a cloud of dust. "Who is it?" Again the silent shape of the boy, wrapped in his *patou*. The woman's arms fall wearily to her sides. "What do you want now?" The boy holds out a few notes. The woman doesn't move. Doesn't say a word. The boy heads for the passage. The woman comes out to meet him. They murmur a few inaudible words to each other and slip into one of the rooms.

To start with, there is only silence, then gradually some whispering . . . and eventually a few muffled groans. Then once again silence. For quite a while. Then a door opening. And footsteps rushing outside.

・ ・ ・

As for the woman, she goes into the toilet, washes herself, and returns shyly to the room. Finishes her cleaning, and leaves.

Her footsteps ring out on the tiled floor of the kitchen, accompanied after a while by the hum of gas, spreading its sonic layer around the house.

Once she has made her lunch, she comes to eat it in the room, straight out of the pan.

She is soft and serene.

After the first mouthful, she suddenly says, "I feel sorry for that boy! But that isn't why I let him in . . . Anyway, I hurt his feelings today, and almost drove the poor thing away! I got the giggles, and he thought I was laughing at him . . . which of course I was, in a way . . . But it was my fiendish aunt's fault! She said something awful last night. I'd been telling her about this stammering boy, and how he comes so quickly. And . . ." She laughs, a very private, silent laugh. "And she said I should tell him . . ." The laugh, noisy this time, interrupts her again. ". . . Tell him to fuck with his tongue and talk with his dick!" She guffaws, wiping away tears. "It was terrible

of me to think of that right then . . . but what could
I do? As soon as he started stammering, my aunt's
words flashed into my mind. And I laughed! He panicked . . . I tried to control myself . . . but I couldn't. It
just got worse . . . but luckily," she pauses, "or unluck-
ily, my thoughts suddenly took a different turn . . ."
She pauses again. "I thought of you . . . and suddenly
stopped laughing. Otherwise it could have been a
disaster . . . one mustn't hurt young men . . . mustn't
take the piss out of their thing . . . They associate their
virility with a long, hard dick, with how long they can
hold back, but . . ." She bypasses that thought. Her
cheeks are all red. She takes a deep breath. "Anyway,
it's over . . . but that was a narrow escape . . . again."

She finishes her lunch.

After taking her pan back to the kitchen, she returns and stretches out on the mattress. Hides her
eyes in the crook of her arm and lets a long, thoughtful
moment of silence go by before confessing some more:
"So yes, that boy made me think of you again. And
once again I can confirm that he's just as clumsy as
you. Except that he's a beginner, and a quick learner!
Whereas you never changed. At least with him I can
tell him what to do and how to do it. If I'd asked all
that of you . . . my God! I'd have gotten a broken

nose! And yet it's not difficult . . . you just have to listen to your body. But you never listened to it. You
guys listen to your souls, and nothing else." She sits
up and shouts fiercely at the green curtain: "And look
where your soul has got you! You're a living corpse!"
She moves closer to the hiding place: "It's your blasted
soul that's pinning you to the ground, my *sang-e saboor*!" She takes a deep breath: "And it's not your stupid soul that's protecting me now, that's for sure. It's
not your soul that's feeding the kids." She pulls the
curtain aside. "Do you know the state of your soul
right now? Where it is? It's right there, hanging above
you." She gestures at the drip bag. "Yes, it's there, in
that sugar-salt solution, and nowhere else." She puffs
out her chest: "*My soul feeds my honor; my honor protects
my soul.* Bullshit! Look, your honor has been screwed
by a sixteen-year-old kid! Your honor is screwing
your soul!" She grabs his hand, lifts it up. "Now, it's
your body's turn to judge you," she says. "It is judg-
ing your soul. That's why you're not in physical pain.
Because it's your soul that's suffering. That suspended
soul, which sees everything, and hears everything,
and cannot react at all, because it no longer controls
your body." She lets go of the hand and it falls back
onto the mattress with a thud. A stifled laugh pushes
her toward the wall. She doesn't move. "Your honor is

nothing more than a piece of meat now! You used to use that word yourself. When you wanted me to cover up, you'd shout, *Hide your meat!* I was a piece of meat, into which you could stuff your dirty dick. Just to rip it apart, to make it bleed!" She falls silent, out of breath.

Then suddenly she stands up. Leaves the room. She can be heard pacing up and down the passage, saying, "What's the matter with me now? What am I saying? Why? Why? It's not normal, not normal at all . . ." She comes back in. "This isn't me. No, it isn't me talking . . . it's someone else, talking through me . . . with my tongue. Someone has entered my body . . . I am possessed. I really do have a demon inside me. It's she who's speaking. She who makes love with that boy . . . she who takes his trembling hand and puts it on my breasts, on my belly, between my thighs . . . all of that is her! Not me! I need to get rid of her! I should go and seek counsel from the hakim, or the mullah, and tell them everything. So they can drive away this demon lurking inside me! . . . My father was right. That cat has come to haunt me. It was the cat that made me open the door to the quail's cage. I am possessed, and have been for years!" She flings herself into the man's hiding place, sobbing. "This is not me talking! . . . I am under the demon's spell . . . this isn't me . . . where is the Koran?" Panicked. "The demon has even stolen the Koran! The demon did it! . . . And the damned feather . . . she took that too."

She rummages around under the mattresses. Finds the black prayer beads. "Allah, you're the only one who can banish this demon, *Al-Mu'akhkhir*, *Al-Mu'akhkhir* . . ." She tells the prayer beads, "*Al-Mu'akhkhir* . . . ," picks up her veil, "*Al-Mu'akhkhir* . . . ," leaves the room, "*Al-Mu'akhkhir* . . . ," leaves the house, "*Al-Mu'akhkhir* . . ."
She can no longer be heard.
She does not return.

As twilight falls, somebody walks into the court-yard and knocks on the door to the passage. No one replies; no one opens. But, this time, the intruder seems to stay in the garden. The sound of cracking wood, and of stones being bashed together, floods through the walls of the house. He must be taking something. Or destroying. Or building. The woman will find out tomorrow, when she returns along with the first rays of sunlight shining through the holes in the yellow and blue sky of the curtains.

. . .

Night falls.

The garden goes dark. The intruder goes off.

Day breaks. The woman returns.

Very pale, she opens the door to the room and pauses a moment to check for the slightest sign of a visit. Nothing. Distraught, she walks into the room and up to the green curtain. Pulls it slowly aside. The man is still there. Eyes open. The same rhythm to his breathing. The drip bag is half-empty. The drops are falling, as before, to the rhythm of the breath, or of the black prayer beads passing through the woman's fingers.

She lets herself fall onto the mattress. "Did somebody repair the door onto the street?" She is asking the walls. In vain. As always.

She picks herself up, walks out of the room, and, still bewildered, checks the other rooms, and the cellar. She comes back up the stairs. Into the room. Confounded. "But no one has been here!" She collapses onto the mattress, in the grip of a growing weariness.

No more words.

No more movement, except the telling of the prayer beads. Three cycles. Two hundred and ninety-seven beads. Two hundred and ninety-seven breaths. No mention of any of the names of God.

Before embarking on a fourth cycle, she suddenly starts talking. "This morning, my father came to see me again . . . but this time to accuse me of having stolen the peacock feather he used as a bookmark in his Koran. I was horrified. He was furious. I was scared." The fear is still visible in her gaze as it seeks shelter in the corners of the room. "But that was a long time ago . . ." Her body sways. Her voice becomes definite: "It was a long time ago that I stole it." She stands up suddenly. "I'm raving!" she murmurs to herself, calmly at first, then fast, nervously. "I'm raving. I've got to calm down. Got to stop talking." She can't stay in one place. Keeps moving around, chewing on her thumb. Her eyes dart around frenetically. "Yes, that fucking business with the feather . . . that's what it is. That's what is driving me crazy. That bloody peacock feather! It was only a dream, to start with. Yes, a dream, but such a strange one. That dream haunted me every night when I was pregnant with my first child . . . I had the same nightmare every night. I saw myself giving birth to a boy, a boy who had teeth and could already speak . . . He looked just like my grandfather . . . That dream terrorized me, it tortured me . . . The child used to tell me that he knew one of my biggest secrets." She stops moving. "Yes, one of my biggest secrets! And if I didn't give him what he wanted, he would tell that secret to everyone. The first night, he asked for my breasts. I didn't want to give them to him because of his teeth . . . so he started screaming." She covers her ears with trembling hands. "I can still hear his screams today. And he began to tell the start of my secret. I ended up capitulating. I gave him my breasts. He was sucking, and biting on them with his teeth . . . I was crying out . . . I was sobbing in my sleep . . ."

She stands by the window, with her back to her man. "You must remember. Because you kicked me out of bed that night too. I spent it in the kitchen." She sits at the foot of the curtains patterned with migrating birds. "Another night, I dreamt of the boy again . . . This time, he was asking me to bring him my father's peacock feather . . . but . . ." Someone knocks at the door. The woman emerges from her dreams, from her secrets, to lift up the curtain. It's the young boy again. "No, not today!" the woman says firmly. "I am . . ." The boy interrupts her with his jerky words: "I . . . m-m-mended th-the d-d-door." The woman's body relaxes. "Oh, so it was you! Thank you." The boy is waiting for her to invite him in. She doesn't say anything. "C-c-can . . . c-c-can I . . ." "I told you, not today . . ." the woman says wearily. The boy comes closer. "N-n-not . . . n-n-not to . . ." The woman shakes her head and adds, "I'm waiting for someone else . . ." The boy takes another step closer. "I . . . I d-d-don't w-w-want . . ." The woman cuts him off, impatient: "You're a sweet boy, but I've got to work, you know . . ." The boy tries hard to speak quickly, but his stammer just gets worse: "N-n-not . . . n-n-not . . . w-w-wo . . . rk!" He gives up. Moves away to sit at the foot of a wall, sulking like a hurt young child. Helpless, the woman leaves the room so that she can speak to him from the doorway at the end of the passage. "Listen! Come this afternoon, or tomorrow . . . but not now . . ." Calmer now, the boy tries again: "I . . . want t-t-to . . . s-s-speak . . . t-t-to you . . ." In the end, the woman gives in.

They go inside and ensconce themselves in one of the rooms.

Their whispers are the only voices echoing through and underlining the gloomy atmosphere engulfing the house, the garden, the street, and even the city . . .

At a certain point, the whispering stops and a long silence ensues. Then suddenly, the violent slamming of a door. And the boy's sobs departing down

the passage, across the courtyard, and finally fading into the street. Then the woman's furious footsteps as she marches into the room yelling, "Son
of a bitch! Bastard!" She stomps around the room
several times before sitting down. Very pale. "To
think that son of a bitch dared spit in my face when
I told him I was a whore!" she continues with rage.
She stands up. Voice and body stiff with contempt.
Walks toward the green curtain. "You know that
guy who came here the other day with that poor
boy, and called me every name under the sun? Well,
guess what he does himself?" She kneels down in
front of the curtain. "He keeps that poor little boy
for his own pleasure! He kidnapped him when he
was still a small child. An orphan, left to cope on
his own on the streets. Kidnapped him and put a
Kalashnikov in his hands, and bells on his feet in
the evenings. He makes him dance. Son of a bitch!"
She withdraws to the foot of the wall. Takes a few
deep breaths of this air heavy with the smell of gunpowder and smoke. "The boy's body is black and
blue! He has burn scars all over—on his thighs, his
buttocks . . . It's an outrage! That guy burns him
with the barrel of his gun!" Her tears tumble onto
her cheeks, flow down the lines that surround her
lips when she cries, and stream over her chin, down

her neck and onto her chest, the source of her howls.
"The wretches! The scoundrels!"

She leaves.
Without saying anything.
Without looking at anything.
Without touching anything.

She doesn't come back until the next day.

Nothing new.
The man—her man—is still breathing.
She refreshes the drip.
Administers the eyedrops: one, two; one, two.
And that's all.

She sits down cross-legged on the mattress.
Takes a piece of fabric, two small blouses, and a
sewing kit out of a plastic bag. Rummages in the kit
for a pair of scissors. Cuts up bits of fabric to patch
the blouses.

From time to time, she glances surreptitiously at
the green curtain, but more often her eyes turn anxiously toward the curtains with the pattern of migrating birds, which have been pulled open a crack to

make the courtyard visible. The slightest noise draws her attention. She looks up to check whether or not someone is arriving.

And no, nobody comes.

As every day at noon, the mullah makes the call to prayer. Today, he preaches the revelation: *"Recite in the name of your Lord who created, created man from clots of blood. Recite! Your Lord is the Most Bountiful One, who by the pen taught man what he did not know.* My brothers, these are the first verses of the Koran, the first revelation given to the Prophet by the angel Gabriel . . ." The woman pauses and listens carefully to the rest: ". . . at the time Allah's messenger withdrew to meditate and pray in the cave of Learning, deep in the mountain of Light, our Prophet was unable to read or to write. But with the aid of these verses, he learned! Our Lord has this to say about his messenger: *He has revealed to you the Book with the Truth, confirming the scriptures which preceded it; for He has already revealed the Torah and the Gospel for the guidance of mankind* . . ." The woman goes back to her sewing. The mullah continues: *"Muhammad is no more than an apostle; other apostles have passed away before him* . . ." Once again, the woman stops her patching and concentrates on the words of the Koran: "Muhammad, our prophet, says this, *I have not the power to acquire benefits or to avert evil from myself, except by the will of God. Had I possessed knowledge of what is hidden, I would have availed myself of much that is good and no harm would have touched me . . .*" The woman doesn't hear the rest. Her gaze wanders among the folds of the blouses. After a long moment, she lifts her head and says dreamily, "I have heard those words before, from your father. He always used to recite that passage to me, it amused him hugely. His eyes would shine with mischief. His beard would tremble. And his voice would flood that sweaty little room. He would tell me this: *One day, after meditating, Muhammad, peace be upon him, leaves the mountain and goes to his wife Khadija to tell her, 'Khadija, I am about to lose my mind.' 'But why?' his wife asks. And he replies, 'Because I observe in myself the symptoms of the insane. When I walk down the street I hear voices emanating from every stone, every wall. And during the night, a massive being appears to me. He is tall. So tall. He stands on the ground but his head touches the sky. I do not know him. And each time, he comes toward me as if to grab me.' Khadija comforts him, and asks him to tell her the next time the being appears. One day, in the house with Khadija, Muhammad cries, 'Khadija, the being has appeared. I can see him!' Khadija comes to him, sits down, clasps him to her breast and asks, 'Do you see him now?' Muhammad says,*

'Yes, I see him still.' So Khadija uncovers her head and her hair and asks again, 'Do you see him now?' Muhammad replies, 'No, Khadija, I don't see him anymore.' And his wife tells him, 'Be happy, Muhammad, this is not a giant djinn, a diw, *it's an angel. If it was a* diw, *it would not have shown the slightest respect for my hair and so would not have disappeared.'* And to this, your father added that the story revealed Khadija's mission: to show Muhammad the meaning of his prophecy, to disenchant him, tear him from the illusion of devilish ghosts and shams . . . She herself should have been the messenger, the Prophet."

She stops and sinks into a long, thoughtful silence, slowly resuming her patching of the little blouses.

She does not emerge from this silence until she pricks her finger with the needle, and shrieks. She sucks the blood and goes back to her sewing. "This morning . . . my father came into my room again. He was holding a Koran under his arm, my copy, the very same one I had here . . . yes, it was he who took it . . . and so he had come to ask me for the peacock feather. Because it was no longer inside the Koran. He said it was that boy—the one I let come here, into my home—who stole the feather. And that if he comes I must make sure to ask him for it." She stands up, goes to the window. "I hope he does come."

• • •

She steps out of the house. Her footsteps cross the courtyard, stop behind the door that opens onto the road. No doubt she takes a quick look into the street outside. Nothing. Silence. No one, not even the shadow of a passerby. She turns away. Waits outside, in front of the window. Silhouetted against the background of migrating birds frozen midflight on the yellow and blue sky.

The sun is setting.
The woman must go back to her children.
Before leaving the house, she stops by the room to carry out her usual tasks.
Then leaves.

Tonight, they are not shooting.
Beneath the cold, dull light of the moon, the stray dogs are barking in every street of the city. Right through till dawn.
They are hungry.
There are no corpses tonight.

As day breaks, someone knocks on the door to the street, then opens it, and walks into the courtyard. Goes

straight to the door into the passage. Places something
on the ground and leaves.

As the last drip of solution makes it into the dropper and flows down the tube into the man's veins, the
woman returns.

She walks into the room, looking more exhausted
than ever. Her eyes are guarded, somber. Her skin pale,
muddy. Her lips less fleshy, less bright. She throws
her veil into a corner and walks over, carrying a red-
and-white bundle with an apple-blossom pattern. She
checks the state of her man. Talks to him, as she always
does. "Someone came by again, and left this bundle at
the door." She opens it. A few grains of toasted wheat,
two ripe pomegranates, two pieces of cheese, and,
wrapped in paper, a gold chain. "It's him, it's the boy!"
An ephemeral happiness flits across her sad face. "I
should have rushed. I hope he comes back."

As she changes the man's sheet: "He will come
back . . . because before he dropped by here, he came
to see me at my aunt's house . . . while I was in bed.
He came very gently, without a sound. He was dressed
all in white. He seemed very pure. Innocent. He was
no longer stammering. He had come to explain to me
why that fucking peacock feather was so important to

my father. He told me it was from the peacock that had been banished from Eden alongside Eve. Then he left. He didn't even give me a chance to ask him anything." She changes the drip bag, adjusts the timing of the drops, and sits down next to her man. "I hope you don't hate me for talking to you about him and entertaining him here in the house. I don't know what's going on, but he's very—how can I say?—very present for me. It's almost the same feeling I used to have about you, at the beginning of our marriage. I don't know why! Even though I know that he too could become awful, like you. I'm sure of it. The moment you possess a woman, you become monsters." She stretches out her legs. "If you ever come back to life, ever get back on your feet, will you still be the same monster you were?" A pause, as she follows her train of thought. "I don't think so. I convince myself that you will be changed by every-thing I'm telling you. You are hearing me, listening to me, thinking. Pondering . . ." She moves closer to him. "Yes, you'd change, you'd love me. You'd make love to me as I want to be made love to. Because now you have learned lots of new things. About me, and about your-self. You know my secrets. From now on, those secrets are inside you." She kisses his neck. "You'd respect my secrets. As I shall respect your body." She slips her hand between the man's legs, and strokes his penis. "I never touched it like this . . . your . . . your quail!" She laughs. "Can you . . . ?" She slips her hand inside the man's trousers. Her other hand drops between her own thighs. Her lips skim over the beard; they brush against the half-open mouth. Their breath merges, converges. "I used to dream of this . . . always. As I touched my-self, I would imagine your cock in my hands." Little by little the gap between her breaths becomes shorter, their rhythm speeds up, overtakes the man's breathing. The hand between her legs strokes gently, then quickly, intensely . . . Her breathing becomes more and more rough. Panting. Short. Heavy.

A cry.
Moans.

Once again, silence.
Once again, stillness.
Just breathing.
Slow.
And steady.

A few breaths later.
A stifled sigh suddenly interrupts this silence. The woman says "Sorry!" to the man, and shifts a little. Without looking at him, she pulls away and moves out of the hiding place to sit against the corner of the wall.

Her eyes are still closed. Her lips are still trembling. She is moaning. Gradually, words begin to emerge: "What's gotten into me now?" Her head bangs against the wall. "I really am possessed . . . Yes, I see the dead . . . people who aren't there . . . I am . . ." She pulls the black prayer beads from her pocket. "Allah . . . What are you doing to me?" Her body rocks back and forth, slowly and rhythmically. "Allah, help me to regain my faith! Release me! Rescue me from the illusion of these devilish ghosts and shams! As you did with Muhammad!" She stands up suddenly. Paces around the room. Into the passage. Her voice fills the house. "Yes . . . he was just one messenger among others . . . There were more than a hundred thousand like him before he came along . . . Whoever reveals something can be like him . . . I am revealing myself . . . I am one of them . . ." Her words are lost in the murmur of water. She is washing herself.

She comes back. Beautiful, in her crimson dress embroidered with a few discreet ears and flowers of wheat at the cuffs and hem.

She returns to her spot next to the hiding place. Calm and serene, she starts speaking: "I didn't go and seek counsel from the hakim, or the mullah. My aunt forbade me. She says I'm not insane, or possessed. I'm not under the spell of a demon. What I'm saying, what I'm doing, is dictated by the voice from on high, is guided by that voice. And the voice coming out of my throat is a voice buried for thousands of years."

She closes her eyes and, three breaths later, opens them again. Without moving her head, she glances all around the room, as if seeing it for the first time. "I'm waiting for my father to come. I need to tell all of you, once and for all, the story of the peacock feather." Her voice loses some of its softness. "But first I need to get it back . . . yes, it's with that feather than I'm going to write the story of all these voices that are gushing up in me and revealing me!" She becomes agitated. "It's that fucking peacock feather! And where is the boy? What do I bloody want with his pomegranates? Or his chain? The feather! I need the feather!" She stands up. Her eyes are shining. Like a madwoman. She flees the room. Searches the house. Comes back. Her hair a mess. Covered in dust. She throws herself onto the mattress opposite the photo of her man. Picks up the black prayer beads and starts telling them again.

Suddenly, she screams, "I am *Al-Jabbar*!"

Murmurs, "I am *Al-Rahim* . . ."

And falls silent.

. . .

Her eyes become lucid again. Her breath returns to the rhythm of the man's breathing. She lies down. Facing the wall.

Her voice gentle, she continues: "That peacock feather is haunting me." She picks a few flakes of peeling paint from the wall with her nails. "It has haunted me from the beginning, from the first time I had that nightmare. That nightmare I told you about the other day, the child harassing me in my dream, telling me that he knew my biggest secret. That dream made me afraid to go to sleep. But the dream gradually wormed its way into my waking hours as well . . . I used to hear the child's voice in my belly. All the time. Wherever I was. At the baths, in the kitchen, in the street . . . The child would be talking to me. Harassing me. Demanding the feather . . ." She licks the tip of her nail, turned blue by the remnants of paint. "In those moments all I cared about was making it cease. But how? I prayed for a miscarriage. So I could lose that bloody child once and for all! All of you thought I was simply suffering the same neuroses as most pregnant women. But no. What I am about to tell you is the truth . . . what the child said was the truth . . . what he knew was the truth. That child knew my secret. He was my secret. My secret truth! So I decided to strangle him between my legs, as I gave birth. That's why I wouldn't push. If they hadn't knocked me out with opium, the child would have suffocated in my belly. But the child was born. I was so relieved when I regained consciousness and saw that it wasn't a boy—as in my dream—but a girl! A girl would never betray me, I thought to myself. I know you must be dying to find out my secret." She turns around. Lifts her head to look at the green curtain and slithers toward the man like a snake. As she reaches his feet she tries to meet his vacant eyes. "Because that child was not yours!" She falls silent, impatient to see her man finally crack. As always, no reaction, none whatsoever. So she becomes bold enough to say, "Yes, my *sang-e saboor*, those two girls are not yours!" She sits up. "And do you know why? Because you were the infertile one. Not me!" She leans against the wall, at the corner to the hiding place, looking in the same direction as the man, toward the door. "Everyone thought it was me who was infertile. Your mother wanted you to take another wife. And what would have happened to me? I would have become like my aunt. And it was exactly then that I miraculously bumped into her. She was sent by God to show me the way." Her eyes are closed. A smile full of secrets pulls at the corners of her mouth. "So I told your mother that there was a great hakim who worked miracles with this kind of problem. You know the story . . . but not the truth! Anyway, she came with me to meet him and receive amulets from him. I remember it as if it were yesterday. All the things I had to hear from your mother's mouth on the way. She called me every name under the sun. She was yelling, telling me over and over that this was my last chance. She spent a lot of cash that day, I can tell you. And then I visited the hakim several times, until I fell pregnant. As if by magic! But you know what, that hakim was just my aunt's pimp. He mated me with a guy they had blindfolded. They locked us up together in the pitch dark. The man wasn't allowed to talk to me or touch me . . . and in any case, we were never naked. We just pulled down our pants, that's all. He must have been young. Very young and strong. But seemingly short of experience. It was up to me to touch him, up to me to decide exactly when he should penetrate me. I had to teach him everything, him too! . . . Power over another's body can be a lovely thing, but that first day it was horrible. Both of us were very anxious, terrified. I didn't want him to think I was a whore, so I was as stiff as a board. And the poor man was so intimidated and frightened that he couldn't get it up! Nothing happened. We kept far away from each other, all we could hear was our jerky breathing. I cracked. I screamed. They got me out of the room . . . and I spent the whole day vomiting! I wanted to give up. But it was too late. The following sessions got better and better. And yet I still used to cry, after each one. I felt guilty . . . I hated the whole world, and I cursed you—you and your family! And to top it all, at night I had to sleep with you! The funniest thing was that after I fell pregnant, your mother was endlessly going off to see the hakim, to get amulets for all her little problems." A dull laugh rumbles in her chest. "Oh, my *sang-e saboor*, when it's hard to be a woman, it becomes hard to be a man, too!" A long sigh struggles out of her body. She sinks back into her thoughts. Her dark eyes roll. Her ever-paler lips start moving, murmuring something like a prayer. Suddenly, she starts talking in a strangely solemn voice: "If all religion is to do with revelation, the revelation of a truth, then, my *sang-e saboor*, our story is a religion too! Our very own religion!" She starts pacing. "Yes, the body is our revelation." She stops. "Our own bodies, their secrets, their wounds, their pain, their pleasures . . ." She rushes at the man, radiant, as if she holds the truth in her hands and is giving it to him. "Yes, my *sang-e saboor* . . . do you know the ninety-ninth, which is to say the last name of God? It's *Al-Sabur*, the Patient! Look at you; you are God. You exist, and do not move. You hear, and do not speak. You see, and cannot be seen! Like God, you are patient, immobile. And I am your messenger! Your prophet! I am your voice! Your gaze! Your hands! I reveal you! *Al-Sabur!*" She draws the green curtain completely aside. And in a single movement turns around, flings her arms wide as if addressing an audience, and cries, "Behold the Revelation, *Al-Sabur!*" Her hand designates the man, her man with the vacant gaze, looking out into the void.

She is quite carried away by this revelation. Beside herself, she takes a step forward to continue her speech, but a hand, behind her, reaches out and grabs her wrist. She turns round. It's the man, her man, who has taken hold of her. She doesn't move. Thunderstruck. Mouth gaping. Words hanging. He stands up suddenly, stiff and dry, like a rock lifted in a single movement.

"It's . . . it's a miracle! It's the Resurrection!" she says in a voice strangled by terror. "I knew my secrets would bring you back to life, back to me . . . I knew it . . ." The man pulls her toward him, grabs her hair, and dashes her head against the wall. She falls. She does not cry out, or weep. "It's happening . . . you're exploding!" Her crazed eyes shine through her wild hair. "My *sang-e saboor* is exploding!" she shouts with a bitter laugh. *"Al-Sabur!"* she cries, closing her eyes. "Thank you, *Al-Sabur!* I am finally released from my suffering," and embraces the man's feet.

The man, his face haggard and wan, grabs hold of the woman again, lifts her up, and throws her against the wall where the khanjar and the photo are hanging. He moves closer, grabs her again, heaves her up against the wall. The woman looks at him ecstatically. Her head is touching the khanjar. Her hand snatches it. She screams and drives it into the man's heart. There is not a drop of blood.

The man, still stiff and cold, grabs the woman by the hair, drags her along the floor to the middle of the room. Again he bangs her head against the floor, and then, brusquely, wrings her neck.

The woman breathes out.
The man breathes in.

The woman closes her eyes.
The man's eyes remain wild.

Someone knocks at the door.

• • •

The man—with the khanjar deep in his heart—lies down on his mattress at the foot of the wall, facing his photo.

The woman is scarlet. Scarlet with her own blood.

Someone comes into the house.

The woman slowly opens her eyes.

The breeze rises, sending the migrating birds into flight over her body.

My thanks to

Paul Otchakovsky-Laurens

Christiane Thiollier

Emmanuelle Dunoyer

Marianne Denicourt

Laurent Maréchaux

Soraya Nouri

Sabrina Nouri

Rahima Katil

for their support and their poetic gaze